# TO DANCE THE
# HEMPEN JIG

*A Frank Dalton Novel*

*Book 1 in the Frank Dalton Series*

Jonathan Shipperley

*For Dad*

*Sine Metu*
*"Without Fear"*

*As with most positive things in my life, I owe this novel to the inspiration and understanding of my best friend and beautiful wife, Michelle, and the never-ending love of my talented children, Willow, Aidan, Gavin and Anna.*
*Thank you guys, I love you. Always.*

*I'd also like to express my heartfelt thanks to all those that helped me out with this novel. A lot of work went into it and I couldn't have done it without your help. In particular I'd like to thank Dr. Vince Moore, Terry Westhoff, Mathew Pearcy and all my stalwart colleagues that read draft after draft during class at Tiffin University, thanks guys. I also owe a special thanks to my beta readers: Willow Shipperley, Andrea Shipperley, Todd Wardwell, Aaron Foster and Jennifer Elzweig. You guys basically wrote the book for me. Any mistakes are all mine.*

# CONTENTS

Cover designed by Cover Designer
Cover image designed by Paul Fleet/Shutterstock.com

Printed in the United States of America

First Printing: Apr 2018
Kindle Publishing Direct

ISBN-13 978-1-9804602-8-2

# PROLOGUE

"So there I was," Petty Officer Hackman said, looking at Jones, making sure he was still following along. "In the Red Dog Saloon, half a beer still in my hand, when wouldn't you know, in walked-"

"*Mayday. Mayday. Mayday. Come in, Coast Guard...*" The Rescue 21 communications radio crackled to life.

"Well, shit," Hackman said. "I was just getting to the good part. Alright, let's get to work, Jones."

Seaman Jones stared blankly at Hackman and jumped as the radio squawked again.

"The radio, Jones. Answer the radio," Hackman said.

Jones nodded and keyed the radio's microphone. "Vessel hailing mayday, vessel hailing mayday, this is Coast Guard Station Port Aransas, Coast Guard Station Port Aransas, channel one six. What is your position and nature of distress, over?"

The two Coast Guardsman waited for an answer. Jones stared at the communications radio, willing whoever was on the other end to say something. Hackman paced backward and forward in the cramped room, idly tapping his fingers on his pants.

On board a fishing vessel far out in the Gulf of Mexico, wave after wave slammed against the hull as the boat steamed through the turbulent water, seawater roaring over the bow, splattering against the bridge. A nearby lightning strike lit up the lone fisherman standing on the bridge, his reflection a ghostly image painted in the windows, mirroring his terrified white face. He gripped the overhead tighter as the fishing boat pitched and rolled.

A soft incantation came from the fisherman's lips, muttered over and over: I hope we make it, I hope we make it. The red navigation light cast an eerie glow as he fumbled with the radio.

"*Coast Guard! Oh, thank god! This is the commercial fishing vessel Reel Lady, channel sixteen.*" The fisherman braced himself into a corner of the bridge, repositioning his grip on the overhead with one hand as he fumbled the radio with the other. Squinting at the GPS in the dull illumination he said, "*We are an eighty-seven-foot trawler, one hundred miles off the coast of Aransas. Coast Guard our captain-*"

Jones waited a moment for the transmission to begin again. When it didn't, he keyed the mike and said, "*Reel Lady, Reel Lady*, Coast Guard Station Port Aransas, say again your last, your transmission was broken, over." Hackman had stopped pacing, the fright in the fisherman's voice making the hairs on the back of his neck rise.

Powerful floodlights on the vessels superstructure shone bright beacons through the sea spray. The fisherman glanced out the stern windows and gulped, his fingers turning white as he held on tighter. The back deck was awash and the surrounding ocean awake, churning in time with his stomach and he could see the rest of the crew hanging on.

He keyed the microphone again, almost whispering, "*Coast Guard, our captain is missing...I repeat, our captain is missing, he's gone.*"

"Jones, wake up the boat crew and put them on stand-by. Then alert the Air Station. A hundred miles is too far for our vessels, we're going to need air support, they should be able to fly in this weather, but find out," Hackman said.

A loud warbling alarm reverberated around the station. It lasted for about fifteen seconds before trailing off. Jones piped, "Now, ready boat crew lay to the command center, man overboard one hundred miles off shore."

"Jones. Who's the RDO?" Hackman said.

"Mr. Frampton's the response duty officer on tonight."

Hackman picked up the phone and dialed Frampton's number. A moment later he said, "Hackman here, sir, Officer of the Day from Station Port A. We've received a distress call from a fishing vessel with a man overboard situation about a hundred miles offshore. We've put the ready boat crew on standby, but recommend we launch an air asset, as the distressed vessel is too far offshore for our small boats...Yes, sir, I also suggest we divert the Cutter *Glorious* from routine patrol, she's the nearest asset...Yes, sir. I've plotted their arrival time, and the *Glorious* can be on scene in about two hours. Once the air station has a helicopter up, they should be there in about an hour...Yes, sir. Roger, that." Hackman hung up the phone. "Jones. Divert the *Glorious*; tell them they have tactical control of the air station asset. Tell them if they can make contact with the fishing vessel to coordinate a standard search pattern following along the route the fishing boat took."

Jones nodded, changing the channel on the radio to contact the *Glorious* on a secure channel.

Hackman gazed out the window of the communications room. He couldn't see the trawler from here, but he could imagine what they were going through. May God help those fishermen.

3

# ONE

*Hello Sailor*

The palm trees swayed languidly on the night's light breeze, fronds moving in time with waves tenderly lapping along the shoreline. The moon played hide and seek, hidden behind a string of clouds, its absence leaving an inky blackness that smothered the world like molasses.

I was lounging on the starboard bench seat in the stern of my boat, the *Ghost*, moored up at the T-heads in downtown Corpus. I had my feet propped up on the wheel and could just make out the faint strain of a country and western song floating towards me from one of the nearby restaurants. I nursed a beer, too lazy or too tired to grab another, I wasn't sure which.

I couldn't sleep. The gentle waves that usually lulled me, slapping against the hull, weren't working their magic tonight. I was still on leave, a temporary reprieve from the bustle of active duty military life, and much as I enjoyed being free, restlessness was setting in.

The hatch to the main cabin was open a crack, the cool draft from the air conditioning raising goose bumps on my arms. I didn't often leave the air on and the hatch open, but I had a guest down below tonight. Peering through the crack, I could just make out the shape of her curvy form nestled in a cocoon of sheets in the forward berth. It seemed like her chest rose and fell with each breath, almost in time with the swells from the waves. Such a shame.

Earlier that night at my local bar, run by my old friend Pete, she had sat down at the bar beside me, one stool over, and obviously alone. I hadn't been looking for anyone or anything in particular, but after a little while we started to talk, and seemed to hit it off. She had an air of uniqueness about her that I couldn't quite define, and that intrigued me. We went back to my place because it was closer, mere steps from the bar, and perhaps had a little too much to drink.

Now, it felt like we were on the tail end of the relationship, although we'd just met. The air of mystery I thought she had evaporating with each breath. Thinking on it now, perhaps I'd wanted to impress her with my boat, don't know why that was important, it wasn't like me to be so materialistic. Maybe, I sensed that the relationship wasn't going anywhere. Fool reason though.

I took a swig of beer and sighed, I seemed to do a lot of that these days. Sighing that is, although the drinking was vying for a close second place. It was starting to feel like I'd been in the Coast Guard for a zillion years, and I was looking forward to retiring from active duty, maybe moving the *Ghost* someplace else, maybe an island. Do some fishing, drink some beer, write a book. Who knows? I didn't have any fixed plans.

My cell phone rang from where I'd left it inside the cabin on the little desk next to my computer, its shrill noise abrasive in the calm night. I got up and pushed open the hatch some more, climbing down the few steps into the cabin. I walked past the dining table, the silhouette of too many empty wine bottles casting shadows, and silenced the phone as quickly as I could.

"Dalton," I said, quietly into the phone. "Hold on." I glanced into the forward berth. The ringing phone hadn't stirred my guest, but I didn't want to push it. I walked back to the hatch, climbed up a couple of steps, and stuck my head out. "Go ahead."

"Sorry to bother you, Agent Dalton, this is Petty Officer Rogers from the Sector Command Center. I have a marine casualty to brief you on." My gut immediately sank.

"What's going on?" I said.

"Sorry, sir. I know you're not on duty–"

"Actually, I'm on leave."

"Understood, sir. But the SAC specifically asked for you."

Shit. The SAC was the Special Agent in Charge, Mr. Lewis. "The SAC? Okay, let me grab something to write on." I reached down and rummaged blindly through a cubby until I felt a pen and what turned out to be an envelope. Whatever works. I leaned on the hatch so I could write, and sandwiched the phone between my shoulder and ear. "Go ahead."

"Roger that, sir. We've received a report from Station Port Aransas about a commercial fishing vessel, the *Reel Lady*. The vessel called over the radio to say their captain went missing while they were fishing in the Gulf of Mexico. The master is presumed to have gone over the side somehow. The *Glorious* was diverted, and she's on scene along with a rescue helicopter from the Air Station. We're going to have a conference call with you, sir, the chief of response, and the SAC, at minute twenty to go over our options. Mr. Lewis wanted you on the call, sir, because at this point the missing mariner is presumed deceased." I glanced at my watch. I had about forty-five minutes.

"Fine. I'll take the call at the office, I'm not far," I said, and hung up. I needed to get dressed. The deck of the lounge was messy as if a clothing explosion had detonated in the cabin. I gave myself a moment to focus and spotted my pants draped over a chair and shoved a leg in each hole. I picked up a bra I nearly tripped on and rooted around for my shoes. I had time enough to make it to the office, but not time enough to waste.

I walked through to the forward berth and sat on the edge of the bed. I contemplated the best way to do this. I didn't want to be an asshole, there was no need for that, she hadn't done anything wrong. On the flip side, I didn't want to seem welcoming as we had about as much in common as a rabbit and a pineapple. I chose the middle road for now and rubbed her back, giving her a gentle shake to wake her thoroughly.

"Hey honey, you have to get up. I need to go to work," I said, not quite remembering her name.

"Hey," she said, dreamily. She rolled towards me, her hand blindly crawling up my leg. "Ready again?"

I moved her hand and got up, hitting the switch for the dim overhead light, and pulled off the rest of the sheets, taking in her nakedness and making her squeak. Okay asshole it is, then.

"I wish I had time, I truly do." I sort of meant it. "But I have to get to work."

I couldn't leave her on my boat; I didn't know her well enough. Besides, although attractive - call me callous, I call it realistic - I knew I'd never see her again. That old rabbits and pineapple thing. The more we'd spoken last night the more apparent it had become.

I sighed. "Listen. I've got to go, but you can stay here." I made a show of looking at my watch. "For another couple of hours. After that, my wife is due back from her trip, and she won't be too pleased to see you sleeping in her bed."

Her eyes went wide as she inhaled sharply and scrambled out of bed, wrapping the sheet around her. Her hair was all messed up from sleeping, but on her, it didn't look untidy, it looked good. She grabbed her clothes I held out for her and headed for the bathroom. If only we had more in common. Anything really.

Over her shoulder, she said, "You're a fucking asshole." She slammed the bathroom door behind her.

I can't say I blamed her for being upset, when she went to sleep everything was fine. Anyway, she had to go now because if she stayed, she'd find out I wasn't married. Shit just tumbles out of my mouth all by itself sometimes, the filter not quite engaging. Just make that a double asshole with a side of fries.

There was some banging and muttered cursing, taps running and toilet flushing. She stormed out of the bathroom, making me wince as she battered open the door.

"Look," I said, trying to soften the abrupt ejection. "The least I can do is offer you a ride home."

She gave me the finger as she pushed past me and stamped through the cabin and up the stairs to the back deck, giving me a nice view of her perfectly formed rear. What was wrong with me? Get it together, Frank.

It was a damned shame, but some people were not destined for futures together. I wasn't looking for something long term, but I at least liked to have a conversation once in a while. The boat rocked on its moorings as she stepped off, and I heard her calling for a cab on her phone.

I made coffee while I waited for her cab to arrive. I may have been an asshole like she said and I was thinking, but I at least wanted to ensure she got home safe. Maybe not a complete asshole then?

From the stern, I had a clear view of the marina parking lot, so when the coffee brewed, I moved there and took in the air. I'd only taken a few sips when a brightly lit cab pulled in, and she slid into the back seat. Satisfied she was in competent hands, I stepped down to the galley, rinsed out my mug in the sink, and made sure everything was secure. I retrieved my badge and P229 Sig Sauer from the safe I kept under the bed, strapped the pistol to my side, slipped on my jacket and hit the deck.

I drove fast, but not recklessly. It was still early enough in the morning that the roads were clear, but not late enough that the drunks were spewing out from the bars. I wanted to get to work quickly; I didn't want to be another statistic.

I pulled into the Sector underground parking garage and waited patiently for the guard to come out. After a minute that felt like ten, I beeped my horn. A muffled curse came first, followed by a chair scraping on the floor. A rumpled security guard shuffled out from the guard shack, yawning. He cast his bleary eyes over my badge I was holding out the window before he nodded and raised the barrier, waving me through. I parked and ran up the stairs to the fifth floor. It was quiet this early in the morning, and I easily threaded my way through the sea of cubicles to my office. I sat down at my desk, pulled up to the computer and rattled the keyboard to wake it up. The screen came to life, and I logged on, shoving my ID card into the reader. Once I was in the system, I navigated over to e-mail and found the one the command center had sent with the access codes for the telephone conference. I punched the numbers into the phone and grabbed a cup of coffee from the galley while it was connecting. I sat back down as roll call was starting.

"Mr. Lewis, are you ready for the brief?" Petty Officer Rogers said.

"Go ahead, Pete."

"Thank you, sir. Okay, at 2130 yesterday the eighty-seven-foot commercial fishing vessel *Reel Lady* reported via the Rescue 21 system that their master was missing. They were close to a hundred miles offshore at the time, and the weather on-scene was...standby." I heard some rustling coming from the other end. "The weather, according to the National Weather Service, was seas of six to eight feet, winds from the north at fifteen knots and gusting to thirty-five, patchy fog and intermittent thunderstorms. According to the vessel's crew, they initiated man overboard procedures at once. We launched the MH-65 Dolphin helicopter, designation Rescue CG 6043, from Air Station Corpus Christi, and diverted the cutter *Glorious* from its routine patrol to assist."

"Understood. Go on, Pete."

"Based on the *Reel Lady's* automated track line we were able to help them correct their course and successfully back-track based on the set and drift of the tidal conditions. At 0020 the master was sighted face down in the water by the crew of the fishing vessel. They pulled him aboard, but unfortunately, he was unresponsive. The *Glorious* was nearby conducting a search on the same course, and sent their small boat over to the *Reel Lady* after they called in."

"What about the helicopter?" Frampton said.

"Rescue 6043 had to return to station, sir, at 2345, they were bingo status, flying on fumes. The plan was to refuel and head back out but was stood down when the missing fisherman was found. We ran his particulars through the flight surgeon, but she determined with the amount of time the fisherman was in the water, and the fact he was found face down, it was too late for CPR."

"Petty Officer Rogers, this is Agent Dalton. Let me see if I have this straight. What you're saying is that the fishing vessel that reported the master missing was also the one to recover him?"

"That's right, sir. The crew didn't know the exact time the master fell in the water, so we're estimating about four to five hours based on when they last saw him. Survivability for the water temperature wasn't an issue, but he wasn't wearing a life jacket or a Gumby suit," Rogers said.

"How come they didn't know when he fell in the water?" I asked.

"That's not entirely clear, sir. They said they noticed he was missing from the bridge when one of the crew went below to cook dinner."

"Okay, where's the master now?" I said, taking a swig of coffee.

"He was on the *Reel Lady*, but they transferred him to the *Glorious*. The *Glorious* is going to transfer him to the Medical Examiner when they get back to base. They have an ETA of around noon," Rogers said.

"Very well, thanks, Pete," Lewis said.

"If I could sir, there is one other item of note. When we ran the vessel registration through the Marine Information database, we got a hit for an expired lookout."

"What was the lookout for?" I asked.

"Hold one, sir." Rogers typed something in the background. "It says the lookout was posted because the *Reel Lady* had been involved in drug smuggling. They found two bales of marijuana in a false hold about five years ago, but...scanning the report here...it looks like they've been clean since then. That's why the lookout was expired."

Some deep rumbling conversation came through the speakers from the other end of the line, no doubt plotting my demise.

"Agent Dalton?" Lewis said.

"Yes, sir."

"I want you to take the lead on the investigations side of things. Get down there and figure out if this is just an accident or if there was anything more going on. Nose around a little, see what you can come up with."

"Yes, sir," I said, reaching for the off button on the phone, just a second too late.

"Oh, and one other thing," Lewis paused; probably knowing I wouldn't like what he was going to say. "I need you to take Agent Carter with you."

I didn't say a word, but I could feel Lewis holding up his hand on the other end of the line as if to stop me.

"Now don't give me excuses. I know she's headstrong and thinks she knows everything, but not without reason. She did graduate from FLETC, the FBIs training academy down in Georgia, with flying colors, after all...She has a good heart, she just needs a little guidance. I'm making it your job to guide her. See that she stays out of trouble and learns a thing or two, will you?"

I sighed to myself. "Yes, sir." Jessica Carter was headstrong, arrogant, and didn't listen. Welcome back to work.

# TWO

## *Carter Sparks*

"Carter? I'm Dalton. Frank Dalton. We spoke on the phone last night."

I'd arranged to pick up Carter at a small park and ride at a local coffee shop near downtown. It seemed unnecessary to have her come all the way into the office; she lived on the way to Aransas and the *Reel Lady*.

I held my hand out to her, and we shook.

"Get in, and I'll brief you on the way." I opened the passenger door of the eco-friendly government sedan for her, and she muttered brusque thanks.

Even dressed in civilian clothes Carter had stood out among the handful of commuters. Her body language screamed - I'm a Federal Agent and trying very hard not to look like one. New agents were always easy to spot; Carter was no exception. An oversized jacket covered a polo shirt and came halfway down the backside of her khaki slacks. Most rookies thought a baggy shirt or large jacket would hide their weapon; instead, it drew attention, especially in the mugginess of South Texas. Her jet-black hair was pulled back in a bun so tight it looked like it might hurt and dark sunglasses rounded out the Federal Agent ensemble. She gave me a tight look, lips pursed together as she slid into the seat.

I pulled out of the park-and-ride and onto route 181 and merged onto the Nueces Bay Causeway towards Portland. The squirrels in the eco-box protested when I floored the accelerator. They eventually gave in, and I shot over the bridge without killing us. I took small but perverse pleasure in trying to break the little engine that couldn't.

"So Jessica, I wanted to go over a few things before we get there."

"Such as?" Carter had a sensual voice. It was deeper than expected, husky and sexy, like a singer from a '20s jazz club.

"Well, for starters, like how we're going to run this investigation."

"I'm going to take the lead," she said.

I paused for a moment, considering how best to reply. "That's certainly one option."

"Why would I let you take the lead?" she said, almost snorting. "I outrank you."

Oh boy, it's going to be like that, is it? I clenched my teeth, gripped the steering wheel tighter and counted to ten before I replied.

"Sure, sure you do. Thing is, this is a pretty sensitive case." I glanced at Carter and carried on quickly. "I get where you're coming from, all your training, Academy time and so on. The SAC tells me you did really well down at FLETC."

"But."

"But you need some field experience to go with all that training to round you out. You might have excellent technical abilities and book smarts; you don't yet have the proficiency to go along with it. Listen, I was on leave when I got the call about this. The SAC asked me to help, to give you some guidance."

I knew as soon as I said guidance I'd said the wrong thing. Out of the corner of my eye, I saw her staring blankly at me, her face impassive. I concentrated on driving. Queen palm trees flew passed, ominous clouds dark and pregnant overhead. I turned off the highway at the exit for Aransas Pass; there wasn't another car in sight for miles. I sped up, dust billowing behind me. I couldn't remember the last time it had rained; everything had dried up and turned to dust. When it did rain, it was all gooey sludge until it dried again.

When she finally spoke, her words were monotone. I sensed she was seething underneath. "I can handle a sensitive case, Dalton."

I glanced at her. Whatever look I had on my face must have shown through.

"No, I can. I've done a ton of interviews and interrogations. Mr. Lewis asked *me* to help *you* in this case, not the other way round. He said we needed to work together and my high scores for fieldwork would be invaluable. I think perhaps you mistook what he said. "

"Did I? I know you have high scores, Carter. Like I said, I get it, but this case is a little different. This isn't a classroom where if you fuck up no one gets hurt. This is the real world. We...shit—"

A gray sedan barreled out of a side road, appearing from nowhere. I yanked the steering wheel and swerved, the tires protesting as I stomped on the brake and we skidded to a stop inches before impaling a palm tree. The sedan accelerated away.

"Shit. Did you see that fucking guy? Did you see?" I looked at Carter. "Shit. Are you okay?"

Carter was gasping and rubbing her right shoulder. "I'm fine. Shoulder hurts, is all."

"Shit. Sorry."

"Not your fault. I'll be okay. The seat belt did its job."

"Do you need to go to medical?"

"I said I'll be fine. Let's just go."

I looked around. "Fucking guy's taken off already. Sorry. He came out of nowhere. Did you get a look at him?" I put the car into reverse and maneuvered away from the tree.

"No. I didn't see him."

"Guy came out of nowhere," I said.

"I know. You said that already."

"Okay." I took a deep breath to steady my nerves. I sat there for a second, collecting myself.

"Are we going to sit here all day?"

I ignored her and gently coaxed the squirrels back to life, pulling onto the road.

After a minute or two of silence, my eyes moving from mirror to windshield to mirror I said, "Alright...Where were we?"

"We were at the point where you were trying to tell me why I can't do the job I've been trained to do," she said, still rubbing her shoulder.

"Yes. No. It's not like that. The reason the command wants me to take this is because they're treating the death as suspicious."

"And?"

"And when they ran the captain's associations, it came back with a hit on a fellow called Timmy 'Batman' Black."

"Batman? Really?"

"Really. Not like the superhero, though, more like an anti-hero. Timmy was called Batman because he liked to close his business deals with a baseball bat if they weren't going his way."

"Jesus."

"No, he was never involved. Just Batman," I looked at Carter but didn't get a reaction. I continued. "That's one of the reasons the command called me in. I've dealt with these types of people before. They don't mess around, and they don't like us much either, or any Feds for that matter. I do need your help, though."

"Glad I can do something," Carter said.

I ignored her. "While I'm talking to these guys, I want you to keep your eyes open. I don't think there's any danger, they're not completely stupid, but I want you to read their body language, see if we can isolate who's lying, if anyone, or who's more likely to tell us the truth."

"I didn't think there was anything suspicious about the death. I thought the master of the boat fell overboard. Slipped or something," she said.

"It's the 'or something' we're looking into. You're probably right, this could be routine, and we'll go home tonight and think nothing of it. However, we're mandated to look into every maritime death, and based on the Batman connection we need to look just a tiny bit closer than usual."

She nodded. "You have any history on the crew?"

"No. Nothing popped up. All I know is they reported the captain missing, and it took about six hours to find him. This could all be a tragic accident; we just don't know yet. So, can we work together? Will you follow my lead?"

I glanced at Carter. Her face didn't give away too much. I hoped she saw it my way.

"Yeah. Sure. I'll be your little bitch."

Guess not. "Fuck, Carter. What's your problem? You're just out of school. You don't have any field experience. You've been in the Coast Guard, what, five minutes? I've been in nineteen years. I've been doing this job for the last ten. I'm experienced. I know what I'm doing. Why the attitude? What's eating you?" I didn't give her a chance to respond. "You know what? Don't fucking answer, I don't want to hear it."

I was seething. Fuck. This is all I needed. I knew she was going to be trouble. A rookie agent with a big fuck-off chip on her shoulder about God knows what.

The rest of the journey was in silence.

After driving down a few nondescript side roads for a few miles, the salt air struggling through the vehicle's air conditioning vents, we approached the port town of Aransas. Hulks of derelict fishing vessels dotted the landscape, rusting and sad, remnants from past hurricanes and storms. The occasional liquor and check-cashing store dotted both sides of the street, their garish neon lights enticing the downtrodden, all competing to take your hard-earned wages.

I rolled the windows down, and immediately the incoming slug of humidity battled with the outgoing air. The cooled air lost quickly, and the rotting stench of fish rode in on a horse of heat and assaulted my senses. I quickly rolled the window back up.

I pulled into the parking lot and the shabby, but still serviceable sign, Reel Fish Reel Quick, swung in a light sea breeze. Reel Fish Reel Quick, was the homeport of the *Reel Lady*. They had a fleet of fishing vessels with catchy titles like *A Hook In*

*Time* and *Catchin' Up.* The *Reel Lady* had been heading into port ever since they recovered their captain. Their arrival was supposed to be sometime in the afternoon, and although I hadn't wasted any time in getting here, she had beaten us to the dock and was moored up. Shit.

I got out of the car, the stench of rotten fish wasn't getting any better, and it clung to the air like moss to stone. My feet crunched on bleached, broken shellfish shells that paved their lot. The passenger door slammed, and Carter appeared as I pulled out my go bag from the trunk.

I think I hated her a little bit. I was annoyed I'd been saddled with such a cantankerous know-it-all. She looked frumpy in her oversized coat. I put her out of my mind and took a look around. There were several nice cars, like really nice, unusual for a small fishing company. Mixed in with the usual beat up cars, trucks and circa 1990s Toyotas there was a Range Rover, a Maserati convertible, a sparkling Audi and a shiny new BMW, one of the large ones, complete with temporary tags. Fishing must be good, must be *reel* good. I looked at my eco-friendly government sedan and sighed. I hoped the squirrels were resting up for the return trip.

Carter jerked me out of my reverie with her dulcet tones. "What are we waiting for, Dalton?"

I looked at her and shrugged. Maybe it was time to be the big man on the campus. "Just taking it all in, Carter. Just taking it all in. Look, I don't want to get off on the wrong foot here. Forget what I said in the car, I was just pissed off. It's been a long day already."

I started to walk towards the dock when Carter spoke up. "So, I've been thinking. About what you said."

I stopped and looked at her.

"I was thinking I am going to take the lead in this investigation."

I looked at her blankly. "No. You're not," I said.

Her nostrils flared, and her cheeks flushed. She swallowed and took a deep breath, forcing it down. She looked at me.

"I thought we sorted this out," I said.

"For you, maybe. Hear me out, Dalton. Like I said, I had time to think. You might think I've only been in the Coast Guard for five minutes, but I spent four long, grueling years at the Academy. Think on that. Four long, shitty years of swabbing and running and marching and classes and on and on. What did you do? Eight short weeks of boot camp about a bazillion years ago? I have enough time in to know when I don't know something. I was excited when Mr. Lewis asked me to help. You have no idea what it's like to be a woman in the service. We have to try twice as hard and be twice as good, just to feel like we're on the same level as a man."

"Now hold on, Carter."

"No, you hold on, Dalton. I'm trying to explain. I'm trying to make this work. I'm not a bitch, even though it might seem that way right now. I realize I have a long way to go, but I thought...I was led to believe..." She waved her hands around. "That this was all mine. This was what I thought was the culmination of long years of hard work. The beginning of something. And what do I find? My feet have been shot out from under me, before we even start, by some guy the SAC asked to guide me. Fuck you and fuck him."

This wasn't the time to argue. This was the time to let her vent. Maybe I was seeing the real Carter. I wondered how many others had ever seen this side of her.

Carter started to run her hands through her hair, realizing at the last moment it was in a bun. "And this fucking jacket. I look like a fucking blimp."

"I honestly hadn't noticed."

"Then you're a lousy investigator."

Carter ripped off the jacket and flung it on the ground stamping on it and grinding it into the seashells. Underneath that jacket was a different person. She pulled her hair out of the brutal bun and shook it loose, a small groan of pleasure escaping her lips. Her hair wasn't black like I thought, but a dark shade of auburn, about shoulder length. Gone was the dowdy and tense rookie, and in its place was...a no-nonsense female Federal Agent. Looking every bit the part.

"Dalton. I need this," she said, hesitating.

Now it was my turn to think. Carter had a reputation for being a bitch. Perhaps I'd let that cloud my judgment. Maybe she did have to act like a tough cookie to get ahead. I could certainly appreciate that.

"Perhaps we've both come about this from the wrong direction. I have the field experience, but honestly, I have no idea what you've been taught. It's been years since I went to school. I'm probably a bit rusty on new policy and guidance as well. How about I teach you how to apply what you learned in school to the real world, and you can educate me on new ways of doing things. Maybe we can learn from each other."

Carter didn't look like she actually agreed, then again, she didn't disagree either. Her internal shield was up again, masking her thoughts.

"Okay?" I asked.

"Sure, we can try that."

She walked off, and I followed her.

The steps up to the office were old and gnarly, and like the sign could have used a fresh coat of paint. The door was plain, wooden, blue paint peeling from years of neglect. I stayed my hand from knocking as I could hear snippets of a loud conversation coming from inside.

"I'm sorry, Jimmy," said one voice.

15

"I told you this wasn't the right trip," said another, curt voice.

I might have learned something valuable, but Carter pushed past me, loudly knocking and swinging the door open before I had a chance to stop her.

"Goddammit," I said.

I walked through the door after her. We were inside a huge warehouse with massive bay doors in the far back, flooding light into the building. Through the doors, several fishing vessels were offloading crates, a forklift moving busily back and forth. After my eyes adjusted from the brightness outside I could see that to the right of the door was a soda machine, and this is where two men were standing, staring at us.

"Hey, guys. Where's the boss?" I asked.

One of them ignored me and walked off. The other shrugged and pointed to a large chair perched on the edge of the loading dock, facing the water.

"Thanks."

We walked over to where they had pointed, our shoes thumping on the stained concrete and echoing off the tin walls of the warehouse. As we got closer, I could see the chair was an executive kind of chair, brown leather, massive. I doubt that thing could have fit behind any sort of regular sized desk. A thick plume of smoke was wafting into the rafters emanating from the fattest cigar I think I've ever seen, being held by the fattest fingers, I've ever seen, from the fattest man, I've ever seen. He looked, seriously, as if he'd been poured into this chair, he filled every possible crack and cranny. I couldn't imagine how he used the bathroom. How do you even wipe your ass when you're that large? I mean, come on.

I pulled out my badge and introduced myself. "Sir, my name is Frank Dalton. I'm a Special Agent for the U.S. Coast Guard. This is Special Agent Carter. Do you have a minute?"

The man continued to puff on his cigar, looking us up and down. His beady eyes flickered over me but lingered on Carter a moment longer. I couldn't tell if he thought she was a threat, was dismissing her, or was just checking her out.

Finally, he spoke. "Forgive me for not getting up. I'm not as young as I used to be." It was true he was losing his hair, what was left was gelled straight back. I placed him not a day past sixty. Not so old. He was wearing a yellow jogging suit, like something that would have been comfortable and fashionable in the '70s. The front of the yellow ensemble was covered in ash, and his wrist jingled with gold bracelets when he reached forward to shake my hand. He had a surprisingly firm shake, and his gold rings dug into my hand, squeezing. He held the grip perhaps a moment too long, showing me who was really the boss here.

"Tim. Tim Black. Pleased to meet you, Agents." He nodded at Carter but didn't shake her hand. So this was Batman, huh? Na na na na na na na na na na na na - Batman! echoed inside my head.

"I'm very sorry for the loss of your captain, Mr. Black. I understand the crew did everything they could for him."

"It is what it is." He shrugged, more ash falling on his voluminous stomach. He didn't seem to notice. "Fishing's a dangerous business. People get hurt." He had a staccato way of talking as if the effort to get the air out of his lungs was too much for him.

"Were you on board when it happened, sir?" I said.

Black stared at me for a moment.

"Me?" Black waved at his stomach, as it jiggled in front of him like a large tub of lemon Jell-O. "No. No, I wasn't on board. I don't fish anymore." He flapped his hands at one of the moored vessels at the dock. "You'll want to talk to them. Tell them Mr. Black said it was okay. They'll speak with you. You can use my office if you want. For privacy. Talk to Ricky. He's the first mate."

"Of course. Thank you for your help, sir."

Black continued to puff on his cigar, never moving from his spot as we walked outside to the *Reel Lady*.

On the dock, gulls floated lazily in the afternoon sea breeze, waiting to swoop in and pounce on some scraps. The waterfront was chock full of fishing boats, some moored up three deep waiting to offload their catch. Aransas wasn't known for what you would call the best fishing fleet in the world. Boats were dented and dinged, paint faded and peeling. It wasn't like the marina where I live, all glossy and picture perfect. This was a working port, where real people chose to sail in weather most of us wouldn't go outside in. These were working boats, ran hard and looking like it. Fishermen were a proud bunch, and rightly so, it was a hard life and a hard job, not something they would give up for anything else.

I looked at the *Reel Lady* and suppressed a shiver. It would be super easy to slip over the side of one of these boats, far out to sea. A quiet splash. Coughing and spluttering, trying to catch a breath amid the waves. Head bobbing, barely above water, yelling at the crew, but no one to hear you over the racket of the engines and fishing gear. You can see them, but they're not looking for you. Not knowing you're in the water. Watching your only chance at survival steam away from you, and knowing that you only have a small window. A small chance someone might notice you're gone and raise the alarm. You tread water but know it's only a matter of time. No life jacket. Out of shape. You start to slip under. So tired. So tired.

It would be super easy to slip over the side, late at night, far out to sea. It would be super easy to be pushed too. Late at night, far out to sea.

# THREE

## *Jimmy Was a Racecar Driver*

"What do you think, Carter?"

She glanced at me, shrugged and then stared at the *Reel Lady*. "I don't know. There's not much to think about. We haven't spoken to anyone."

"Good point. Let's go find this Ricky then."

The *Reel Lady* was a hulk of a vessel. She was only eighty-seven feet long but up close looked much larger. Her superstructure was a nice shade of rust, marred only by the original white peeking through, and her hull was a cool blue, long faded by salt and sun. Dents and scrapes were apparent everywhere; she was no showboat. Four men huddled together on the stern, talking quietly and smoking. We made our way over to them, mindful of large crates of shrimp whizzing above our heads, suspended on teensy tiny hooks, held in place by a rusty green crane. The men scattered when we got close, except for a tall, skinny man who was leaning on the deck railing. He took a drag of his cigarette and threw it over the side as he looked at us, challenging.

"Hey, sir. Looking for Ricky. Is that you?" I asked. I had to raise my voice to be heard from the dock, over the whirring and clanking of the crane.

He nodded once. "That's me."

"Ricky, my name is Frank Dalton, this is Jessica Carter, we're investigators with the Coast Guard. Can we come aboard, so we don't have to shout at each other? We just need to ask you a few questions about what happened last night."

Ricky nodded at me, and we climbed aboard using a makeshift gangway made of a couple of two-by-fours and a long stepladder. Not the safest gangway I'd ever used, but it did the job.

"Pleased to meet you," I said. We shook hands. He had a hard grip, hands rough and calloused from work. "Mr. Black said we should talk to you. First, though, let me say, that we're dreadfully sorry about the loss of your captain. I know it must be tough."

Ricky's eyes flittered between us and over our heads, into the warehouse. His eyes veiled as if they were shutters, banging closed on a stormy day.

"Had you known the skipper long?" I said.

Ricky's face remained impassive. "You'll want to talk to Jimmy. He's the one that noticed Willis was missing."

"Sure. That sounds good, who's Jimmy?" I said.

"Deckhand."

"Mr. Black said we could use his office for the interviews. Do you have any problem with that?"

"That's fine. It's back over there," Ricky waved his hands at the warehouse. "I'll send Jimmy over."

"Thanks. Appreciate it," I said.

Ricky nodded, walked to a hatch in the superstructure, and bellowed inside for Jimmy. For such a skinny man his voice was pure baritone when he yelled, like the deep rumbling bass of a tuba.

Once Ricky was out of earshot, Carter said to me, "What the fuck is that smell?"

I breathed deeply and smiled. "That, my dear, is the smell of money. Or rotting fish. Sweat. Saltwater. Low tide. Take your pick. It is pretty awful, isn't it? You never get used to it, though, you just learn to tolerate it."

"I can't wait."

Jimmy slowly shuffled into view through the hatch, mopping his brow with an old dirty rag, sweat dripping down the front of his coveralls, chest heaving.

Ricky jerked his head in our direction and Jimmy looked from Ricky over to us and then back to Ricky. Jimmy mumbled something to Ricky I couldn't catch, and then Ricky shrugged. Jimmy stared for a second and then lumbered over to us.

"Jimmy?" I said.

Jimmy nodded. "S'right."

"I'm Frank, this is Jessica. Mr. Black said we could use his office to talk. Shouldn't take more'n a few minutes." I smiled a quick, tight smile to Jimmy. "Perhaps you could show us the way?"

Jimmy clambered over the side of the *Reel Lady* and motioned for us to follow. He walked straight through the random puddles of fish run off seemingly oblivious to the slop, while Carter and I dodged around them.

He led us to a small cramped office, invisible unless you knew it was there, tucked into the dingy back of the warehouse. Stale cigarette smoke and fish gut stink permeated the air of the room. Jimmy squeezed his bulk behind a small desk that took up over half the space. When he sat down, he unzipped his overalls part way to reveal a sweat and food stained white T-shirt. His large stomach eased itself onto the desk, and he sighed in relief and motioned me to sit, ignoring Carter's stare. I took out my pad to take some notes, while Jimmy took a long drag from a cigarette he had just lit. Carter glared at him and coughed, but he didn't even raise an eyebrow.

"Okay Jimmy," I said, "why don't you lead us through the events that happened yesterday."

Jimmy didn't say anything for a moment, so I prompted him again. "So what happened?"

"Right. Well, I went up to the bridge to see if the captain wanted a mug of tea. He liked tea in the afternoons. He wasn't there. I looked out the bridge windows over the transom, but couldn't see him. I'd just come from the galley, and he wasn't there. I thought he might have gone for a piss."

"Weren't you worried no one was driving the boat?" asked Carter.

Jimmy stared at her for a second before answering. "No, Miss. I wasn't. Not at the time. The boat was on autopilot. It wasn't unusual for the captain to take a breather for a minute or two."

"And what time was this?" I asked, trying to get the conversation back on track.

Jimmy thought for a second before answering. "About four in the afternoon, after that I went back down below to prepare the evening meal."

"And what was for dinner?" Routine questions always helped establish a baseline; no one was going to lie about what they had for dinner. I could gauge Jimmy's body language and compare it later to questions in which he might not be so truthful.

"Dinner was—"

"Never mind dinner," Carter said. "Why didn't you call the Coast Guard for help," she shuffled through some notes, "for another two hours?"

Jimmy stared at Carter like she had two heads. So did I. I broke the tension and tried a different tack. "Jimmy," I said, to get his attention away from Carter and back on me, "what happened after you prepared dinner?"

Jimmy turned back to look at me, taking the last drag on his cigarette and stubbing it out in the overflowing ashtray on the desk. He blew the smoke in Carter's direction.

"I went up to the bridge to see if the Cap wanted any grub."

"And did he?"

"He wasn't there. I looked around. We was still on course, and the autopilot was still on, but it was strange he wasn't up there by now."

"Okay. What happened next?"

"I went back down to the galley and asked the guys if they'd seen him, they were the ones working on deck while I was cooking."

"And what are their names?" I asked.

"Ricky, you just met him, George, and Paul."

"What time was this?"

"About five-thirty. We always had dinner at five-thirty."

"Alright. Had the guys seen the captain?"

"No. They said they thought he was on the bridge. When I told them he wasn't and hadn't been earlier, Ricky, he's the first mate, he tells me and the rest of the crew to search the boat. Ricky goes up to the bridge, and I can feel the engines start to slow down."

Jimmy began to twitch. He was nervous, but I couldn't tell if he was lying, tired, scared, or all three. "Tell me, Jimmy, what's your usual routine on board. You know, before any of this happened. Take me through a typical day."

Jimmy lit another cigarette, the action calming him. After a moment he said, "Normally, I help out on deck. We all do. The Cap'—"

"I can't see the relevance in this," Carter said, looking at me. She turned to face Jimmy, "Tell me what happened when you found the master of the vessel."

"Excuse us, Jimmy, me and Carter need to confer for a minute." I took hold of Carter's elbow and ushered her out of the small office and down a narrow passageway to gain some privacy.

"Get off me, Dalton," she said, taking my hand off her elbow.

"What do you think you're doing?" I hissed at her.

"Dalton, you're not asking the right questions," she whispered back, holding up her hand. "We need to know what happened to the captain. Who gives a rat's ass what his usual day is like?"

"Finished?" I said.

She nodded.

"First, we are not interrogating the man, we're interviewing him. Second, he's not guilty of anything yet, we're just trying to find out what the hell happened, and every time you jump down his throat, it takes us two steps back. These men have just been through a tough ordeal. Maybe they did top the captain, but we'll never find out unless we build a rapport. We need to use a kid glove approach. Understand?" Carter didn't say anything and walked back to the office.

"Sorry about that Jimmy," I said, entering the room behind Carter, but stopped when I saw a woman squeezed in next to Jimmy behind his desk. I couldn't tell you if I'd stopped talking because I was more impressed with her looks, or the fact she'd managed to squeeze in next to Jimmy. She had intense blue eyes, piercing, even through the haze of smoke, topped by a shock of golden hair. A cute button nose perched above an upturned mouth, as if she was always one step away from having heard the world's best joke.

"I'm Dalton, this is Carter," I said, reaching over the desk and offering my hand.

"Mr. Dalton, Miss Carter," she said, shaking my hand, "my name is Jamie Lancaster from Lancaster, Lancaster, and Mitchell. I'm representing the crew, and I'd appreciate it if you wouldn't ask them any more questions without me or representation from my firm present." She handed both of us a card and shook Carter's hand, "And I would like a word with all the crew first before we continue."

"Of course," Carter said.

"No," I said. All three of them looked at me. "I don't mean to be a pain, Miss," I glanced at the card, "Lancaster. I don't mind you being present when we interview the crew, but I can't let you talk to them alone. Not until we're done."

"May I remind you, Mr. Dalton, that I represent the crew, and as their legal—"

"Sorry," I said, glancing at Jimmy. "Can I talk to you outside for a moment, Miss Lancaster?" I didn't wait to see how she squeezed back around the desk, I didn't need the distraction. I marched back up to the cozy spot where I'd just talked to Carter. Carter trailed behind.

As soon as she reached me, I said quietly, "Miss Lancaster, let me be very clear. The Coast Guard is here to try and find out what happened. As such, we control the investigation, who we talk to and when. You're more than welcome to be involved in the interviews with the crew, but you can't represent them all, as that's a conflict of interest."

"Mr. Dalton, this is highly irregular." She looked at Carter for confirmation I was off my rocker.

"No, it's not," I said. "This is standard practice for an administrative investigation. This isn't a criminal investigation; no one has been arrested or charged with anything, so they don't need counsel. If you want to go ask someone, be my guest, but I'm not hanging around while you call. These people have been through enough, without this lasting all day." I looked Lancaster in the eyes. She huffed and went back to the office, and I was right on her heels until Carter pinched me by the elbow, holding me back.

"Can I have a word?" she said.

I was going to ignore her, but something stopped me, maybe it was the look on her face.

Carter inhaled and held her breath for a second before starting. "I know you're not my friend."

I snorted.

"But I want to try and make this." She waved her hand between us, "I want to make this work, this partnership. I want you to explain to me why the lawyer can't be in the room." She looked at me plaintively.

"Okay." I resisted the impulse to check the time on my watch. "It's simple. As far as we know the crew hasn't done anything wrong. But we have a dead body. We have to figure out how it happened, and our best way of doing that is to try and put the crew at ease and ask simple questions. It's not a criminal investigation at this point, just civil, so it's not like you see on TV." I ran my hands through my hair. "Listen. We have to get back in. If you follow my lead and don't interrupt, I'll coach you through it later."

"Alright. I'll try," she said. "I really do want this to work. And I really do want to learn."

I looked her in the eye and thought she was sincere. "Okay. Let's go in."

"Jimmy," I said, as we entered. I needed to shake things up a bit, "I'd like to get back on board the *Reel Lady*, get a feel for the layout, take some photos."

Jimmy looked at Lancaster. She shrugged.

"Sure," he said.

Standing on the stern of the vessel, looking up at the bridge, it was hard to imagine that just yesterday waves were spraying the windows, and all hell was breaking loose. The crew holding on to avoid slipping, searching the waves, massive spotlights beaming through the night. I shook my head and came back to the present.

The crew were smoking again and huddled together talking quietly and watching me. I walked over to them with my entourage in tow.

"Jimmy. Can you walk us through where everyone was?"

"I can do that," Ricky said, his deep baritone cutting through the quiet gossip of the crew.

"Thanks, Ricky. Okay. Why don't we start with where everyone was last night?"

"Yeah. Sure. I don't see why it's important, though. Cap' Willis just slipped over the side while he was cleaning some fish."

"How's that?"

"The overboard flap gets stuck, up there on the side of the bridge. See it?" Ricky pointed to a piece of plastic secured to the side of the bridge, about ten feet up.

"He used to clean fish while we was on a run, in that sink up there. The guts and what have you are supposed to fall over the side out a flap. Sometimes it gets stuck. He was probably reaching round when he slipped." Ricky pointed at a section of open deck near the bridge that was secured with a single line, right next to the sink. "Sometimes the crew take a piss right there. Easier than going down below. One time I slipped, and nearly went right in. There's nothing to stop you. I reckon I was lucky that night. Luckier than the Cap' anyway." The rest of the crew mumbled in agreement.

"So that's what you think happened?" Carter asked.

"Yeah. Seems as likely as anything else."

"What was the weather like Ricky?" I made a note to check the NOAA weather report when we got back.

"Wasn't too bad."

One of the crew snorted. We all looked at him at the same time. "That's Paul. Pay him no mind. He's new. Only been on the two trips. Ain't that right, Paul?" Ricky said.

Paul looked down as he spoke. "Yeah. I s'pose. Seemed rough to me, though. I was hanging on for life when I called the Coast Guard."

"That was you, Paul? Called the Coast Guard?" I said.

He looked up, saw everyone still staring, nodded, and looked down again. "Yeah. That was me."

I filed that away.

"So, Ricky. Humor me. I have a ton of paperwork to do, you know? I have to have exact times for whatever went on. Keeps the old man off my back. So why don't we start with where you were and what you were doing, before any of this all happened."

"Yeah, sure. Not much to see. We were trawling." Ricky pointed to the outriggers, now secured upright. "The outriggers were down, nets were out. Looking for shrimp."

"Who was with you?" I said.

"It was me, George, and Jimmy. Then Jimmy went inside to make supper. Paul was sleeping."

"What time was this?"

Ricky scratched his stubble, "Maybe around five. We usually have supper sometime 'fore six."

"And the captain was on the bridge?" I asked.

Lancaster, silent up to this point said, "You don't have to answer that Ricky. You couldn't possibly know where the captain was."

"Sure," he said, ignoring her. "The cap' was on the bridge. While we work the nets, he drives the boat. Same way we've always done it. No reason to think he was anywhere else."

Lancaster walked away, pulling out a phone, no doubt to call her higher-ups. "Ricky, which way is the galley?"

"Forward, through the hatch. You want to see it?"

"Yes, please."

Ricky walked the thirty feet or so of the deck from where we were on the stern to the galley door, knocking the dogs loose with his right hand so we could go through. The door was really a watertight hatch, so it was dogged down to keep it shut tight. I stepped over the lip of the door and followed Ricky into a short passageway that ran into the galley, my shoes sticking to the floor as we neared. The galley spoke of rough days at sea. There was a brown, crusty stain running down the side of the stove, the fridge had countless dirty fingerprints around the handle, and a dent in the door that looked like it was usually kicked closed. The sink was stainless once upon a time, but that time had long since passed, and a few dirty dishes lay piled up inside. The whole place stank of rancid grease; the air was thick with it, and every time I swallowed, lumps went down my throat. A small table secured to the floor in the opposite corner with bench seats finished off the kitchen.

I looked back at Jimmy, his bulk squeezed into the narrow passageway. There was no way Jimmy was getting past Carter, so I turned and spoke to him over her head, "Jimmy, you said you were cooking dinner?"

"'S'right."

"And then you went to see if the captain wanted tea?"

"Yeah."

"Which way did you get to the bridge?"

"I went—"

"He went up the ladder here, through the other side of the galley," Ricky said, cutting off Jimmy.

I turned to Jimmy, "Is that right?"

Jimmy glanced at Ricky before he answered. "Yeah. Yeah, it is."

The ladder looked narrow, "Alright, let's go up."

Ricky went up, followed by me, Carter, and then Jimmy. The others had stayed out on deck. If they'd ever had a meal in the galley, they probably didn't want to spend any more time in there.

It was crowded on the small bridge, and I eased myself over to the wheel so I could look at the instruments. "Ricky, can you turn on the GPS for me, and power up the rest of your electronics?"

"Sure. It'll take a moment to come up," Ricky said, flipping breakers and pushing buttons.

25

I looked out the bridge windows. The dry salt spray made the windows hazy, but I could still see all around. It would have been easy for the captain to see the crew working on the stern deck. Come to think of it, it would have been easy for the crew to see the captain too. I took a couple of steps to the rear hatch.

"Ricky, is this the cleaning station you were talking about?" I gestured to a dirty sink, partially covered by an old block of wood, streaked in fish guts, with a short, blunt looking knife attached to the sink by a string.

"Yeah. That's right. The flaps behind the sink get stuck sometimes," Ricky said moving to the sink and pushing on the rubber flaps. "When you're cleaning fish, or shucking scallops, the guts an' shells an' what have you are s'posed to go over the side, like this, but sometimes they get caught. The only way to fix it is to reach around and yank the flaps."

"Show me."

Ricky reached around the open side of the bulkhead with his right hand, hanging on with his left, caught hold of the flaps and gave them a quick tug. As if to prove his point a couple of loose scallop shells fell into the water below.

"That's quite a ways to reach round, Ricky. You guys do that underway?"

"Yeah. It's the only way to loosen the flaps, like I said. Captain coulda been reaching round and slipped."

"You're a shrimper, right? A trawler?"

"S'right."

"So how do you get scallops up in the nets? Aren't they stuck down in the mud?"

"Get all sorts of things in them nets. Shrimp, fish, scallops. Catches stuff we sort out, throw back. Sometimes the Cap' would keep some bits and pieces for dinner."

The GPS beeped, and I looked back to see the electronics powered up.

"You've got some really sweet navigation gear here, Ricky. A lot more'n most fishing boats I've been on."

"We go a lotta different places. Need to know where we are. Where we're going. Got to get home too."

"No doubt. Alright, can you pull up your track line on the electronic chart for me?"

"Yeah. But Paul's more of the electronics guy. Hold on, and I'll get him." Ricky walked back out to the cleaning station and shouted in that booming base again, "Paul, can you help out Mr. Dalton? I've got to use the head."

Paul looked up at the bridge from the deck and shuffled over, climbing the outside ladder. He'd been talking to the lawyer.

"Hey, Paul."

"Agent." Paul nodded at me but didn't offer to shake hands.

"Paul, Ricky tells me you're the electronics guy; can you bring up your track line on your electronic chart for me, please?"

Paul shrugged, leaned over the console and pressed a few buttons. A few moments later I was looking at a line on an electronic chart that showed me where the boat had been. I pointed to an area that looked like a toddler had scribbled in crayon. "Is that where you started the search?"

Paul shrugged again, "Guess so," he said. I took a couple of close-up shots of the screen with my camera. It would be useful to compare it to the track line the intel guys would get for me.

"Do you have an AIS system on board?" I asked.

Paul gave me a blank look.

"You know," I said, "it records where you've been, and sends out beeps so other vessels can tell who you are on their radars. Like on an airplane?"

"I don't know about that, sir. This is only my second trip, and I'm just getting used to all what everything is."

"That's alright." I slipped my bag off my shoulder and pulled out a small thumb drive. "I'm just going to slot this into the laptop here, and download your—"

"You can't do that."

I turned and looked at the lawyer. She had climbed up the outside ladder and was glaring at me.

"Actually I can, Miss Lancaster. Like I said before, this is just a fact finding mission, I can take any evidence off this boat that's pertinent." I turned back around and slid the thumb drive into the back of the laptop.

"My boss, Mr. Lancaster Senior told me you cannot take any evidence off of this vessel."

I didn't turn around and spoke to her over my shoulder while I tapped at the keyboard. "Well then. He's wrong as well. Listen. I don't mean to be a pain in the ass, but you guys really need to brush up on your Admiralty Law. I'm not the lawyer here, but I seem to know more than you do. If you keep getting in my way and impeding my investigation, I will have Agent Carter here escort you off the vessel."

Lancaster tried to retreat gracefully down the ladder, but it's hard in heels and on the phone at the same time. She almost made it, but messed up the last step and did a little dancing, bobbing movement trying to regain her balance. Actually, it didn't look that bad really.

The data finished downloading, and I popped the thumb drive out and slipped it back into my bag. I took a few more photos of the bridge layout and the view from the bridge windows; you never know what might be relevant later.

"Alright, Paul. So you called the Coast Guard last night right?"

Paul nodded.

"Did you call from in here?"

"Yeah. I was scared. I thought we were going to sink, it was so rough, the waves were pounding, and we'd just lost the captain."

"So you were sleeping when he disappeared?"

"Yeah. I'd just worked the last shift and was getting some shuteye. Or trying to. It was so rough I wasn't resting well."

"Did you hear anything? Anything strange go on before you hit the rack?"

"No. Not really."

I looked at him. "Not really, or no?"

"No. Nothing happened."

"Okay." I rubbed at my face. "Carter, do you have anything?"

She looked at me for a second, trying to gauge if I was testing her. "Yes. I do. Paul, what was the captain like? Did you get along with him?"

"He was all right I guess. Didn't talk to him too much, you know. This was my second trip, and everyone told me to just stay out of his way." Paul said.

"Why'd they want you to stay out of the way?" I asked.

"I dunno," Paul said. "I think they just wanted me to keep clear as I was the new guy."

"Well, apart from that, how was the captain? Did the other crew get on okay?"

"I—"

"You shouldn't be talkin' 'bout stuff you don't know, Paul," Ricky said, walking back up the ladder from the galley. Ricky looked at me. "You done with him?"

"Yeah, I think so, thanks. He was a great help."

"Is that it then?" Ricky said, "I've got things to do, so's the crew."

"Almost. Give me a minute here with Carter, and I'll catch up with you out on deck."

"Sure."

When Ricky and his pals had shuffled out, I scanned the bridge once more. I wasn't sure what I was looking for, nothing looked out of place, I just had a feeling something wasn't quite right. Like when you're walking down a dark alley and the hairs on the back of your head rise up and scream at you that there's a crazy person running up behind you with a big ass knife, but then you turn around, and it's just a cat. That feeling. There was just something not quite right. Something fishy, *Reel Fishy*, I punned to myself.

"Carter. What do you think?"

"I don't know. Ricky doesn't seem to want the crew to talk for themselves."

"Yeah, I saw that. I'm not sure if he's trying to keep secrets or if he's just controlling. I don't think there's a lot more we can get here now; we can always come back later. Why don't we have a quick look in the engine room, and the other spaces, snap a few more photos and call it good? We should probably check in with the Medical Examiner as well, to see if she has anything yet."

"Yeah, okay."

We walked down through the galley and found the captain's cabin. There wasn't anything that immediately stuck out, but we gave it a quick once over, just to see.

"Oh, look at this," I said. I pulled out a new looking iPhone 6 from underneath the single mattress. Ricky was hovering in the doorway watching us.

I waved the phone at him. "Seen this phone before, Ricky?"

"No."

"Well, since it was stuffed under the mattress, it must have been the captains. Carter, can you sort out an evidence receipt for me?"

"Sure." she said.

"I strongly object to you taking any potential evidence from this vessel," Lancaster said.

"Oh hello, Miss. Lancaster. I thought you'd left already." I smiled at her.

She didn't smile back; the cute, almost joking curve of her mouth I'd noticed when we first met was turned into a face I bet her Mama wouldn't have approved of.

"No. I'm still here. Listen, it's one thing taking some computer track lines or whatever, but taking a phone, essentially a mini computer that could have company proprietary information on it, is another. I cannot allow you to leave the vessel with that phone." She stood as if to block me, even Ricky got out the way.

"Miss. Lancaster. Once again, we are conducting an investigation into the circumstances of the death of Mr. Willis, the captain. We have the authority to use anything that may help us to discover those circumstances—"

"But he simply fell overboard, how much information—"

"As I was saying. The Coast Guard investigates every death on board of all commercial vessels. There is no evidence as of right now that anything other than the obvious happened, but that does not preclude us from pursuing our investigation. If you want, I would be happy to talk this over with you at the office, and show you the applicable regulations and so on. Perhaps tomorrow?" I smiled at her. I think she could tell I wasn't sincere.

I took the receipt that Carter had filled out and gave her a copy.

"After the investigation is finished you can have this item returned, along with any other evidence we seize," I said. "Now if you'll excuse us. Ricky? You still here?"

I poked my head out into the corridor. I could see Ricky just slip around a bulkhead, and decided to follow him. Carter was right on my heels. I thought he'd headed down the ladder into the engine room, but when I looked down the steps it was dark. I fished my flashlight out of a pocket, flicked it on and climbed down, shining the light around the engine room.

"Ricky? You in here?" I didn't hear anything, but when I shone the light into the far corner, I saw something move and heard Carter's sharp intake of breath.

I moved the flashlight back to where I thought I saw movement. "Hey. Who's in here? U.S. Coast Guard, come out into the light," I said.

A wraith appeared in the circle of my light and stood motionless. I almost backed up a step but stopped myself as I realized it wasn't a wraith but a man. A man so pale he could have passed for dead, his eyes deeply sunken and black, a long beak-like nose.

# FOUR

## *George and the Mechanics*

"Who are you?" I said.

"George," he said, in a rasping whisper.

"George. Why don't you come on out where I can see you? Keep your hands in view buddy, don't reach for anything and no sudden movements."

"Okay," George said, and he made his way silently over to where we were.

"What were you doing back there in the dark, George?" I said.

"Maintenance. On the engine. Lights went out. Was just looking for the switch when you came down."

"Alright, George. Let's go up top where we can talk," I said as he reached us. "After you."

We sat at the small table in the galley. George was one side and Carter and I the other. It was cramped, and my leg was touching Carter's.

"George, what do you do here on the boat?" I said.

"I'm the mechanic and deckhand. Mostly deckhand," George said.

"What were you doing when the captain went missing?"

"I was working the nets on the back. With Jimmy and Ricky."

"When was the last time you saw the captain?"

I couldn't tell if George was thinking or not, as his expression never changed. He didn't seem to blink either. Maybe he was a wraith after all?

"I don't recall. I don't really keep track of what the captain's movements are...were...above my job description."

"Right," I said. I looked at Carter, hoping she'd pick up the lead.

"How well did you get on with him?" Carter said.

George shrugged. An almost infinitesimal movement of his shoulders. At least I think it was a shrug.

"Never had any complaints."

"What do you think happened to the captain?" I asked.

Another small shoulder movement. "Don't know. Not my place to guess. Maybe he slipped."

"And maybe he didn't?" I asked.

George didn't say anything. He didn't move. He didn't blink.

"You done?" Ricky said, entering the galley. Ricky had broken the moment, and I wasn't going to get anything useful out of George. I wondered if he had been waiting, just out of sight. I looked at Carter, and she nodded.

"Yeah. I think so," I said. "Ricky, George. Is there anything else you believe that we might need to know, that we may not have asked you guys?"

George did his almost shrug, Ricky shook his head.

"Well, thanks for your time, gents. Once again, I'm sorry for the loss of your captain. We'll be in touch if we need anything else." I shook hands with both of them. "Oh. One last thing. When do you guys plan on going fishing again?"

"Don't know," Ricky said. "You'll have to check with Mr. Black. He runs the shop."

"Alright, I will. Thanks again."

We left the *Reel Lady*. Mr. Black grunted at us as we passed his warehouse seat that they'd be fishing again in two days. I filed that away. We slung our bags in the trunk, and I slid behind the wheel, starting the car to cool it down but not driving anywhere. I was trying to figure out what to say to Carter. In the end, I decided just to get on with it.

"Let's talk," I said. "I know we got off to a rough start this morning, but I appreciate your help. Once you got your rhythm, you were asking some good questions. On that note, do you have any questions for me, about what we did, or what went on?"

Carter turned in her seat to look at me and was silent for a moment. I gave her time.

"There was one thing I didn't understand. Why were you so interested in what they had to eat and what their routine was? I thought we were investigating a death."

"We are, and we were. That's a good question, though. Broadly speaking, when we interview someone we're trying to build a rapport, trying to make them feel comfortable. They're much more likely to open up if they think we're on the level with them or have something in common. It's also useful to gauge their body language on easy questions, then or if, they're not telling the truth we have something to compare. It's not foolproof, but it's a useful skill to develop." I took a swig of lukewarm coffee I'd left in the car. "There are some classes you can take, if you'd like, to help with interviewing, that you wouldn't have got at the Academy."

"Thanks." Carter looked at her feet, making a decision. "Listen, Dalton. I know I wasn't helpful in the beginning, I just, I just like to know what's going on. I thought I was going to be in charge, and then you tell me you're here to babysit. It just...it just pissed me off. I'm really not like this. I worked so hard at the academy, and then when Mr. Lewis called me I was so excited, I guess I let it get to my head a little, so when you said you were running the show, I just flipped my lid. I'm sorry. You've been nothing but helpful."

I studied Carter for a second. It takes a lot of guts to admit when you're wrong. I admired the hell out of that.

"Apology accepted. I believe you. And thank you for clearing the air. I think we can make this partnership work. I wasn't joking when I said you could teach me some new things, and if you work with me, I promise to always keep you up to speed when I can. Deal?"

We shook hands. "Deal."

I looked out the window. "I don't see much going on here. Let's head over to the ME's office and see what Doc Hutchins has come up with."

I turned on the radio, and the lonely wail of a techno '80s band I couldn't recall, warbled from the standard G-ride speakers. After a minute Carter leaned over and turned it off.

"You're showing your age," she said and buried her nose in her phone. I wasn't sure about that but said nothing. I didn't feel old. Did Carter have a sense of humor?

The Medical Examiner's Office of Corpus Christi was nothing like you'd imagine from watching movies. It wasn't dank and dark and depressing, nor was it all glass, gleaming polished stainless steel and swish sound effects like a CSI episode. Instead, it was an unassuming brick building, pleasantly painted and landscaped, set back from the local police station. From the 5th floor, you could see the Corpus Christi Bay on one side and downtown from the other. The Shining City by the Sea. We, however, stayed on the main floor. I guess it was easier to wheel the dead bodies in if you keep it all on one level.

Doctor Kelly Hutchins was an odd bird for a Medical Examiner. She was a whirling dervish of bustling activity, wrapped up in a diminutive package, and despite the frenzy, her compassion belied her size. I'd seen her move from defending the cause of death on the witness stand as an expert witness in front of high-powered attorneys to hugging relatives that had come in to identify their lost ones. In a word, she was the consummate professional, well, in two words. I'd known her for years, and she'd been the ME well before I'd ever come along.

"Hey Doc, how are ya?" I said.

"Frank! Goodness, I haven't seen you in ages. I'm doing great. How've you been love?" She hugged me, and I was simultaneously wrapped in her arms and enveloped in the lingering smell of disinfectant coming from her lab coat.

"Can't complain. Doc, this is Jessica Carter, my new partner. Carter, this here's the best ME in all of Corpus."

Hutchins snorted. "Pleased to meet you, Jessica. Pay no mind to Frank here. I'm the only ME in Corpus, and Frank's getting old."

"I told him that in the car," Carter said.

"Did you now," Hutchins said, raising an eyebrow. "And what did Frank say?"

"He didn't say anything. I think he's probably going deaf too."

"Oh," Hutchins said, clapping her hands together, "I believe that we'll get along splendidly, Jessica."

I rolled my eyes. "Ladies. Can we get down to business?"

"Party pooper," Hutchins said, "Oh, okay. So I'm assuming you want to talk about the dead fisherman?"

"You assume correctly. What can you tell us?"

"Follow me."

We walked over to the shiny steel refrigerated racks, and Hutchins consulting a clipboard found the right numbered drawer and pulled it open, a sheet-shaped body sliding out. The faint odor of decay came with it. It wasn't as bad as people make out, but it wasn't something I'd want to breathe in all day. Mind, I hadn't been there for the actual autopsy. That could get pretty whiffy.

"Captain Frederick Lucius Willis, age 49, found in the Gulf of Mexico by the crew of the *Reel Lady*," Hutchins said.

"Yeah. That's right. The crew said he must have slipped over the side."

"Did they? I suppose he must have got in the water somehow, but I don't think he slipped, that's your job to figure out, though. Here, let me show you."

Hutchins pulled back the sheet, exposing Willis and the familiar Y incision, the hallmark of every medical examiner's investigation.

"His organs appeared normal, except for his liver, which was enlarged, indicative of someone who's lived a life hard from the bottle. Add to that, his skin was yellowing, which makes me believe he was in the first stage of liver failure." She raised his right arm and pointed to the left. "He was also an intravenous drug user, the track lines are prominent on both arms."

"What did the tox report say?" I asked.

"Patience, young man. I'm getting to that," Hutchins said. She rapped my knuckles with her clipboard as I tried to read it upside down.

"His blood pathology report suggested that he'd recently injected opiates into his system."

"So he was high and fell overboard," Carter said.

"Well. I don't think so."

"What do you mean?" I asked.

"The amount of opiates in his system would leave me to believe that he was still functioning, all be it at a diminished capacity, and although his lungs did show some water intrusion, I can tell you he wasn't breathing when he fell in the water."

"So if he was high as a kite, he'd still be breathing and would have drowned had he fell in the water, which would have shown up in his lungs?" I said.

"Exactly. You know, the offer to be my assistant still stands."

"Another day, Doc."

Hutchins looked at her clipboard again. "My report suggests he was in the water, but he didn't drown."

"What are you saying? That he was dead when he entered the water?" Carter said.

"Yes."

"So what was the cause of death then?"

"Asphyxiation."

"He was strangled?"

"Not exactly. Look here, at his neck. There are no ligature marks or post-mortem bruising, so he wasn't strangled." Hutchins pulled out a small penlight from her top pocket and pried apart one of Willis's eyelids. "But if you look at his eyes, see the marks?"

I leaned in closer and pulled on my reading glasses.

"Old." Hutchins and Carter said together.

I ignored them, trying to see what the Doc was pointing out.

"Deaf." They both said in unison.

I ignored them again. "What am I looking at?"

"Those little red marks are petechiae, basically broken blood vessels that show up during suffocation," Hutchins said.

I leaned back and took off my glasses. "Let me get this right. He was high but didn't OD. He was in the water but didn't drown, but he was asphyxiated or suffocated somehow. Thanks for the puzzle. Anything else?"

"Yes," Hutchins said. "And perhaps this is the most interesting. It's hard to tell, but I don't think he died on board the vessel."

"Why not?"

"Time of death. It's a bit more exact than stuffing a thermometer into him like you're cooking a ham, so I extracted part of his tissue and ran an analysis through the mass spectrometer and gas chromatograph. The results lead me to believe he was frozen for a number of days."

The silence stretched out for a moment while I absorbed this little nugget. "Shit. He was killed on land and dumped," I said.

"It certainly looks that way," Hutchins said.

I blew out a breath and rubbed my face. "Okay, Doc. Any other little tidbits?"

"No, I think that's about it." Hutchins snapped her nitrile gloves off and shook hands with Carter. "It was a pleasure to meet you, dear. I hope you'll drop by again?"

"I'd like that," Carter said, nodding her head. "Just on better circumstances."

"Oh. Of course. Sometimes I forget as I'm in here all the time. Frank, Nice to see you again too, dear. Don't be a stranger."

"I won't Doc, I won't," I said.

"And be kind to Jessica, teach her the right way. Not the way you had to learn."

I looked at her, then Carter. "Sure Doc, sure."

We made our way out into the sunshine, and I took a moment to lean into a conveniently placed palm tree and breathed the fresh sea air. Although it was humid, it made a pleasant change from sucking in the artificial air inside the morgue. I had the utmost respect for Kelly Hutchins. I didn't know how she did it, day after day, looking at death and destruction.

"What did she mean in there, when she said to teach me the right way?" Carter said.

The back of my neck itched. Sometimes I wish I still smoked. "Well, you don't want to be taught the wrong way, do you? Come on, Carter. Looks like we have a bad guy to catch."

We jumped in the car and drove back to the office, parking the Econo box in the underground parking lot.

I was just grabbing a cup of coffee that looked suspiciously like the coffee I had made last night when my boss walked in, Assistant Special Agent in Charge Tobias Smith. That was a super mouthful, so I either referred to him as the ASAC or by name.

"Frank. Long day. Talk to you guys when you get a chance?" Smith said.

"Yeah, Toby. I'll grab Carter and catch up with you in the conference room in a minute if that's okay?"

"Sure thing. No rush."

I wound through the cubicles and found Carter making googly eyes at a puppy someone had brought in.

"Cute dog," I said, "Carter, the ASAC wants to see us. Can you grab the case folder off my desk, and I'll meet you in the conference room?"

I beat Smith to the meeting and sat down in an ergonomically challenged chair that someone had probably ordered for hundreds of dollars more than it was worth, and a moment later Carter came in pulling up the next most uncomfortable chair and sat next to me. She handed me the folder, and Smith walked in.

"So what have you got for me?" Smith asked.

"Well, at first splash it seemed like the captain of the *Reel Lady* fell overboard. The crew recovered him a few hours later, deceased. We interviewed the crew and Mr. Black—"

"What did Batman have to do with it?" Smith said.

"Oh, you know him too?" Carter asked.

"I think the whole Coast Guard in South Texas knows about Mr. Black," Smith said. "He's famous, or at least infamous, should I say? Frank, did you bring Carter up to speed on why we call him Batman?"

"I did. He was well behaved today, though. But here's the thing. We interviewed the crew, your usual selection of half deadbeat fisherman, but nothing super unusual. That was until we went to see the ME."

Smith smiled. "How is the good Doc? Been a while since I saw her."

"She's good. Feisty as ever. She says Willis didn't drown, though. She thinks he was frozen and died sometime well before he was found. So we're looking at murder one. The crew's looking good for dumping him at the least, but we've got to figure out where he was iced, so to speak, before we can arrest them."

Carter and Smith both groaned. "Is he always so punny?" Carter asked.

"Always, that's why I keep him around. Has nothing to do with his investigative skills," Smith said. "Okay. Nice work you two. Keep me up to date. I'll brief the SAC and let him know what's going on, he may need some more details so that he can brief the Director, but we can handle that later. If you need anything, you know where you can find me. Needless to say, this is your top priority."

We drove back to the *Reel Lady*. Batman's chair was where we had last seen it, but no Batman. I guess after they had finished off-loading the vessel he didn't need to sit there and watch anymore. The vessel looked deserted when we climbed aboard, although I wasn't announcing our presence. I had a feeling someone was watching, though.

"Where is everyone?" Carter said.

"They'll be out as soon as I do this," I said. I reached for the hatch to the fish hold, the most likely place I thought they could have stowed a frozen Captain Willis.

"Need help?" Ricky's baritone rumbled from his skinny body. If I looked closely, I thought perhaps I could see his ribs vibrate as the words came out.

I winked at Carter.

"Yeah. Ricky, I need you to open the hatch to the fish hold for me."

Ricky hesitated and then bellowed for Paul to come out. "Bring the T-bar with you when you come out." There was a muffled acknowledgment from inside, and a moment later Paul came out with said T-bar.

"We don't use the fish hold much," Ricky said. "What are you hoping to find?"

"I'm not hoping to find anything," I said, "but we didn't look in here when we came aboard this morning, and I just remembered I can't complete my paperwork until we have a quick look in all the spaces."

"You'll be wanting to look in the laz and bow locker then too, I suppose?"

"Yeah. That sounds good. Thanks for offering."

Ricky grumbled something, but I let it go. Paul popped the hatch open, and after it had aired out for a minute, I let Ricky go down first. If the air was foul, I didn't want to be the first down there.

"All good, Ricky?" I said. I heard a rumble of thunder from below that I took to be his affirmative and climbed down into the hold. I had my four-gas meter attached to my foot, so if there was anything nasty down there my foot would beep and vibrate. My foot stayed silent, so I figured I was okay. That and Ricky was still standing.

The fish hold was a space about twelve feet by twenty and down about ten, and followed the contours of the hull. I saw an old rusting anchor and a few coils of line hanging from wooden hooks; various boxes were strewn around, spare parts for the engine most likely.

"You don't keep fish down here when you're underway?" I asked Ricky. I could see Carter's flashlight bouncing around as she came down the ladder, blocking the light from the overhead hatch.

"No. Use it as a storeroom mostly." Ricky waved his hands around. "Engine parts, damage control stuff."

The floor was damp, and it smelled of mold and mildew. When the hatch was closed it didn't look like there was any ventilation. Carter cleared the ladder but slipped as she made her way over to me.

"Easy," I said, as I caught her from slamming her ass on the steel floor. "Okay?"

She gave me a brief smile. "Yeah, thanks. Slippery."

I shined my light around looking for any evidence that Willis had been stashed in here, but there was nothing to see. It looked just like a dank storeroom. I could have called our CSI guys, but they had to come down from Houston, and there was so much crap in here it would take months and months to sift through this. I knew we couldn't hold the *Reel Lady* that long unless we came up with something a bit more conclusive.

There was a hatch leading from the stern bulkhead of the fish hold into the lazarette, and I got Ricky to undog it for me. I poked my head inside and shined my light around. Apart from the steering ram and rudderpost, there wasn't enough space in there to hide anything.

We made our way back up the ladder and then forward to the bow locker, but there was nothing there but some old anchor line and more spare parts.

"Ricky, can you do me a favor? I need to talk to all the crew; can we meet up in the galley? Shouldn't take more'n a few minutes."

"Sure. Jimmy's not here, though, he's on a parts run," Ricky said.

We met in the grease stricken galley, and I looked at Paul, Baritone Ricky, and Wraith George. Paul was the only one staring at me.

"So, there are a few inconsistencies in your captain's death, and I just wanted to see if any of you had any ideas why?"

I nodded to Carter on a prearranged signal, and she slid out some documents from a folder. They didn't have anything important written on them, I just wanted to see if we could shake something loose.

"It says here you reported the captain missing at 2130 and then you found him," Carter shuffled the papers in her hand, "at 0020. Is that right?"

Nods from around the table. "If you say so. I wasn't watching the clock. Too busy, you know?" Ricky said. Wraith George didn't move. Perhaps he was asleep with his eyes open. Couldn't tell.

Carter continued. "When you recovered him from the water, you reported he was already deceased, and that he must have slipped, perhaps when he was cleaning fish, although no one saw him. Still right?"

More nods. I didn't want to tip my hand that we knew he was previously frozen, but something had to shake loose.

"Paul," I said. "When was the last time you remember seeing the captain?"

"Well I—"

"Paul didn't see much of the captain. Paul was busy out on deck most of the time, or sleeping." Ricky said.

"Thanks, Ricky. I was talking to Paul, though. Is that right Paul? Surely you saw the captain driving the boat, or for meals?"

"I—" Paul said.

"Already told you that—" Ricky said.

"Carter. Could you escort Ricky and George here outside for a moment please?"

"Sure. Come on you two," Carter said.

Ricky glared at Paul on the way out, and Paul looked down. There was definitely something going on here.

I sat down across from Paul. "So when did you see the captain last, Paul?"

Paul rubbed his face. "Well. It's like Ricky says, I was working a lot on this trip. And sleeping."

"So you didn't see him for meals?"

Paul thought about my question. When the answer came to him, I could see it surprised him. "Actually no. George said he wasn't feeling well, and Jimmy took all his meals to the bridge or to his cabin."

"Well, what about when you were working on the back deck. Surely you could see him on the bridge? Or when he was cleaning fish?"

"Sure. Sure I did."

Knowing that was impossible, I pressed Paul.

"Are you sure you actually saw his face, actually saw him? Or could it have been someone else?"

"Why...why would it have been someone else?"

"Did you see his face?" I said.

"Well. Now that you mention it, I don't think I ever did. His back was always turned when he was on the bridge, and I never did see him for meals."

"Did you ever go up to the bridge on that trip?"

"Well sure, I stood watch and stuff, but I never relieved the captain, it was always usually Ricky who was on watch before me."

I looked Paul right in the eye. "Let me float this one by you. Is it possible that the captain was already deceased when you went out fishing the other day?"

"Can't see how...Why would you say such a thing?" Paul said.

"Listen, Paul. It's entirely possible that Captain Willis was not alive when you set sail—"

"But."

"Hear me out," I said, raising my hand to ward off Paul's questions. "I'm telling you this because I think you're honest with me, and I want to be upfront with you. We believe Captain Willis was murdered before your trip and dumped when you were out to sea."

"No. That's stupid. Wait. You...you don't think I could have anything to do with that? Then why would we rescue him? Why wouldn't we just lose him altogether? No. It doesn't make sense."

"I can't answer why just yet. Possibly to make it look like an accident. We don't know. I do know, though, that I think you're one of the good guys. I don't believe you're mixed up in all this."

Paul shook his head. "No. I'm definitely not mixed up in this." Paul rubbed his face and took a deep breath, blowing it out. "Jesus. I can't believe this. The guys have been so kind to me. How can I tell them you think they tossed the captain?"

"Well, that's the thing, Paul. You can't say anything—"

"Oh come on."

"No really. You can't tell them a thing. If they think you know, I can't guarantee your safety."

"Fuck. I don't want to be here anymore." Paul made to move from the table.

"Sit down, Paul. You have to be here. I'm sorry, but I've put you in an awkward situation. If they think you told me something—"

"But I didn't," Paul said.

"But if they think you did, your life could be in danger too. You have to act normal, go about your daily routine. If it gets too much," I handed Paul my business card, "call me. My cell is on that card; you can reach me anytime. If anything comes up, at all. Call."

"Fuck," Paul said again.

I hated doing this to Paul, but it was the only lead I had at the moment. "Listen. I'm going to call the other guys in here and talk to them one at a time too. No one will know what we discussed, and if everyone is quizzed, it'll look normal."

"What'll I tell them if they ask about what we talked about?"

"Tell them the truth, except for what I said. Just say I was asking when was the last time you saw the captain and so on. I'll ask them the same questions."

I went out to the back deck to check on Carter. I was sorry to have excluded her, but I needed her to keep the rest of the crew busy. I filled her in on the details of my conversation with Paul, and we both spoke with Ricky and George, one at a time in the galley. By the time we were done, Jimmy had come back from his parts run, so we spoke with him too, just to keep it looking normal. None of them had anything useful to say, which was about what I'd thought I'd get from them.

We got back in the car and drove towards the office. It was getting late in the day, and I was looking forward to going home.

# FIVE

## *Dalton's Dungarees*

"So... Frank," Carter said, "tell me something about yourself. Why did you join the Coast Guard?"

I groaned. "I don't know. I needed a good job at the time I guess."

"No, really. That sounds like the standard answer you give at parties."

"Parties? I don't go to parties," I said.

"You know what I mean. That's your canned response. I'm interested. Really. Why did you join?"

"What can I say? I like blue."

Carter sighed and looked out the window. I thought about it and figured the truth was worth a shot. "Okay. I'll bite. My great-great-great granddaddy's name was Frank Dalton. I guess he was the first Frank Dalton. He was a Deputy U.S. Marshal back in 1887, and from what I can gather he was a good man, but he got shot in the gut and died when he went to arrest Dave Smith, a suspected horse rustler. His partner, Deputy J.R. Cole was with Dalton, but no one thought that it was going to get rough."

"Where was this?"

"Oh. Out in the Wild West, someplace in Kansas called Coffeyville. Unfortunately, as they rode up to the door, Smith came out and blasted both of them with a shotgun. Deputy Cole managed to get away and brought back a posse, rounded up everybody in the house, Smith too, and hung 'em."

"That's some story."

"All true. Look it up. What I think is more interesting is that Frank was the oldest Dalton brother. After he'd died, there was nothing to keep his younger brothers in check, and they formed the Dalton gang. Terrorized railroads and robbed banks. They were quite famous in their time. Eventually they all got caught in a gunfight by the local law."

"So you're famous."

I snorted. "No, not me. They were. Or infamous at least. Anyway, I joined the Guard because I feel like law enforcement's in my blood."

Carter glanced over at me.

"It's more than just morals, though," I said. "I can actually feel when I do something right or wrong. And sometimes I can feel it in other people too."

"Now you're having the new girl on. You're teasing me."

I held up my hand in a Boy Scout salute. "No, scouts honor. I can sometimes feel...stuff. Stuff that isn't quite there. I don't know. I'm rambling. How about you. Why'd you join?"

"I needed a good job at the time," Carter said.

"That's my line." I smiled when I glanced at her.

"I guess I felt obligated. After 9/11, everything changed. I felt like I wanted to do something to help. I didn't want to join the Marines or Army. I dunno. I've always liked the water and felt what with the Coast Guard being so small, I could have more of an impact, get more field time maybe."

"Well, that's true. You should be able to pretty much stay in the field if you stay as an Agent. A lot of people can't handle it, though. We have our fingers in a lot of different pots, it is still the military, and some people can't handle the responsibility and rules."

"Don't forget the high paycheck," Carter deadpanned.

"Right. That too. How could I forget?"

I dropped Carter off at the park-and-ride where I'd picked her up that morning. I told her I'd call her if anything came up, and drove myself back to the office. I checked with our DOMEX digital forensics guys, but they hadn't had any luck with Willis's phone yet. Tomorrow they said. Maybe.

I drove home with the windows open. It had been a day of smells, and I wanted to wash them away. I pulled into the marina parking lot at the T-heads where Ghost was docked and decided to swing by Pete's Bar.

"Hey, Pete. How've you been?" I said as I walked through the door.

Pete squinted against the brightness of the open door. "Frank, long time no see. How did it work out with the lady last night?"

"I don't want to talk about it."

"That good , huh? Alright, what'll you have?"

"Oh, the usual."

"Always one with the words, this man," Pete said to the mostly empty bar.

The bar overlooked the marina, and I could almost see the *Ghost* from the bar. Half of the bar was open to the outside, palm trees dotting the area. It was really more of a beach shack, placed in a marina. There was an old jukebox in the corner, and Pete didn't serve anything fancy, just beer and shots, strictly functional he liked to say. He catered to the liveaboard boating community and the occasional transient tourist and knew what they wanted. They wanted simple and simple was what they got.

I eased myself onto a barstool about the same time a bottle of Pete's local brew slid its way down the bar to me, falling neatly into my outstretched hand.

"Pete. You're a life saver," I said, taking a long swig.

"Tough day?" Pete asked.

"No, not really. A long day is all. And I met my new partner."

"Oh yeah. What's he like?"

"She."

Pete grinned. "Should've known. What's she like? Nice?"

"I don't know to tell you the truth. She's only been in the Guard about ten seconds, so it's hard to say. She started off trying to throw her little Ensign bar around, but I think we worked through that. She's listening and willing to learn which is great. Has a cute voice too."

"That all that's cute? Just her voice?" he said, slapping me on the back. "Relax. I'm kidding. Can't an old man...Oh, never mind. Seriously, though, it's great that she has you to learn from. I remember taking you under my wing all those years ago."

"Ha." It was true. I'd had a rough time initially when I'd joined. It was well and truly the Old Guard. You do it my way or the highway mentality. If it wasn't issued to you in boot camp as part of your sea-bag, and fill in the blank here - spouse, kids, debt, whatever - then it didn't belong in the service. Back then no one cared about your life outside of the Guard. Your life was the Guard. If you had marital problems, or your kids were sick, it was just tough shit. That's a hard nut to crack for any new enlistee. Thankfully, most of that bullshit has changed, hence the Old Guard moniker.

After I'd transferred to my second unit, Pete was there. An old salt, but fair. He wasn't like a lot of the others. He showed me the ropes, and how it could be, how it should be. He retired shortly after that, but we kept in touch, and after I'd transferred to Corpus, I moved Ghost here.

Pete attended to the other two customers in the bar, and then came back over to me. "So what's the case you're working on with your partner, what's her name?"

"Jessica. Jessica Carter. It's a murder case. A guy fell off a fishing boat, but it looks like he was killed earlier and then dumped. It's got some complications."

"Oh yeah?" Pete said. "Anything you can elaborate on?"

"I'll tell you this. Batman's involved somehow."

"Shit. He's got his fingers in everything." Pete knew him well; Batman was notorious among the boating community. Nothing substantial ever seemed to stick to him, and he'd stayed out of jail.

"Finished with that?" Pete asked, pointing at my beer.

I drained the last dregs. "You know it. Last one, though, I've got to get an early night, busy day tomorrow."

"Okay, Frank. This one's on the house. Old times."

"Pete. You're never going to get rich. You say that every time."

"Don't want to get rich. Would have opened a bikini bar if I wanted to get rich. Let's just say I still appreciate your company."

"Alright, thanks." I threw some money on the bar anyway. "Take it easy Pete. I'm taking this one with me."

Pete waved from across the bar, already deep in conversation with another customer. I did a quick double take as it had looked like George the Wraith at first. It wasn't but could have passed for his brother, the deep sunken eyes. I made a mental note to ask Pete about him next time I was in.

Two minutes later, I had bounced down the dock and across to the *Ghost*. I know it's only a small boat, but I always got a feeling of deep calm when I stepped aboard. Perhaps the previous owner was a Zen master or shaman or something. Whoever it was I enjoyed the tranquility they'd bestowed upon my boat, and it felt special. Comforting.

I went below and made myself a ham sandwich, and took it back to the stern to enjoy the last of the sun and the rest of my beer. Tomorrow was going to be a long day, and I turned in early. I didn't see Wraith George's doppelganger watching my boat from the shore, but I figured out later it had to have been him.

I swung by the DOMEX lab when I got to work, as Mark Malone, the tech guy, had left me a post-it note. He'd signed it Eminem after his initials, but no one I knew called him that. Carter hadn't shown up yet, so I walked over alone.

"What have you got, Mark?" I said.

"Did you see my post-it note on your desk?"

"No. Just thought I'd drop by."

Mark looked a little deflated, but that didn't stop him from playing a little rendition of Would the Real Slim Shady Please Stand Up on his phone. I ignored that too.

"Well. That iPhone you gave me? We managed to do a chip off and retrieve some of the data."

"A chip what?"

"A chip off. Come on, I must have explained this to you before? How long have you been working here anyway?"

"I could swear I have no idea what you're talking about. Please elaborate."

Malone muttered to himself and shook his head, but continued. "Basically, we take the phone apart, isolate the memory chip by heating up the phone to melt the solder, and then we can extract the data. Ringing any bells?"

"No. Go on."

"It takes a while for this to happen, for the data to transpose. It's like watching you type on the screen, so I don't have everything yet."

I let that pass. "I thought iPhones were unhackable?"

"We're not hacking it. We're fooling it. We use that and another program called Celebrite. It's from the Israelis."

"Figures. What did you have to do, bribe a Mossad Agent?"

Malone looked shocked. "No of course not. I—"

"Just kidding, Mark. Lighten up."

"Right. Of course." Malone faked a laugh. "How silly of me. You and your Special Agent humor."

I sighed. "So what did you get?"

"Right." Malone pushed his spectacles further up the bridge of his nose. It was a tell that he was concentrating. "Come over here, and I'll throw them up on the big screen."

For whatever else Malone might be, he was a tech genius. The department budget didn't really stretch to a lot of new technology, too many crusty old Admirals stuck in the dark ages of wooden ships and typewriters. Somehow, Malone had managed to get the DHS to fund him a small grant, as long as he shared the results with other government agencies. Something he would have done anyway.

Malone waved his hand, at least that's what it looked like to me, from the computer screen to a giant, almost transparent screen hanging from the ceiling. At the same time, the lights dimmed, and the giant screen came to life, with streams of hex data scrolling through.

Malone watched the data scroll for a moment and then with another swoosh of hands, stopped the data on a sixteen-digit hash. I didn't really understand what it all meant, but I didn't have to, that's what Malone was for, and I appreciated that.

"This hash represents one of the photos we took off the phone," he said.

"Okay. Let's see it."

A photo appeared of what looked like a group shot of several men. "Can you enhance that?" I asked.

"Can Eminem sing?"

"I couldn't say."

The image pixilated, enlarged and then cleared up. I was staring at the faces of a trimmer, younger Batman Black, the unfortunate but vastly healthier looking Captain Willis, and a still wraith-looking, sunken-eyed George.

"Shit," I muttered.

"You know them?"

"Can you enlarge those containers they're standing around?"

The containers came into focus. They looked like shipping crates, and there must have been half a dozen in the photo. One box was open, and there were three empty slots. The other slots were full of ominously dark rifles, and Batman, Willis, and George looked like they were holding the three from the crate.

"Yeah. I know them." Looked like the three compadres were not only old buddies but gunrunners too.

"Can you print me out a series of those shots Mark, please?"

"Sure can."

"Did you find anything else of interest?" I said.

"No, not really. Just some family shots. I can print those up too if you want."

"Yeah. You never know. Did you manage to get an idea of where the phone's been?"

"Working on it. I told you it was slow. Usually, we can identify where the phone's been by looking at the geocache data on the photos and if he accessed any GPS apps. He might have deleted all the data from the phone, but nothing is ever truly gone. I don't have it yet. But I will."

"Thanks. Remind me to use a burner phone when I go to the dark side."

"That doesn't work either."

I looked at Mark. "I'm kidding."

"Oh, of course. Special Agent humor again."

I left Mark and swung by Carter's desk. She still wasn't in so I called her when I got to my desk.

"Carter," she said, on the first ring.

"Hey," I said. "Where you at? You're running late."

"Yeah, I know. Sorry. I had a couple of errands to run." She sounded a little flustered.

"Are you okay?"

"What? Yes. Yes, I'm fine. Thanks. Listen, I'll be there in two minutes." She hung up. I would have followed up with her, but the other line rang.

"Special Agent Dalton, Investigations."

"Frank?"

"Yeah," it took me a second to place the voice. "Pete? What's up?" Pete never called me.

"Can you swing by when you get off shift? There's something I want to talk to you about."

It was early for Pete to call; besides, I don't think I ever remember him calling me at the office.

"We can talk now if you want."

"It'll be better in person, Frank. Listen, I don't want to worry you, it can wait until your shift is over, I just wanted to catch you."

"Alright, if you're sure it can wait. I'll catch up with you this afternoon. At the bar?"

"Yeah. That's great. Thanks, Frank. Later."

Another intriguing phone call. I was thinking about what Pete might want when Carter flew through the door and headed to her desk. I got up and walked over.

"Hey," I said.

Carter jumped.

"Sorry. Didn't mean to scare you," I said.

"It's okay. It's nothing. Forget it."

I turned her wheely chair around, so she was facing me, and sat down on the edge of her desk. "What's going on?"

"It's nothing. Really."

"Look. You're late. You're short with me on the phone, and you're really jumpy. We have a lot to do today, and I need your head in the game."

"I'll be fine," she said staring at the floor.

I thought about it for a second, taking her whole demeanor in, something wasn't right. "Keep your jacket on. Follow me."

"Where are we going?"

"Just follow me."

We walked downstairs, and across the street, to a hole in the wall coffee joint, I favored, aptly named Jitters. It wasn't gourmet six dollar a cup coffee, nor was it a skinny macchiato flavor top or whatever the hell people ordered. All you got was a big, strong, steaming mug of house coffee. But it was good. I told Carter to get a table in the back while I got two mugs. I gave her the mug that was slightly less chipped and sat down across from her.

I let her sip on her coffee for a bit until she'd calmed. "Now," I said, "What's going on. If we're to be partners, we speak the truth to each other, and we trust each other. If we can't talk to each other and trust each other, we won't work well in the field. I need to know you. You need to know me. I need to know you've got my back."

"I have your back, Dalton."

"Call me Frank."

She smiled a little. "Jessica."

"Okay, Jessica. What's going on?"

"I don't want to be a burden."

"You'll never be a burden, as long as we're open and honest. Go ahead. I'm listening, not judging."

Carter sipped some more of her coffee. "This is good."

"I know. Stop stalling. What gives?"

"It's my Mom. She's not doing well."

"I'm sorry to hear that," I said. I was, truly. I gave her time to talk. To gather her thoughts. After several false starts, she began to tell me the story.

"My mom and I were really close when I was younger, but...but after my brother had died we just drifted apart. I didn't see it at the time. I was angry. Angry at her, angry at the world, how unfair it all was. I was only twelve, my brother was sixteen. He'd just gotten his license. It was a drunk driver. He came out of nowhere. T-boned him. From what I remember he didn't suffer, it was over quick."

"I'm so sorry, Jessica." I reached across and briefly held her hand, gave it a squeeze.

She sat back, pale. "My dad couldn't handle it, and he left shortly after my brother died. His leaving added to my teenage angst, but I didn't really get on with him anyway. It hit my mom hardest, I think. She was left all alone with just bitchy me. It took years for my mom and me to reconnect. I went through a teenage rebellion that I'm sure was hell for my mother, probably more than would be normal... I was a wreck. I started to hang out with the wrong crowd." She paused for a minute to use a napkin and wipe her eyes. The world shrunk to the space around us. "It wasn't until I was seventeen, a year older than when my brother died that I sorted out my life..."

She fell silent for a moment. When she didn't look like she was going to continue I said, "You were about to tell me how you got your life together."

"Right." A deep breath. "You're going to find this stupid..."

"Try me. I have a significant capacity for what some people think is stupid," I said, thinking about my Zen boat.

"One night...I had a vision...of my brother. I don't know if it was truly my brother, or if it was my fucked up subconscious, or what, but it felt like my brother, you know? He told me to cut out the shit, sort my life out. He told me how lucky I was that I was actually alive, and a year older than when he died. He said he would totally swap places with me, just to see a sunset, to feel the breath of the wind on his face..." I handed Carter another napkin. "Whatever it was, it had the right effect. Maybe it was the right time, maybe it was fate, I don't know. But I did turn my life around. I got back on my feet. I quit the lowlifes I'd been hanging with, and I tried to be a better person. It took a long time, but I did it. I also reconnected with my mom. She's such a good person that she forgave me instantly. She's been my rock and my biggest fan. After all, it's just the two of us now."

Carter blew her nose into the napkin, and I gave her a moment while I refreshed our coffee from the barista.

"Thanks," she said, as I sat down again.

"So what happened this morning?" I said.

Carter sighed. "My mom has Alzheimer's. She's starting to forget who I am, keeps asking where Billy is. Frank, it's been years since he died, but she doesn't remember. The hospital called me this morning as I was coming into work. She'd had a particularly bad night, and they asked me to go in. Although she doesn't always remember me, I seem to calm her down. When I got there, though, she didn't know me. She kept screaming, over and over and they had to sedate her. It was just a terrible morning all around."

"I'm so sorry, Jessica. You know, you can always talk to me if you need to."

"Thanks, I appreciate it, but we've just met. It's not the sort of thing you just dump on someone you've just met. Besides, I didn't really know how you'd react. And I didn't want to come off needy on my second day after our rocky start."

"There's nothing needy about it at all. We're a team now, and we look after each other. Listen, why don't you take off for the day, sort out what you need to and come back in tomorrow. I can handle what's going on."

"Really?"

"Yeah, Go. I've got it."

Carter sighed again, straightened her shoulders some and lifted her head up. "I'd love nothing more than just to crawl back into bed, but I can't. I need to work. It'll keep my mind off of what's happening with my mom. And besides, we have a murderer to catch don't we?"

"Okay." I smiled. "I actually do need your help. But if you need to take off later or whenever just let me know."

"Yes, boss."

I put our empty mugs on the counter, and we walked back across the street. I filled her in on what Eminem had shown me.

"Guns? How old was that photo do you think?"

"Eminem said it was hard to say. He could tell it was a photo of a photo, so there's no telling when it was initially taken. The copy was made a few months ago. Judging by the way Batman looked though it had to be at least ten years ago."

"Do you think they're still running guns?"

"Again, hard to tell. We didn't see anything on the *Reel Lady*, but who knows? We could check out some of their other vessels, put a look-out on them, see if any of the Cutters pick something up."

Back at the office, we grabbed another Econo box G-ride from the underground lot, and sped out powered by rubber bands and will power. Captain Frederick Lucius Willis was divorced, but I wanted to go see his ex. They would have been married about the time the gun running picture was taken, so I wanted to see if she knew anything, perhaps she had a score to settle?

# SIX

## *What the Butler Doesn't Know*

We drove in what I always felt was a northerly direction, but what the car told me was east, along the beautiful and winding Ocean Drive. On my left, the bay sparkled in the sunlight, dotted with the occasional shimmering sail on the horizon; on a good day, you could see clear across the Bay to Aransas. Both sides of Ocean Drive were home to multimillion-dollar houses, condos, and the occasional small hotel; palm trees lined the middle of the street, and it was a pleasant drive to Willis's ex-wife's house.

We arrived at the Rivas estate just off Ocean Drive and drove through an ornate entrance gate down a long winding driveway, the tires crackling and crunching on the shingles. In front of us were two stories of tastefully sprawling house, with massive double front doors opening onto a wraparound porch. The buzz of a weed whacker came from a small team of landscapers over to the left. We parked in the front, walked up several steps to the porch and rang the bell, the chime rumbling somewhere deep inside.

"Nice house," Carter said.

"Not too shabby. A little out of my price range," I said.

A moment later, an honest-to-God butler appeared at the door. He was dressed in a tuxedo with tails and was wearing white gloves. The inside of the house was a step up from the porch, and the butler looked down on us imperiously.

"Can I help you, sir, madam?" he said.

I held out my badge. "I'm Special Agent Dalton, this is Special Agent Carter, we're here to see Mrs. Rivas."

The Butler barely glanced at our badges. Instead, he said, "Is Mrs. Rivas expecting you?"

"No, we just dropped by. However, I'm sure she'll see us. Please tell her it's about her ex-husband."

"Mr. Dawson?"

"Err, no. Captain Willis."

Butler-man raised an eyebrow, the only indication he was surprised. "If you'll follow me to the library, I'll inform Mrs. Rivas that you're waiting."

"Say, how many exes does she have anyway?" I said, following Jeeves into the house.

"I wouldn't presume, sir." Jeeves left and closed the double doors of the library behind him.

"Damn, Carter," I said, looking around. "A library. In a house."

"I know, right?" she said. "I don't think the public library I went to as a kid had this many books."

I walked around the library admiring the furnishings and rubbing my finger across the spines of several books. At one end of the library was a leather couch and three leather armchairs, next to a fireplace. For the library's large size, it still felt cozy. I turned as I heard the doors open and in strolled a vision of white. She was dressed in a white chiffon dress, a cross between a pool cover up and something you'd see at a nightclub in Miami. There were just enough layers to tastefully cover her lady bits, and she walked like she was floating, even though I could see heels that went on forever.

She glided over to us and stretched out her right hand to shake. In her other hand was a martini glass half full of clear liquid, two large olives skewered on a stick, and an unlit cigarette in one of those holders they used to use in the '20s.

"Mr. Dalton?" she said, as she shook my hand. She had a firm grip. No limp fish there.

"Special Agent," I said. "This is Special Agent Carter." She shook hands with Carter.

"Forgive me, Special Agents. Roberts forgot to mention that part; he's getting somewhat on in years."

"That's quite alright Mrs. Rivas—"

"Oh please. Call me Julia. Shall we sit?" She gestured to the leather seats. She sat on the couch, folding herself into its comfort, flicking her feet up underneath her. Carter and I sat on leather chairs. I tried to perch on the end so I could write notes but kept sinking into the chair. I could feel who was getting the upper hand already.

"Mrs. Rivas," I began. She stared at me. "Sorry, Julia. Did Roberts say why we were here?"

"He said it had something to do with my nefarious ex-husband, Freddie. Did something happen to him?"

"What makes you say that?"

"Well, I'm not a Special Agent, but I can't imagine they make house calls just to say hello."

"You're right, Julia. I'm sorry to inform you that your ex-husband Frederick Lucius Willis was found yesterday in the ocean. I'm afraid he didn't make it."

Rivas didn't look phased. "I'm not surprised. Mind if I smoke?"

"It's your house," I said. "Why aren't you surprised?"

"Be a dear and get me that ashtray off the mantelpiece?"

I got up, found a heavy glass ashtray above the fireplace, and handed it to her. She balanced it on the armrest and retrieved a lighter from the hidden depths of her bra, taking a long drag as she lit up.

"It's been so long now; I don't suppose there's any harm in telling you. Freddie was always living on the edge when we were married." She blew out a long stream of smoke. The library didn't smell stale, so she either didn't smoke much or Roberts was a whiz with the Febreze. "I suppose that's what attracted me to him, he was a bit of a rebel, and I was a little rich girl looking to act out. It was a mutual attraction. He traveled so much back then too that every time he came home, the sex was new all over again." She smiled tightly at me, perhaps wistfully. "I'm sorry to hear of his demise, but we hadn't been married for years, and I hadn't seen him for longer than that. Tell me, was that Mr. Black figure involved?"

"Why do you say that?"

"Oh come on, don't be difficult, dear. He was always hanging out with that ne'er do well. I can't imagine he would have left his business partner."

"So they were partners back then, Mr. Willis and Mr. Black?"

"Much to my disgust, yes. That was the one thing I didn't like about Freddie. His association with that man and that henchman of his, Jeffery or Julian or something like that."

"George?"

"Yes. That's him. Dreadful man. I always thought he looked like he was dead or dying, the way he could stare at you without blinking."

I nodded. "What was it about Mr. Willis's relationship with those two you didn't like?"

"Have you met them? What was to like? No, Freddie was always a bit fly by night, but I don't think he truly turned into a bad apple until he got involved with them. You know do know Mr. Black's reputation, don't you?"

"We're familiar with it." I glanced at Carter; she was furiously scribbling notes. She didn't seem to be sinking into the chair. I'd have to remember to ask her why.

"Yes. Well, you see that was the last straw. Freddie told me he had to run a few errands for Mr. Black. I was terribly upset because we were invited to a private art exhibition that night, a new up and coming artist, I hear he's doing rather well now. Anyway, I'd just bought a new dress, and I hated to disappoint... I know that sounds all sorts of frivolous, but it was important to me."

"Freddie tell you what errands?"

"No, and I never asked, not at the time. I was too furious. I saw Black in the car when he picked up Freddie; I heard the tires crunching on the gravel and looked out the window. That George was in the back too. They sped off, and I didn't see him for three days. When he came back, he smelled like he hadn't showered in three days too."

"Have you always lived here?" Carter asked.

"Yes. It's the family house. Daddy was a whiz in the stock market, did rather well for himself and retired here when he was still in his forties."

"What happened after Freddie got back?" I said.

"Well. I made him delouse in the shower; he stayed in there for what felt like a week. When he finally came out all pink and scrubbed, I sat him down in here and demanded he tells me what was going on. He ummed and ahhed and hedged for a while until I threatened to cut him off from this lifestyle."

"What did he say?" I said.

"He actually laughed at me. Can you believe that? He laughed at me."

I shook my head. I'm not sure I could imagine anyone ever laughing at her.

"He said he didn't need my damn money, said he had a sweet deal going with Mr. Black. The trip he'd just taken was the first of many, and he was going to be stinking rich. As if to prove it, he pulled out two huge rolls of cash and threw them at me. I was shocked. I asked him if it was drug money, I couldn't think how he would have made that much money so quickly, and he just laughed again. He said it was better than drugs. He was getting stuff that people wanted, although he used a more vulgar word. I told him to get out. He told me to watch myself. I threw the money back at him, screamed at him to get out. He left. That was the last time I saw him. I kept tabs on him for a little while after that, it was stupid of me, but I did still love him. That wore off about the same time I found out Mr. Black was beating up people with a baseball bat. I just couldn't condone what either of them were doing after that. I knew Black must be connected, and now he had his hooks in Freddie. I just never realized how awful and evil Black was."

"You don't know where he got all that money?"

"No. I believed him when he said it wasn't drugs. But really, I have no idea what it could be. It was a lot of money he had with him, though."

"Do you think your butler might know?"

"Roberts? I couldn't think why he would. They didn't speak to each other. Freddie thought it was pretentious that I had a butler, and I don't think Roberts liked Freddie's brash behavior."

After a few more questions that didn't go anywhere I thanked her for her time. "Oh anytime, darling," she said, and we left.

I drove back along Ocean Drive deep in thought, heading for downtown. I didn't see the gray sedan pull out and follow us until I slowed down for a light. I happened to look in the mirror and the car peeled out from behind me, tires chirping on the smooth tarmac, and took a sharp left turn as the light turned red.

"Did you see that car?" I asked Carter. She shook her head and glanced out the window where I was pointing. "I think that was the same one that nearly drove us off the road yesterday." Carter looked closer at the car as it was speeding off. I thought about following it, but I wouldn't be able to catch up with it now, not in this car - didn't have time to wind the rubber bands.

"Why would it be following us? We didn't even know what was going on yesterday," she said.

"We didn't know what was going on, but someone else did. We've been two steps behind this thing from the start. Remind me to switch out this vehicle when we go out again, we need something with a bit more oomph."

"You should write these things down. You're giving me so many things to remind you about; I don't remember what they all are."

"What good are you if you can't remember stuff?" I said, teasing.

"What good are you? You're the one asking me."

"Touché. Really, though. We do need a better car."

When we got back to the office, there was another post-it note on my desk. I think we kept the post-it note company in business in this office. I followed the note's directions and went in to see the lieutenant, grabbing Carter on the way.

"Hey, Tobias," I said.

"Frank, Jessica." He nodded at us. "I have the SAC on the line, and he wanted to get an update on what's going on with your case. Let me put him on speaker. Are you still there, Mr. Lewis? I have Agents Dalton and Carter with me."

"Hello, Frank, Carter. How's the case going?"

"Good afternoon, Mr. Lewis," I said. "Honestly, this case has a lot of twists and turns. It's a lot more than just a dead fisherman."

"I know you were on leave, Frank and have been thinking about retirement some, sorry to put this on you but I needed someone to get a round turn on this before it got out of hand."

"Not a problem, sir. At this point, we know Mr. Willis didn't drown, and we know that Mr. Black is involved, but we're still in the preliminary stages of the investigation and are trying to run down all the leads we have. I have to say up front that Agent Carter has been a huge help."

"Glad to hear it. Keep up the good work, Carter. Do you have anything specific you can tell me for the Assistant Director's brief tomorrow morning, Frank?"

"Nothing conclusive at this point, sir, although our DOMEX tech retrieved some old photos from the captain's phone that had been deleted and it confirmed a long-running relationship with Mr. Black and others in the crew. The picture we saw appeared to show that Mr. Black and Mr. Willis were gun runners."

"Now, that's interesting," Lewis said. "Are you sure we had the authority to take the phone?"

"Yes, sir," I said.

"Very well. Have you alerted the ATF and our partner agencies?" Lewis asked.

I chose my words carefully. "Although we don't have a lot to go on right now, we're still the lead agency, and I'd like to keep it that way for as long as possible, sir."

"Of course, Frank. I just want you to be aware that if Willis and Black were running guns that could take this investigation out of our jurisdiction. We might have to hand the information over and take a step back."

"Yes, sir." Shit. I really didn't want to give this one up just yet.

"For now, though, I want you to continue. Keep me updated on what you find out, and we'll play it by ear."

"Yes, sir," I said, relieved.

"Good work, Frank. Listen, I have a meeting I'm running late for, but keep me up to date, and if anything important happens, call me directly, don't go through the chain."

"Roger that, sir."

I walked back to my desk and thought over what the SAC had said. Something wasn't ringing true, but the thought refused to surface and hovered in that unique region in the back of your head, where you know something is going on, but can't quite place your finger on it. No matter. When the time was right, it would come out.

I checked my e-mails for a few minutes, letting the details of the case percolate around my head. I was pretty sure Batman had murdered Willis but I didn't know where or why and it could just as easily have been one of the other crew. In fact, Black probably didn't get his hands dirty at all. I still wanted to think Paul was straight with me, though. I hadn't heard from him, so had to assume he was still okay.

My phone vibrated in my pocket. It was a text from Pete. *Don't forget to drop by, when you get a chance*, it said. It reminded me of the way he was on the phone this morning and as I didn't have any new information on the case I figured it would be a good time to go see him.

I went to the secure locker that held all the keys to our G-rides and punched in the code 1790 to open it. I rooted through for a second and selected something a little more fitting. Grabbing Carter, we went down to the garage. I pressed the lock button on the key fob so I could find the behemoth I'd chosen, and soon we burst out into the sunlight, the engine roaring in a black Dodge Ram Crew Cab with a 5.7L V8 Hemi, and tinted windows. I screamed around the corner and settled into the short drive to Pete's, filling Carter in on our old friendship.

I pulled in front of Pete's and noticed one of the windows was boarded up.

"What's up with the window, Pete?" I asked as we went in. Pete was drying a few glasses with a dish cloth and putting them up behind the bar.

"Oh, nothing. Wind slammed it closed, and it cracked earlier. Is this Jessica?" Pete smiled at Carter and came out from behind the bar, throwing the rag over his shoulder. He took her offered hand in both of his. "Extremely pleased to meet you, Jessica. Frank was just telling me all about his new partner last night."

"He was?" she said, turning to me and smiling.

"Don't get too excited, Carter," I said. "I just told him I had a new partner, is all."

"Oh that's not all," Pete said. "What he didn't say was how utterly gorgeous you were."

"Pete, you old flirt. Stop," I said.

"No, please go on," Carter said.

"Oh where to start, where to start," Pete said looking Carter up and down.

"How about you start with why you called me down here, Pete," I said.

Pete sobered immediately. "Yes. Right. Can I get you two a drink? Coffee, soda?"

"I'm good. Stop stalling. What gives?"

"Okay, okay. You remember that guy that was in here when you left yesterday."

"I remember," I said, thinking of the George lookalike.

"Well, he was asking about you."

"Asking what?"

"Where you live, when you come in, what time you go to work."

"He was shaking you down for information," I said.

"Yes, he was. But he wasn't doing it directly. He was subtle. I must be getting old. I didn't put two and two together for a little while. Not until he came back this morning."

"What did he want this time?"

"He had the audacity to try and shake me down. He told me he'd be coming around much more, and he thought we could come to a nice business arrangement. I told him where to go."

"Is that when he broke your window?

"No. He didn't break it. Well, in a manner of speaking he did. I shoved him when it was obvious he was trying to shake me down. I might be old, but no one's going to hold me upside down and collect my loose change. When I shoved him, he tripped and landed against the window."

"Seriously? Jesus. Are you okay?"

"Me? I'm fine. I should have waited 'till he was outside. I liked that window."

"What did he do after that?"

"That's the strangest thing," Pete said scratching behind his ear. "He didn't say a word. Just got up, shook himself off and walked out."

"Where'd he go?"

"No idea."

"Did you call the cops?" I asked.

"I called you."

"Come on, Pete. You know I'm not a cop. We used to do the same job."

"You're all I need."

"Fine, do me a favor, though, and file a report. If he ever comes back, you'll have documentation."

"He won't come back, but sure, I'll call it in if it makes you happy."

"It does. Was there anything else?"

"No. No, I don't think so. I just wanted to let you know he was asking questions about you."

"Thanks, buddy. I'll see you around."

"See you, Frank. And Frank?" I turned. "Look after Jessica."

I stared at Pete, "Of course," I said. Strange thing to say.

"Enchanted, Jessica."

"Bye, Pete. Pleased to meet you."

We walked back to the truck, but instead of getting in I pocketed the keys.

"Come on," I said to Carter. "I want to show you something." I walked with her down to the marina.

"Where are we going? Shopping for a boat?" she said, looking around.

"Not quite. I want to show you *Ghost*."

Carter looked at me. "Is that a boat?"

"Yeah, a small one. She's a 47 foot Gulfstar Sailmaster. Two cabins, two heads, galley, living room. I live aboard."

"She doesn't sound that small."

"No, I guess not. I suppose it depends what you compare her to."

We walked along the boardwalk to where *Ghost* was moored up, and I stepped on. As soon as I laid a foot on her, I knew something was wrong. I signaled Carter to stay quiet, and drew my gun. Moving carefully so as to not rock *Ghost* and alert anyone on board, I carefully pushed open the hatch and eased down the steps to the main lounge. If I went forward someone could come up behind me from the master cabin, so I had to check that first. I edged over to the port side and crouching down shimmied closer to the cabin door. Entering low so I was less of a target, I poked my head through the door and hastily back again. No shots. No one was in there. I entered the cabin and nudged the head door open with my foot. Shower, sink, toilet. Nothing else. I let out a deep breath I'd been holding and made my way back to the lounge. Confident now no one was going to sneak up on me from behind, I crept forward toward the other cabin. I passed through the galley. There were very limited places anyone could hide. I peripherally took in the mess around me. Someone had definitely been here. I followed the same procedure in the forward cabin as I had in the stern. Nothing. I blew out another breath, and made my way back to Carter.

As I poked my head out of the hatch I saw Carter on the boardwalk. She'd drawn her gun, giving me cover.

"Hey, all clear," I said.

Carter stood up and holstered her weapon. "What's going on?" she asked.

I felt my cheeks redden. "You'll think this is weird, but the moment I stepped foot on *Ghost* I knew the Zen had gone."

"The what?"

"Zen. *Ghost* had a lot of Zen. Well, I call it Zen. I'm not really sure what it is. I just know that whenever I come aboard, I always feel safe and secure, like a big fluffy blanket hugging me." I shrugged. "Stupid, I know. But when I stepped on her just now, I didn't feel it, and knew something was wrong."

"It's not stupid. I saw my dead brother, remember."

"Yeah."

"So was somebody here?"

"Yeah. It looks like someone was looking for something. Here," I said, holding out my hand to her for balance. "Come aboard."

Carter stepped lightly onto *Ghost* and peered through the hatch. "Frank, I didn't know you were such a neat freak."

I grimaced. The boat was trashed, draws were opened and dumped, paper strewn all over. The place had been completely ransacked.

"What do you think they were looking for?" Carter said.

"I don't know. I don't think it was a coincidence that guy was asking Pete all those questions, though. And we've been followed by whoever that is in the gray sedan. I think they've just upped the game."

"Can I use the head?" Carter asked.

"Sure, it's just through there," I said, pointing.

Carter went to use the head, and after a moment called out to me. "Frank, I think you need to see this."

I followed Carter and opened the door to the head a little wider to see. Someone had left a message written in red lipstick on the mirror.

"Back off, Dalton," I read aloud. "That's Cryptic."

"You mean you don't always have that written on your mirror?"

"No. I usually go with don't burn the toast again, or something like that." I went to the fridge and found my beer stash was still intact. Thankful for small mercies I grabbed one and handed another to Carter. I then went and checked underneath the main cabin bed. My safe was intact. They either weren't good at searching or were interrupted.

"Do you mind giving me a hand cleaning up real quick? I'll buy you a beer," I said.

"I hate to give you the same advice you just gave Pete, but don't you think we should call this in? The mirror is a clue, after all, and if someone's threatening you..."

"Fuck." I ran my fingers through my hair while I thought. "You're right of course, but I don't want those CSI assholes rooting through all my shit. Let me take some photos of how things are now, and the mirror, we'll tidy up a bit and give the office a call."

We did the best we could. Carter kept asking me where this thing or that thing went. She held up some skimpy black underwear she found tucked up in a corner. "Frank, you wear some weird underwear for a guy."

"Those aren't mine. And I don't know how they got there."

"Duh! I know they're not yours. And you don't have to pretend to be a saint. We all have lives outside of work."

"Well. She's not coming back anyway." I'd seen to that. Carter didn't say anything, and pretty soon the place looked as good as it ever did. I'd have to find that Shaman now so I could get the Zen back on my boat.

# SEVEN

## *Up in Smoke*

We drove back to the office, and I filled in Smith.

"What about surveillance at the marina?" he said.

"CCTV? I thought about it. They have cameras, but as far as I know, they don't work. They're more of a deterrent for vandals and weekend boaters, so most of them are pointing at the transient docks than the liveaboards. I'll check with the marina manager when I go home, though, see if they have anything."

Smith didn't have any other thoughts, so I went in search of Eminem.

"Hey, Mark. I've got some images on this CD I want you to take a look at when you get a chance, not urgent, though," I said, handing him the CD.

"Afternoon, Frank. What are they of?" he said, throwing the CD on his desk.

"Someone broke into my boat and wrote some shit on my mirror. I took some photos and put them on that disc. I don't know who did it, so I don't have anything to compare the writing to, but maybe you can turn something up? It may or may not be related to this case. Speaking of, did you get any more photos off of that phone?"

Mark turned and waved me back over to his super tech screen or whatever it was.

"No, not yet. It takes a while for the chip off to do its magic. If you could put a good word in about budget, and we got faster computers it might help."

I waved him off. "You're preaching to the choir, buddy. Heard of sequestration? Continuing resolution? The whole military is broke."

"So it would seem if you're the best we've got."

"Ha ha." I nodded at the screen. "What have you got?"

"Right. I've been going through the records of Mr. Willis, and he seemed to be the owner, CEO, CFO, partner and so on of a whole slew of companies. Ones that don't actually exist."

"Shell companies, then. What was he doing? Laundering money?"

"It would seem so. At least a portion of the companies I looked at are set up that way, linked to an offshore bank in the Caymans. The rest of them appear to be related to accounts that track the movement of shipping containers, or at least several large cargo and container vessels."

"Willis had cargo and container vessels?"

"Again, hard to say exactly until I do some more digging, but his name does seem to crop up quite a bit. Along with your Mr. Black too."

"Figures. Anything I can pin on Black?"

"Right now all I have is supposition. Nothing illegal to be the CEO of a lot of companies, just unusual. But if you know what we know, then you can bet your bottom dollar it was probably illegal in some way."

"Those ships. Can you get names or doc numbers for any of them? I don't suppose any of them run under the U.S. flag do they?"

"I haven't got the names or doc numbers for all of them yet, but I did get partial details on a 450-foot cargo ship sailing out of Grand Cayman and pulling into Ingleside soon. She should be with the pilots right about now. None of them are U.S flagged, though. It fits with having his accounts in the Caymans, could be an easy way to transport cash."

"Isn't all that stuff done by wire transfer these days?"

"Sure. But if you're making off the book deals, it would be easier to keep with cash. Less traceable than wire transfers, and the beauty of the banks down there is that they don't ask questions. It's illegal to move more than ten grand in cash in or out of the country, but if you have your own transport vessel..."

"What's she called?"

"The *Bold Endeavor*."

"Cute."

An hour later Carter and I were on a Coast Guard 45-foot Response Boat out of Station Port Aransas en route to the *Bold Endeavor*. We had teamed up with some of the enforcement guys and were going to piggyback off their boarding. They had bigger guns than we did.

We had them anchor before pulling into port, so nobody could leave. Pulling up on the leeward side of the freighter the wind was minimized and we climbed aboard using the Jacobs Ladder. I hated climbing up those things. I'm not particularly scared of heights but scaling what feels like a thousand feet straight up the side of a steel boat on nothing more than a rickety rope ladder freaks me out.

By the time I got to the top, the enforcement guys had already completed an initial safety assessment, which means they'd had time to search the accessible spaces on the vessel and make sure no one was going to jump out and kill us with a machete or whatever. Carter and I were there more to check out the cargo, see if anything looked out of place than security.

There were several containers on deck, stacked three high, but the majority of the shipment seemed to be break bulk in the cargo holds. We popped open some of the containers, but the contents matched the cargo manifest that Customs had provided us with, nothing unusual.

I asked one of the deck hands to take us to the captain. He offered to take us up in the elevator, but from experience, I knew the things were super slow and were meant for one person. We'd all be crammed in, with sweaty sailor at the controls. That wasn't in my game plan, so we opted to take the long way round via the stairs. We plodded up a mountain, following the aroma of unwashed seaman-absolutely no pun intended-until he motioned us into a small room with a large table.

"I get captain. Wait here," he said.

So we did.

"Welcome to the good life, Carter," I said. She went to sit down, but I told her to stand. "It'll undermine any authority you have if you're sitting. A lot of cultures don't take women in positions of power well, so it's wise not to make it easier for them to ignore you."

The captain entered the room, preceded by the rancid odor of dirty sailor. I think this was sweaty stink number five, a great classic, mixed with pungent cigarette breath. I moved as far away in the cramped room that I could manage. It wasn't far enough. The captain was a swarthy man, about 5'10", looked as if he shaved once a trip, and changed his shirt at the same time.

I came straight to the point. "Captain. What did you pick up in the Caymans?" I asked.

The Captain shrugged and sat down, gesturing for us to do the same. "Water, coffee, Coca-Cola?" he said.

We both shook our heads, and without looking, he rattled off something quick in a language I couldn't catch, to a sailor behind him who nodded and ran off quickly as if his life depended on it. Which it might. I repeated the question a little slower to get the captain's attention again.

"The manifest, it is here," he said, shoving some papers across the table. He tapped at a column with his nicotine-stained fingers. "Here and here."

"Right," I said glancing at his rat-a-tatting fingers.

"Is this a regular run? Cayman to Corpus?" Carter said.

The captain paused for a moment, not looking at Carter.

"Answer the question," I said.

"No. Is not regular," he said stretching each syllable, making it sound like reg-ooh-lar.

"What was the reason for this trip?" I said.

He shrugged again. "I go where cum-pan-e say. They say go here, I go here. They say go there, I go—"

"There. Got it, thanks," I said. I showed him a photo of Willis. "Captain, you know this man?"

A shake of the head.

"How about this man?"

The captain blanched, and his hand trembled ever so slightly as he shook loose a Marlboro from a soft pack. "No. Never seen."

I'd shown him a picture of Mr. Black. It was evident he knew who the man was. Also obvious he was scared. I knew Black and Willis were getting their guns in the country somehow. These freighters seemed like a logical place. On a 400 something foot ship though there could be a thousand hiding places. Our best bet was to watch the vessel and see where the cargo went. There was nothing more I could get out of the captain. I tried a couple of different tacks, but he didn't budge. Black scared him more than I did.

Once again, we headed back to the office, both deep in thought. I kept an eye out for anyone following us, but this time didn't see anything suspicious. The traffic was light, and I took a circuitous route braking at green traffic lights and speeding up at red ones to see if I could shake anybody loose. It was quiet.

I was at my desk nibbling a ham sandwich I hadn't had a chance to eat at lunch when the duty officer called.

"Sir, there's a Miss Lancaster from Lancaster, Lancaster, and Mitchell here to see you."

I was surprised that she was here after our less than auspicious meeting the day before, so I was curious what she wanted. I hoped it wasn't to complain about the investigation. I told the duty officer to send her up, and I met her at the elevators and escorted her to one of the interview rooms.

"So to what do I owe the pleasure, Miss Lancaster?" I said.

"Mr. Dalton. It appears I owe you an apology."

"Really? To what end?" I asked.

"Can I sit?"

"Of course. Please do."

Lancaster pulled up a chair to the table and delicately sat down, placing her briefcase on the table and opening it, pulling out a folder. I sat down across from her.

"I had a chance to review some of the applicable rules and regulations in regards to marine investigations, and I have to say that everything you did was perfectly in line. I appreciate that you didn't evict me from the vessel, even though you could have done," she said.

Lancaster sounded contrite. I was used to dealing with lawyers, but it was a surprise, a first I think, for a lawyer to apologize to me. Usually, they were just pig-headed, so my appreciation for Lancaster went up a couple of notches.

"Well, thank you. Apology accepted. I can assure you that I never have, and never would do anything beyond the bounds of my authority. You have to admit though that we do have pretty broad authority so I can understand why it confuses people. Real life isn't like TV."

"Yes, I know now. You can board any vessel at any time for any reason and take whatever you deem necessary to conduct your investigation."

I smiled. "You make it sound like we all wear jack boots. But yes, that does about sum it up. Surely that wasn't the only reason you came here, though?"

"No." She opened the folder she'd pulled out, glanced at it and then pushed it over to me. "I thought seeing as though I made a bit of an ass of myself, I could offer you an olive branch and show you these documents. I actually would rather cultivate relationships with law enforcement than abuse them."

"What's in here?" I asked.

"It's Mr. Willis's last will and testament. I know you're trying to fully investigate what happened, and I thought this might help. Our firm was retained as executor, as Mr. Willis did not have any living relatives and while I can't show you anything confidential without a subpoena, I can share the gist of it."

I leafed through the folder. Some of the papers were loose and appeared pretty old. A lot had messy lawyerese penciled across the top, mostly indecipherable to me.

"Miss Lancaster thanks for this, I can't tell you how much I appreciate it. I don't really know what I'm looking at, though, could you give it to me in a nutshell? In English, as it were."

This time she smiled that cute upturned smile I'd caught a glimmer of the first time I'd met her. It was nice to see on her face. "In Mr. Willis's last will and testament dated June 5th, 2003, he bequeathed all his worldly possessions to his wife."

"Wait. 2003? He didn't have a more up to date will?"

Lancaster shook her head.

"Then that would make his wife Julia Rivas?"

"Julia Willis back then, but yes. The will is valid. Mrs. Rivas is the sole heir."

"How much are we talking about?"

"Mr. Willis had approximately two point three million dollars in his checking account."

I stared at her. "Two point three million?"

She nodded. "Yes. But that's not all. He also had a house in San Antonio he left her, market value of three million give or take ,and a small beach condo in North Padre Island, valued at just under a million. Various other small accounts, but they're the biggest."

I added it up and mentally whistled. "So he left his now ex-wife around six million dollars in cash and assets."

"Yes."

"Jesus. Makes you wonder why he was working on a fishing vessel, doesn't it?"

"I did find it unusual, but I'm not the investigator. Maybe he enjoyed the sea?" She smiled at me again.

"Did he leave his business partners anything?" I asked.

"No, it doesn't look like it."

"Why would he leave his ex-wife all that money? They got divorced years ago from what she told me, and haven't spoken in just as long. Are you sure this is his most up to date will?"

"I couldn't say why he left her the money, but this is his will, fully notarized at my office. There can be no question of its authenticity."

I rubbed my face. This was becoming a really long day. "Alright. Thank you, Miss. Lancaster for the information. Can I get a copy of this?"

"It's yours."

She gathered her things back into the briefcase, and we shook hands. I escorted her back to the elevators making small talk about the weather and other nonsense. I was vibrating with excitement and all but pushed her into the elevator when the doors dinged and opened. As soon as they closed, I hurried over to Carter's desk.

"Grab your bag. We need to go talk to Mrs. Rivas again, there's something she wasn't telling us." I filled her in on the conversation with the lawyer.

"Are you sure she knows about the will?" Carter said.

"Miss. Lancaster told me that Mrs. Rivas would have been aware that she was the sole beneficiary. With that much money, it shouldn't have slipped her mind. Makes me wonder why Willis never changed it."

"Maybe he was still in love with her."

"Maybe. Or maybe he never expected to die quite so soon. It does give her motive, though. I don't care how loaded she looks, six million is a lot of fish."

I gunned the V8 out of the parking lot, and we set off for the short distance to her house. As we turned down her street a gray sedan burst out of her driveway, barely made the turn and started to head our way, slowing when it saw us.

"Is that the same car from before?" Carter said.

"It looks like it. He came out of Rivas's drive." I turned the visor down, lit up the blue lights, and turned the siren on. The car stopped two hundred yards in front of us. Even squinting I couldn't see inside the sedan because it was heavily tinted. I slowed the truck but continued rolling forward, silencing the siren but keeping the lights on.

"Carter get your—"

The sedan punched it in reverse, smoke billowing from the rapidly spinning tires. The acrid stench of burning rubber blew through the AC vents. I jammed my foot down on the gas, and the truck responded effortlessly, closing the gap.

Without slowing, the sedan executed a J-turn, going from reverse to forward with no loss of speed, and was now hurtling away from us. It screeched around the next corner, and I lost sight of it behind a wall. I increased speed, hitting the siren again, and barreled after it. I didn't realize the sedan had stopped as soon as it had gone round the corner. I smashed into the back of it, airbags deploying in the truck with an explosive thump. The back of my head hit the headrest as the force of the airbag drove it backward, my teeth mashed down on my tongue and the coppery bitterness of blood flooded my mouth. I fought off the airbag, trying to get it out of my face. I needed to see what was going on. I heard the airbag go off again.

"What the fuck? Carter you okay" I said.

Carter didn't respond.

The airbag exploded again. I was confused, but adrenaline kicked in, and I realized it wasn't the airbag that was still exploding.

"Carter get down, we're taking fire." I pushed at her to get down, releasing her seat belt. She slid down to the passenger well, unconscious. I took cover. Several shots pinged off the side of the truck and one hit the window, glass shattering into a patchwork of fragments but holding together.

I crawled over to Carter's side, staying low, and pushed her door open wide, sliding out to the ground. I pulled out my service weapon. I couldn't see who was shooting at us but figured it was whoever had been driving the sedan. I left Carter on the floor of the truck, so she was protected, and felt around for any wounds but didn't see anything obvious. Hopefully, it was just the airbag that knocked her out.

I inched around the door and raised my head over the hood. A shot pinged off the engine block, and I ducked again, but now I had the general location of the shooter. I checked my weapon and returned fire; popping off three shots in rapid succession.

I heard a loud hiss from somewhere that seemed out of place, and then another shot clunked into the truck. Thank God we still didn't have that econobox, we'd never have survived the crash let alone the gunfire, it would have gone straight through the thin metal.

I fired again, but this time ducked down low under the truck. No one fired back at me, and then I heard a car start up and peel out. I ran out after it, just to see the flicker of its brake lights as it rounded a corner.

"Shit." I fumbled my phone out of my shirt pocket and called the incident into the duty officer along with a description of the car I'd seen, but I hadn't had a chance to get the plate. I also asked them to call an ambulance for Carter.

I carefully pulled her out of the car and gently positioned her on the ground, folding my jacket and placing it under her head. Her eyes opened and slowly came into focus.

"What, what happened?" she said.

"Oh, nothing. You missed all the fun is all."

"What's going on?"

"Nothing much. We were involved in an accident. I called for an ambulance, they should be here soon."

"Ambulance? I'm fine." Carter attempted to get up but winced when she raised her head.

"You're not fine, and you're going to stay right there until you get checked out."

I could hear the ambulance approaching, the wee-wah of the siren, but then the hiss I'd noticed from earlier drowned out the siren. A roaring like a plane taking off on full thrust slammed against my ears, and then I felt a deep rumble in my ribs as they rattled together. The concussion wave rocked the truck and blasted safety glass at us from the remaining truck windows. Car alarms up and down the street warbled and chirped.

"What the fuck was that? Carter stay down."

I stood up and saw a huge funnel of fire and smoke hit the sky. It was coming from the direction of Mrs. Rivas's house.

"Stay here. Wait for the ambulance. Call for back up if you can. And a fire truck," I shouted over my shoulder.

I ran back around the way we'd come, sprinting as fast as I could. I turned in Mrs. Rivas's driveway, arms pumping, legs going. Fragments of burning and charred paper were falling around me, and I dodged them as best I could. I ran round a bend in the driveway and was nearing the house, when a piano for Christ's sake, fell from the sky and landed right in front of me. It collapsed in a heap of sizzling wood and sonorous chimes. The adrenaline punched in. I didn't have time to be startled, just ran around the thing and kept on going.

My steps faltered as I got closer and saw the house, I slowed and stopped. Where before a magnificent sprawl of decadence had stood, now there was only an enormous crater with smoke and flames raging within. The front door was incongruously still intact, closed and upright, supported by part of the framework, but there was nothing else behind it that I could see. The house was just gone. Completely. There was no saving anyone or anything.

I raised my hand as another flare up scorched the sky and I tried to shield my face from the brutal heat. I backed off as the hairs on my arm singed. Behind me, I could hear the wail of sirens coming up the driveway. Either Carter had got through to the fire department, or they were coming anyway. But it didn't matter. The house was gone. And so were Mrs. Rivas and anybody else that was inside. Fuck.

I moved out of the way so the fire department could do their thing and looked for the guy in charge with the red fire helmet. It wasn't a guy, but a girl and I reported to her what I had seen and heard. She asked a few questions which I did my best to answer, and then I went to find Carter. She was sitting in the back of an ambulance at the end of the driveway with a blanket around her.

"Mrs. Rivas?" she said, looking up.

I shook my head. There was nothing to say. Although the official cause of the fire would have to wait for the arson investigator to make a determination, I'd bet my hind teeth this wasn't an accident.

"You okay?" I said.

She nodded. "Just sore. The medics said I could go if I want."

"Let's go then. We can get a ride back to the office. You sure you're okay?"

"Yeah. They said to take it easy for a bit. Might have a headache. If it gets worse call the doctor, etcetera, etcetera."

"You know. This is starting to get out of control," I said, trying not to grind my teeth.

"Do you think it has anything to do with our case?"

I snorted. "Sorry. Yeah, I do. It's all connected somehow. I think it might be time to pull in Black and have a little chat."

Before I could follow up on that, Paul called me. He said he was using an old payphone at a neighboring dock near the *Reel Lady*.

"Mr. Dalton? I don't know how much longer I can do this." He sounded scared.

"What's going on, Paul?"

"I don't know, sir. I think the guys are getting suspicious, they're looking at me funny like...like they know I told you, like they don't trust me anymore—"

Paul was working himself up. "Paul, you need to get a handle, buddy. I understand this is pretty crazy for you—"

"Crazy? You call this crazy? You come aboard and tell me the captain was dumped from this boat while we were at sea. *This* boat. The one I'm on. That he was already dead. And then you tell me the rest of the crew are in on it. You know how easy it would be for them to dump me? And then you ask me to stay here, to act normal. Come on, Mr. Dalton."

"Paul. I get it, buddy. Listen, we're pulling Mr. Black in for questioning right now. I just need you to hang tight, just for a little bit longer. Can you do that for me? Can you hang tight just for a bit?"

I heard Paul sigh as if he had deflated like an old party balloon. He said something I didn't quite catch, and then he said, "Yeah, I guess."

"Okay, Paul. You do that for me, buddy, hang tight. I've gotta go, but call me if you need anything. Anytime, remember?"

All I heard was a dial tone from the phone hanging up. I felt like a shithead. I hoped he was overreacting, but I needed a break in this case. I needed to figure out what was going on. How did Willis make all that money? Why did he give it all to his wife, and why did someone blow her up? Where would the money go now? Was it Batman? Where were all the guns? There were just too many unanswered questions, not to mention who had trashed my boat and shot at us. It felt like forever ago I was hanging out on *Ghost*, getting bored.

It didn't take long for agents to pick up Black for us, but it gave me enough time to change out of my stinky and smoke riddled clothes into something a bit fresher. Carter was waiting for me outside the interview room and looked a lot better, the aspirin must have helped, and we went in together, a united front. We sat down across from Black, and I opened a folder on the desk, taking out the photo we'd found on Willis's phone, and pushed it over to him so he could see it.

"Good evening, Mr. Black. In case you've forgotten my name is Special Agent Dalton, this is Special Agent Carter. Take a look at the photo. Recognize anyone?"

Mr. Black was sporting another foul velour jogging suit. This one was a deadly shade of bright orange and zipped all the way to the top. Black had chubby fingers, clustered with gold rings. He reached for the photo and then hesitated, withdrawing his hands.

"Nice picture. Where'd you get it?" he said, in his staccato clip.

"Do you recognize the people in the picture?"

"Can't say I do. Should I?

I tapped at the photo. "So you're telling me that's not you, Captain Willis and George."

Black glanced at the photo and then regarded me with a steady gaze. He shrugged. "I know those other men, of course. I know me. I just don't recognize them or me. In this photo, that is. Perhaps, perhaps it is photo shopped. The things they can do with computers these days. It's almost like magic."

"And who would do that, and then put it on Willis's phone?"

"Who can tell? In business, one always has enemies. Some people are naturally envious of me."

I shoved a piece of paper across the desk. "Write their names down."

Black didn't move to take the paper.

"What can you tell me about Mr. Willis's will? Did you know he left his ex, Mrs. Rivas, all his money?"

He shrugged again. "Didn't know. Don't care. What Willis did with his money was his concern. He didn't tell me what to do with mine. I didn't tell him what to do with his. What am I in here for anyway?"

"Just a few more questions, Mr. Black. Did you know that Mrs. Rivas was murdered earlier today?"

"No. Now, much as I appreciate the good arm of the law, I have more important things to do. Perhaps you should be out there looking for her killer instead of bothering an innocent businessman like me. "

There was a knock on the door and the duty officer poked his head in.

"Sorry to bother you, sir, but-" he said.

"Really, Mr. Dalton, I thought we had a better relationship," Lancaster said, as she pushed past the officer. "You should have notified me that my client was here."

I smiled tightly at her. She'd changed into a prim and tan pantsuit since the afternoon. I nodded at the officer, and he closed the door. "Mr. Black is not under arrest, we just had a few questions."

"And now he's leaving. Mr. Black. Ready?"

"Of course, Miss. Lancaster. I was just telling Mr. Dalton that I didn't know anything useful."

Mr. Black pushed his bulk away from the table and tipped an imaginary hat to me, the gold on his fingers flashing in the stark light.

"Agents, I hope we don't meet again."

Lancaster escorted him out, and the door closed.

I blew out a breath of frustration and slammed my fist down on the desk, rattling the metal.

"Dammit all to hell."

# EIGHT

## *Serenity for the Soul*

**W**here to turn? What to do? I was in turmoil, feeling angst driven. I knew, absolutely knew that Black and George, Ricky and Jimmy were all involved. Some more than others. I was reasonably sure Paul wasn't. I just didn't know how all the pieces fit together. What caused them to kill Willis and dump his body? Were they hoping it would look like an accident? Why was Rivas blown up? Were they trying to scare me by ransacking my boat and leaving that message, or was it misdirection to hide what they were looking for?

The thoughts spun through my head, round and round. I needed to focus on one element, follow the leads and rabbit trails and either find conclusions or move on. But first, I needed my haven back, and I needed a place to rest. If my head wasn't in the game, I was no use to anyone. *Ghost* may have been physically clean, but I felt its sanctity was blemished, it didn't feel like the old *Ghost* anymore, something was missing.

Good bartenders were always a wealth of knowledge and Pete knew a guy that knew a guy. That guy put me in touch with a local shaman he knew, the real deal, so he said. It was easy to find a crackerjack, advertising on Craig's List, or in the small print at the back of sketchy magazines, but someone who could actually perform? That was much harder. I wanted that safe, secure feeling back on my boat, and I was willing to give it a shot. I'd kept this part of my life separate from work. Telling the guys my boat had lost its mojo didn't fit the image of a law enforcement officer. Mainstream or no-stream was the only way.

Carter had tagged along for the meeting, she said she'd never met a shaman, and I think it piqued her interest. I didn't mind having her with me either. It was only a couple of days since I'd met Carter, but in that short time together I had learned there was a lot to like about her. Although new to the Guard, she could draw on more than I'd initially given her credit for, and despite our rocky beginning, we were working well together. I trusted her. She had my back.

We'd met the shaman at the T-heads; she was not what I was expecting. I was thinking it would be someone adorned with native robes or wearing a bearskin, maybe a long staff, but then I realized how stupid that was. It wasn't Gandalf the Grey I was waiting for, and it wasn't likely a shaman would go walking around with a great big bear suit on, not in the heat of south Texas and not unless you wanted to get thrown in the nut bin. Instead, she was wearing a straightforward, off-white cotton suit. Her only adornment was a small brown leather satchel she carried over her shoulder.

It threw me off when she walked right up to me and said I must be Dalton. It took me a moment to transfer the mental image I had in my head of walking bear rugs with the person standing in front of me.

"I'm sorry," I said, "I'm not really sure how to address you."

Her hair was flaxen and tied up simply in a ponytail. She smiled when she spoke, dimples appearing in the corners of her mouth.

"If we go all formal you can call me Shaman Satinka, but I prefer Tinka. It's simpler. And cuter."

She turned to Carter and took her hand in hers. "And you, my dear. What's your story? No, don't tell me." She paused for a moment. "I sense distress from you. Something else as well, something more...I sense protection."

She closed her eyes for a minute. We didn't say anything. I scratched my nose and felt a bit stupid while nothing seemed to happen.

After a moment more, she said, "I feel someone from your past is looking out for you, someone close. Family? A sibling? Sister? No, a brother."

I got chills down the back of my neck. There was no way she could have known anything about Carter's brother. A tear slid down Carter's cheek, and she just nodded.

Satinka nodded and smiled, still holding Carter's hand. "It is so. I don't usually get such clear images without my cards, but with you, my dear, your brother must be close." Satinka frowned, her forehead creasing. "This might sound trite, but there is a shadow in your aura. It will pass, but a change is coming for you." The frown deepened, and Satinka let go of Carter's hands. "I'm sorry, that's all I have."

"What do you mean?" Carter said.

"There is nothing more. I wish I could give you definitive answers, but it's not always clear. I'm sorry." Satinka turned to me. "Mr. Dalton, I believe you have need of my services. What exactly is it you need me to do?"

"Shaman Satinka-"

"Just Tinka is fine."

74

"Tinka, then. This is going to sound stupid." When she didn't interrupt, I carried on. "When I got my boat, I was told a Yogi or shaman or someone blessed it, or something like that. Maybe it was a sales pitch, but I've always felt weirdly calm and comfortable. Absolutely, safe when I'm on my boat. More than just a secure feeling, something, I don't know, other? It's always been like that, until yesterday. My boat was broken into, I knew the moment I stepped foot on her. The calm has gone, and well..."

"You would like me to replace the sanctity of your vessel?"

"Well, yes. If that's possible?"

"All things are possible. Please, permit me to enter your vessel by myself so that I may draw upon the old auras."

She walked over to the *Ghost*, and placed her hands on the superstructure for a moment, and then walked solemnly aboard. I saw her disappear into the cabin.

"What do you think, Jess?" I asked.

"You know, that's the first time you've called me that."

"I'm sorry. I–"

"No, no. I like it. The only other person that ever called me Jess was my brother. Somehow it feels right coming from you."

I took her hand in mine. "Are you okay? That was some pretty heavy stuff the shaman just said."

"Yeah, that was a surprise. I didn't think shaman were psychic like that." Carter gave my hand a squeeze and let go. "You know what, though? It makes me feel better. Perhaps my brother really is looking out for me from somewhere. He certainly made me get my life back together. Maybe he's my guardian angel." She shrugged.

"I think shaman come in all shapes and sizes. She wasn't what I was expecting either. Maybe that's a good thing." I waved at my boat. "I wonder how long this takes."

Not one for standing around I started pacing. I hoped Satinka could do something. When I glanced back at *Ghost*, I saw clouds of smoke billowing from the open hatch.

"What the..." I started to run towards my boat, but then the Satinka came out onto the stern deck. She waved me off.

"Not to worry," she shouted. "Give me a few more minutes."

I stopped where I was, not sure if I should listen to her. Carter came up to me and placed her hand on my shoulder.

"Trust her. It'll be okay. I have a feeling."

"I hope you're right," I said.

A few minutes later the shaman calmly walked back toward us, carrying something that was still smoking.

"Sage." She held up the smoking bundle. "This is sage. I'm sorry if I alarmed you, it took more than usual. Sage is used to ward off unwelcome spirits and cleanse a place. There were many bad vibes from the people that did this to your boat. But I have replaced what you called your calm. I have also left some feathers above the sink; do not remove them from your boat. It creates a form of protection. However, there is one thing." She paused for a moment and looked me in the eye. "The name of your home. Names are important, they hold meaning, and the old name must change, it has to be changed."

"What should I call her then?"

"That is up to you. It will come. Go aboard, feel her."

I walked down to the old *Ghost*. She didn't look any different. The smoke had dissipated soon after Satinka left. I looked back. Carter urged me on. When I stepped forward, I almost stopped. It was as if I'd walked into a big fluffy blanket, like in those science fiction movies where the actor walks through a portal to another world. Something enveloped me, and a feeling of comfort entwined round my soul. I sat down in the stern, and it came to me. Instantly.

After a few minutes I walked back up to Satinka and said, *"Serenity."*

"Then that shall be her name." Satinka turned to leave.

"Wait," I said. "Thank you. She feels like home again. What do I owe you?"

"Nothing. I do not charge for my services. I take blessings in that I helped you." She turned to leave again, but then stopped. "Perhaps, though..."

"Yes, anything."

"Take my arm, walk with me a ways."

"I won't be a minute," I said to Carter.

I walked arm in arm with Satinka for a minute until we were away from *Serenity*, and then we stopped. She turned to me and placed her hands on my shoulders and said, "Your friend. I feel a bond between the two of you."

"Jessica? I've only just met her."

"It doesn't matter. Your souls talk to each other; I can hear their happy chatter when you two are close. Do not ignore your inner self. She will need your help soon, trust yourself."

"What do you mean?"

"As I said before. I don't always see everything clearly, but she will need you. It is your duty to her, to your souls."

I didn't know how to respond to that. Satinka left, perhaps leaving me with more questions than answers. I didn't believe in a lot of things, but I know she said stuff to Carter that no one could have known. I filed it away in the file that said, to think about when alone with a beer. On *Serenity*.

I walked back. "Jess. What are you doing with the rest of your night?"

"I don't have any plans."

"We've been going a million miles an hour on this case. I think a bit of R and R would do us both some good. Perhaps a brief break will give us a fresh perspective. Would you do me the honor of letting me cook dinner for you aboard *Serenity*?"

She looked at me in the dwindling sunlight as the last rays caught her brown eyes, emphasizing tiny flecks of green.

"I'd be flattered," she said. She gasped when she came aboard. "Oh, Frank. Is this what it felt like before?"

"It's better now. I think the old gal is happy."

I settled Carter in the cockpit seats and poured her a glass of Pinot Grigio I took from the fridge, an old bottle I'd been saving for a special occasion.

"To *Serenity*," I said.

"To *Serenity*."

I went to work in the galley. I cooked my go-to meal, shrimp scampi. It was a family recipe that an old friend had given me a long time ago, and one I could cook quickly and simply. Less than twenty minutes later, I brought two steaming plates out to the cockpit, set on trays. The sun had set, and a warm glow surrounded *Serenity*. The air felt clean and refreshing.

"Oh. My. God. This is freaking delicious," she said.

"You like it? I'm sorry, I didn't even ask if you were allergic to shrimp."

"No. No. This is simply amazing. Frank, you have hidden talents."

"Thanks." We ate in companionable silence, enjoying the view, lights flickering on in neighboring boats, the wink of red and green buoys reflecting off the water. I refreshed our glasses, shaking the last drop from the bottle.

"I've only poured two glasses, the bottle must have shrunk," I said.

Carter giggled. It sounded girlish and womanly at the same time. I liked it, it sounded good on her.

"That's because your glasses are absolutely massive, Frank."

The double entendre was on the tip of my tongue, but thankfully my filter engaged in time.

Carter scooted closer to me. "Do you have a blanket? I don't want to go inside, but it's getting chilly."

I hopped down the steps into the cabin and came back with two fluffy blankets.

"Here," I said, and wrapped one round her shoulders.

"Thank you." We sat next to each other and watched the stars come out. One shot across the horizon leaving a short trail.

"Make a wish," Carter said.

"I already did."

We sat in silence for a while, listening to the gentle splashing of the water and the occasional murmur of conversation coming from some of the other liveaboards.

"Would you like a nightcap?" I asked.

Carter didn't say anything for a moment, lost in thought. "I should probably get going, Frank. I'm sure we have an early start tomorrow. It's been a beautiful night, though."

"Sure? I have some excellent whiskey."

Carter looked torn, while I waited hopefully, but finally said, "No. I have to go. I need my beauty sleep."

She leaned over and gave me a gentle kiss on the cheek. "Thank you again for a super evening."

"Anytime, Jess."

I walked her back to her car, wistful but happy and content.

She leaned out of her car window and said, "Next time, I promise I'll take you up on that nightcap." She blew me a kiss and drove off, waving.

I walked back to the *Serenity*, cleaned up the dishes and settled down for the night. I couldn't wait for that nightcap, maybe our souls really were talking.

The same time the morning light started pouring through my cabin porthole my phone angrily vibrated off the end of my side table and fell to the floor. I groggily picked it up without looking at who was calling.

"Dalton," I said.

"Special Agent Dalton? There's been an accident."

I drove straight to the scene. Carter was there already. She looked pale.

"How bad is it?" I asked.

She didn't say anything. The look on her face told me all I needed to know.

I walked passed the flashing lights of ambulances, the sirens long gone quiet. Passed the Reel Fish, Reel Quick sign, and saw a sheet covering part of what may have been the top of a torso. The rest of the body was firmly wedged under a gigantic crate. Scallops, judging by the words on the side. A massive crate of scallops had fallen from the still swinging rusty looking crane. Fallen on what I was told was Paul. Poor, poor, Paul.

Paul hadn't known what he was getting himself into. I had. But, I thought he'd be safe. Pitiable, foolish, stupid, naïve me. I knelt down next to him. There was nothing the paramedics could have done. They were just waiting for us to release the scene so they could take him to the morgue.

I should have known. I should have pulled him out of there when he called me. While I beat myself up, Carter went around and started interviewing potential witnesses. I could see that no one wanted to talk. No one had to. We all knew why it couldn't have been an accident. Paul was just another unfortunate who happened to get in the way of the massive churning machine that was Batman Black. It hadn't mattered if he knew anything, not at all. It just mattered that he might have known something, might have given the game away. Might have.

In all the worlds of might haves and could have beens, this was the one where Paul's story ended. Goddammit.

I shook myself out of my reverie. I wasn't going to get the bastards like this, feeling sorry for myself. I went in search of the crane operator.

I found him, joking and laughing with Jimmy and Ricky, a steaming paper cup of coffee in his hand. I smacked the cup out of his hand and rammed him into the wall behind him, the metal shutters clanging and vibrating, coffee splattering the wall and sliding down.

I shouted at him, inches from his face, spittle flying from my mouth. "You're a fucking murderer. You worthless piece of shit."

I don't know what I would have done next, probably nothing good. I was blinded by rage, rage for the innocent. I felt fury for Paul who couldn't express his own, and I felt the unfairness of it all. But a hand on my shoulder and soft words in my ear stopped my assault.

"Frank! Leave him. He's not worth your career," Carter said.

I wanted to ignore her. I wanted to smash the laughing, stale-breathed mouth of the crane operator, but most of all I wanted a release from my emotions. Pounding on his face would help. But I didn't give in. I didn't do it.

"We can do this the right way," she said, pulling at my arm. "We can put them behind bars and lose the key. But you can't hit him. Then you'll be off the case. Then you'll have lost, and they'll have won. Don't let them win, Frank. Let's do this together."

I let him go, giving him a final shove.

"Yeah, get lost," he said, trying to save face.

I ignored him. Carter was right. I was better than this. I'd do it the right way; I'd carve their empire apart one piece at a time. I'd do it for Willis and Rivas and Paul and all the other poor souls these fucktards had ever killed.

There was nothing useful for us here. I left with Carter, walking back through the warehouse. Big fat Black was there, sitting in his chair, an unlit fat cigar firmly clenched in his teeth, his massive jowls fighting for space on his face.

He couldn't resist saying to me as we passed, "Such a tragedy Special Agents. Paul was such a nice boy. A good boy."

I wanted to kick him in the head. Instead, I said, "He was good. You got to him too late though, Black. He already spilled. I have a signed affidavit from him back in the office. It won't be long now before we're bringing you in, in cuffs. Enjoy the cigar."

I didn't give him a chance to reply. I could feel his beady little pig eyes staring at us on the way out and refused to give him the pleasure of turning around.

We drove straight back to the underground lot, but I couldn't find an empty space where I usually parked, so I drove down a further two floors than usual. I wanted some space. Some space around me, around the car. We pulled into a spot where the overhead light hadn't been fixed in a week, and just sat in the car.

"It's okay, Frank—"

"No. No, it's not, Jess. I should have protected him. He called me and thought he was in trouble, that they knew, but I just convinced him to stay put. I needed him there. I should have known."

"No one could have known they'd drop a crate on his head. It wasn't your fault, Frank. You didn't do it. Look at me, dammit."

I turned and looked at her. She took my hand and held it firmly. "Avenge Paul, Frank. Let him be the last person these bastards kill. Let's figure out where the guns are coming from, where they're going. Let's nail them. Maybe Mark has something we can work with. Perhaps the ME has something else she can tell us. You can't give up now, then they truly have won, and Paul's death and everyone else's was in vain."

I pulled her hand away from mine and rubbed my face. "Has anyone ever told you how beautiful you are?"

"Not the right time, Frank."

"I mean it."

"Thank you. Come on, let's get to work."

I was about to open the door when something caught my eye. "Hold on, Jess. Don't open the door."

She looked where I was looking. "Is that…"

"Yeah. It is." I had a sick, weary feeling in my stomach after Paul. What caught my eye before we got out now made my stomach turn sour and boil. We'd sat in this dark corner of the lot long enough for anyone coming in not to notice us. The elevator at the end had pinged, the light coming on. That's what had caught my eye initially. Coming out of the elevator was Mr. Lewis, our Special Agent in Charge. Getting out of a parked car was George. Good old wraith-like George. I knew Mr. Lewis well enough to spot him from a distance; I spent lots of time trying to avoid him. The sharp-looking, black tailored suit, was a dead giveaway. George was hard to miss being so tall and rail like thin. They met. Lewis looked around and then handed George a folder. George flicked through it, never saying a word, and then gave Lewis a bulging white envelope. Much as I couldn't quite believe what my eyes were telling me, I'd bet my front teeth that that envelope was full of money.

"That fucking bastard. The SAC's on the take."

"What do you think Lewis gave George?" Carter asked.

"I don't know. Pretty sure it's got something to do with our case, though."

"Shouldn't we go out there and confront them?"

"No. Not right now. It's too dangerous. And what if it's nothing? No, we need to be sure. Let's wait until they've gone, and then see if we can get the security footage for this level."

We waited until it was clear and then headed up to the office. I'd told Carter to keep this to herself. If the SAC was taking bribes, there was no knowing how far this went, or how far into our department. We were on our own for the time being. We couldn't trust anyone.

Carter had some calls to make so I got Mark to show me how to review the security footage. I asked him to leave the room as I viewed it. I trusted Mark but didn't need anyone else in on this yet. On the monitor, I saw us drive in and park, there was a time and date stamp on the bottom of the screen. You could just make us out as we were talking, and then it cut straight to us walking to the elevator.

"That's not right," I said.

I reversed the footage and played it again. Maybe I'd accidentally hit fast-forward or something. The same thing happened, the footage went straight from us in the car to us going to the elevator.

I called Mark back in. "I seem to have screwed something up. The footage appears to be missing a section."

Mark sat down and started typing and then the footage appeared again. Exactly as it had twice before. "What's wrong with it?" I said.

"Wrong with it? Nothing. It's all there."

"No, it's not right. There's a bit in the middle that's missing. Something happened between us sitting in the truck and walking to the elevator. Like two or three minutes are missing."

Mark checked again and then showed me the time stamp. "Look he said. The time stamp never alters. There's you in the car at 0942, and then at 0943 there's you and Carter going to the elevator."

"I'm telling you, Mark, that's not how it happened. Could someone have tampered with this?"

"I don't see how. It's in a secure system. Very few people have access to this, for just that reason."

I had a sinking feeling. "Who has access, Mark?"

"Well. I do, obviously; otherwise I couldn't have shown you this."

"Who else?"

"The SAC does. He has overall authority. It's his unit, after all."

"Could someone have tampered with it, without you knowing? Could they have altered the time stamp, erased some footage?"

"What are you suggesting? I would never—"

"I know you wouldn't. I'm not saying you did, but is it possible?"

"It shouldn't be. If you're positive something's happened to this footage, I'll review it in my lab. Maybe I can figure something out."

"Do it. And Mark. Don't tell anyone. Not even the SAC."

"I have to tell him if he asks—"

"Not even the SAC, Mark. Do you hear me?"

"Yeah. I got it. What do I tell him?"

"If he asks, tell him to come and see me."

I walked out and went to find Carter. We needed a break in this case, needed some luck, something to bust it wide open. When I found Carter, she was just getting off the phone.

"We have it, Frank. We've got a piece of the puzzle."

# NINE

## *Fish Sticks Are Frozen*

"It appears that a Medical Review Officer, a Doctor Keith Scott, down in Miami," Carter said, "was taking bribes in return for reporting positive drug tests on commercial mariners as negative."

"That sounds like more of a case for the Sector guys, Jess. What's that have to do with this case?"

"Let me finish."

I sat down, waving her on and looked around for my coffee cup.

"You're right, it is a Sector case, Sector Miami is dealing with it and reviewing all of Scott's files to see which ones were altered. It's a laborious process as he has files going back for years. The way it worked was simple. Scott was one of a handful of doctors from around the country qualified to make the final determination from a drug test on whether it was positive or not."

"Wouldn't a positive drug test always be positive?"

"Not necessarily. If you had a valid prescription and popped positive, Scott could override the positive result and inform the mariner's employer the test was negative. That would be perfectly legal. Scott however, was taking some of those positive results and suggesting to the mariner that for a small fee, which ranged from a few hundred dollars to a few thousand, he could make the positive result a negative. There was no one to question his authority. He'd make a notation on the chain of custody form, notify the employer the test was negative, and the mariner would keep his job. This had been going on for years until someone wasn't happy with the excellent doctor's service and complained to the authorities."

I spotted my coffee cup on the far side of Carter's desk and reached for it. "Go on, I'm listening," I said.

"Miami is going through all of Scott's files, and whenever they find an altered report, they notify the nearest Coast Guard office where that mariner lives, so the local unit can follow up. One of those reports came to our Sector, and when they ran his name, they found he was a captain on one of Black's boats; this is where we come in."

"I was waiting."

She ignored me. "This boat is a large fish processor; we're talking three to four hundred feet long. They're required to be captained by a licensed mariner and have licensed crews. This guy," Carter pulled a page from her notes, "has been a captain for eighteen years, with an otherwise clean record. He wants to make a deal."

"A deal for what?" I said.

"Well, he thinks he's looking at some jail time or at the very least the loss of his license. You and I know he wouldn't go to jail for failing a drug test, but he doesn't know that. And besides, his license is worth a lot of money to him, if he loses that he loses his job. Some of these guys pull down upwards of two hundred thousand a year. Although his bank records suggest he's up shit creek."

"And you said he works on one of Black's boats?"

"Yeah. Like I said, a big one the, I can't even say the name with a straight face, the *Reel Thing*."

"Where does Black come up with these god awful names? All right, so this mariner wants to make a deal?"

"Joe Deacon is his name, and yes, he does. What do you think?"

"I'm hesitant, but if he thinks he's in serious trouble, it might be worth having a chat with him. Maybe he knows something about Black's operations that could help us. But I still don't get why you're so excited, we have other leads that look like they may be of more value. Don't you think we should follow up on those first? Where does he live, anyway?"

"Out passed Calallen, but you're missing the point, Frank."

She let me dangle for a minute, fishing boats were not my specialty.

"The *Reel Thing* is a fish processing boat, not a fishing boat. Regular fishing boats off-load their catch to the *Reel Thing* and then continue fishing without going back to port. The *Reel Thing* processes the fish and throws them in their reefers; they have dozens of workers on board rotating on twelve-hour shifts. Frank, think about it, the *Reel Thing* is just a huge floating freezer."

Somebody turned up the rheostat on the light bulb above my head, and I finally understood what Carter was talking about.

"Listen," she said. "Black owns the *Reel Lady* and the *Reel Thing*. The two boats could have met up when they were out to sea. It's a perfect cover, and explains how Willis could have been frozen."

84

I looked at Carter and thought how lucky I was to have her as a partner. "Why wouldn't the *Reel Thing* have dumped him themselves?" I said.

"I don't know. Maybe they couldn't, maybe it would have been too obvious. Who knows? It's just a theory."

"No, it's an excellent theory, Jess. I'm glad you stuck with it, I wouldn't have picked up on that. What I'm wondering is why Paul wouldn't have said anything about meeting this fish processor? It could have really helped us. I don't know, maybe it could have helped save his life."

"You can't blame yourself, Frank, or Paul. Could be he was asleep. He said he was down below a lot more this trip than usual; those other assholes didn't want him nosing around. Besides, if that was their regular routine, it wouldn't have struck Paul as unusual."

I slurped some coffee. It tasted like mud.

"You know that's yesterday's coffee, right?"

I hadn't, it explained why it was so god-awful. And cold.

"Where's this mariner now?" I said.

"He's at home. He knows we're coming."

"You think of everything, don't you? Well, let's get there then before this guy ends up dead too."

We drove to Calallen. It was a small town on the outskirts of Corpus Christi, only notable because you had to pass it to get to San Antonio. Nothing much was in Calallen, a few businesses, a couple of hotels, some houses, but mostly a dusty and flat, flat landscape. They say that in South Texas you can see your kids running away from home for a week, it was so flat. I didn't know about that, but I could believe it if I lived out here.

The captain's house was an unassuming ranch, set back from the road. It didn't look new, but had a recent coat of paint, and looked like it was well kept. There wasn't much in the way of grass, but what there was, was trimmed neatly. As we drove down the driveway dust billowed a mile behind us. An old barn stood in the back, the doors wide open. We pulled up it, and a man, his neck almost perpendicular with his body came out, shading his eyes with his hand and staring at us.

"You got this, Jess?" I said.

She didn't blink. "Yep."

We got out of the car and met him about halfway; he was wearing a pair of bib overalls and wiping his hands on a rag.

"Excuse me if I don't shake yer hands," he said, gesturing to the rag, "was working on an old tractor in the barn."

Carter nodded and said, "Sir, my name is Special Agent Carter, this is Special Agent Dalton. Are you Mr. Deacon?"

Deacon nodded. "Figured you must be the Feds. Don't get many visitors round here. Yeah, that's me. I suppose you've come about the drug test results?"

"Something like that. Do you have somewhere we can sit down and talk?" Carter said.

He motioned us to an old picnic table. It was early afternoon, still a comfortable heat and deliciously warm, so it would be nice to sit outside. Carter and I sat on one side, Deacon on the other.

"Sir, do you have your Merchant Mariners Credential on you by any chance?" Carter said.

Deacon patted the top pocket of his overalls. "My license? As it happens, I do. Knew you'd be coming out, so I kept it with me."

He handed it to Carter, and she passed it to me. I flicked through it. The credential looked just like a burgundy colored passport, and inside it had a photograph of Deacon with his address, date of birth and other vitals. This one stated Mr. Deacon was a Master of unlimited tonnage on ocean-going vessels. No restrictions, multiple endorsements for the usual kind. No wonder he wanted to make a deal, this credential was like gold in the world of mariners.

"Mr. Deacon—"

Deacon frowned. "Sorry, Miss, to interrupt. I haven't been a mister for years. I usually go by Deke or Captain."

"Of course. Captain, our partners down in Miami uncovered an illegal operation by a Doctor Scott. Instead of reporting positive drug tests to the authorities, he was selling clean drug tests results. Your name came up."

Deacon nodded and looked down at his hands clasped on the table. "Yeah. I heard."

"Normally, we wouldn't be having this chat; we would just issue a Complaint and revoke your license. It'd be gone. For good. We could also look back at all the other drug tests you were required to take and see how many of those were positive, and how many fraudulent applications you filled out. Perhaps it turns out you don't even qualify to hold a master's credential."

"No. No need for that. I was stupid. It was just a one-time thing."

"In our experience, Captain, opiate users don't generally have a one-time experience. That was what the test said, wasn't it, opiates? How much did it cost you to have Scott alter the report?"

Deacon sat hunched over, defeat written all over his face. "Too much." He rubbed his face with his hands and sighed. "What can I do? I can't lose my license. It's all I've got. Ever since my dear Rachael died things haven't been going right. I need to work. I'm one payment short of losing all this." He gestured at the house.

"I'm sorry about that," Carter said, "But we can't just ignore the issue. It's our job to ensure the waterways remain safe and to take unsafe mariners out of the picture."

"I've never had an accident; I've never used while I was underway. Surely you've looked at my record. I don't have a blemish on it."

"Well, that's partly why we're making this house call. We understand you work on a vessel owned by Mr. Black."

Deacon looked at Carter.

"We're interested in what you might have to tell us about the operation Mr. Black is running," Carter said.

"What's to tell? I run a fish processor. Can't say it's the most glamorous job, but it gets hard to keep a steady job, what with..."

'Right. I'm sure,' Carter said, as Deacon trailed off. "Here's the thing, though. This is how it's going to work. You tell us what you know about Mr. Black's operations, and we'll see what we can do about the drug charge."

"Can I keep my license?" Deacon said, eyeing the credential where I was keeping my hand on it.

"Honestly? Maybe. That's as good as I can go right now," Carter said. And then she threw him a nugget. "But based on what you tell us, if it's good, we can make a deal and you can go back to work. The other option is you lose your license and probably do some jail time. Depends on what you tell us."

Deacon thought for a minute, stood up and walked off. He lit up a smoke and started pacing, talking to himself.

Carter leaned toward me. "What's he doing?"

"It looks like he's weighing his options," I said. "Nice work, by the way."

"Do you think he'll bite?"

I looked at him, walking the same patch of dirt, kicking up dust. I shrugged. "Have to wait and see. Shouldn't be long. Let him walk it out. Don't say anything until he talks."

"Why?"

"It's like working in sales. The first person to speak usually loses the deal. Let it play out," I said.

Deacon finished his smoke and flicked the butt towards the house. He pulled the pack out for another smoke but put it back in his pocket without lighting one. We waited while he sat back down.

Deacon spoke first. Winner, winner, chicken dinner. "I don't know much. I've only been working for Black for a short time. What is it you want to know?"

This was the tricky part. If Deacon thought he was in too much trouble, he wouldn't say a word.

"Like I said, we want to know about Black's operation," Carter said.

"If...if I tell you what I know, you got to protect me from Black. He's a vicious SOB. If he ever finds out I told you anything he'll, well, let's just say I won't be worrying about that license no more."

Carter looked him in the eye. "We understand Mr. Black's reputation. We'll do what we can."

Deacon stood up. "No, that's not good enough. I need some sort of guarantee."

"Sit down Cap'," Carter said. "Listen, if what you tell us is good enough, we aim to put Black and his crew down for quite some time. They won't be able to get to you."

"You don't know Black then if that's what you think. Locking him up won't stop his reach. You know he's connected right?"

"Captain," I said, "why don't you stay put here for a minute, while me and Special Agent Carter confer. Maybe we can talk it through and make a deal."

Carter and I walked back to the truck.

"What do you have in mind, Frank?"

"Let's see what we can do for him. We need to find out what he knows. It might not be anything useful, but the guy's obviously not going to say a word until we can offer him some sort of protection. Let me make a call to Tobias, he's in regular contact with the District Attorney, and he might be able to set something up. I'm not going to lie to Deacon, but maybe we can get him witness protection or something."

I called Smith and gave him the run down. He asked a few amplifying questions, and he said he'd call back in five minutes.

Smith was good to his word, and the call came through promptly. I put him on speakerphone so Carter could hear, and he told us that if what Deacon said was enough to break the case open, we could have a Federal Marshal keep an eye on Deacon. He wasn't going to offer him witness protection, but it was at least something.

We headed back to Deacon who looked like he'd smoked ten more cigarettes in the short time we'd been gone. His hands were shaking slightly, either from nerves or the nicotine overload. Probably a bit of both.

As I sat down, I made a show of looking around and said, "It's pretty quiet out here, Captain."

"Yeah, I like it. Was my Poppa's house 'for he died. Thought I'd be able to live out my retirement here."

"Maybe you still can. I spoke with our boss, the Assistant Special Agent in Charge and he's prepared to provide a Federal Marshal for your protection, twenty-four seven, on the condition that what you tell us is actionable."

"What's that mean?" he said.

"It means that if the information you tell us is good enough to lead to the arrest and subsequent conviction of Black, then we can make a deal."

"Do I have a choice?" he said.

"Sure. We can walk away right now. We'll take your credential with us of course, we can't have a drug addict running around at sea in charge of a vessel. Then after the boys down in Miami finish their investigation, we'll be back with cuffs for you."

Deacon lit another smoke, the last of the pack. He let out a long, thin stream of smoke. "Not much of a choice."

I shrugged. "You tell us what you know, and we'll provide that protection you wanted. Although..."

Deacon looked hopeful.

"You seem like an intelligent man, Deke; you know Black has his fat fingers in a lot of pots. It wouldn't surprise me if he knows we've been talking to you," I said. "But, he doesn't have any idea what you've already told us, so if we walk away from here with nothing, we might just let it slip that you've been super helpful..."

Deacon looked at me, coughed, then spat on the floor. "That's a dick move, agent."

I shrugged. "It is what it is. It's cards on the table time, Deke. What'll it be?"

Deacon rubbed his face as if he was trying to wash away the cracks and crevices of his life, then just stared at the ground.

After a moment, Carter went in for the kill and prodded him gently. "Deke, tell us about the guns."

He spilled the beans, not just a can of beans but the whole damn enchilada. By the time he was done, we had enough to move forward. Finally, a glimmer of hope on the horizon for the good guys. He'd told us how he would liaise with a freighter far, far offshore, out of U.S. waters. There, they would transfer shipments of guns to the fish processor in waterproof crates and store them way down below in the refrigerated holds. Then they'd get covered with fish from the other vessels. That way, if they were ever boarded by Customs or the Coast Guard, all they'd see if they checked the holds were massive mounds of wriggling fish. It was a neat idea; no one was going to search a fish hold full of fish.

"I didn't know they was guns, to begin with," Deacon said. "I knew it was probably nothing legal, no one goes to that much trouble otherwise. But I don't ask no questions. That's the way Black likes it. No questions and no answers. If you work for him, you keep quiet. The pay was good, and I was happy for a while."

"What changed your mind?" Carter said.

"I'm not a crooked man, I've been at sea for years, but I needed the money, and the bank was looking at me hard to pay down the mortgage on this old place. That and the drug problem. I kept it clean on the boat like I said, but it was getting harder and harder and more expensive."

Now Deacon was talking, he seemed more at ease. The way he talked you could tell it was like he'd almost wanted to get caught somehow. It was just our lucky break it came in the way it did.

Deacon continued, "I could maybe turn a blind eye to those crates, but then we started getting these odd shaped packages, maybe once ever' couple a months. They looked wrong, I think I knew what they was, but my mind didn't want to accept it. So, one night, I get a bee in my bonnet and start nosing around. No one's going to question the captain. I went down to the main reefer to see for myself. Don't ask me why, I never should have, and God help me, you have to believe me, I never had nothing to do with it." He paused for a moment to shake out another smoke from a new pack. Hands shaking it took him several tries to light it. When he had it good and going, he continued. "The package was hanging from a hook in the meat locker. I had to look. I knew, but didn't want to be right. Curiosity killed that cat, you know? Anyways, I slit open the package with my knife, it was all plastic on the outside, and underneath was some sort of muslin material. I cut at the top, just cut a little, but it was enough to see."

When he paused for too long a moment Carter prompted him. "And?"

Deacon shuddered. "And it was a face. A human face. Frozen. Looked like she'd been dead a while."

"I'm sorry, did you say she?" Carter said.

"Yeah. P'raps I could have handled it better if it'd been a man, but it wasn't. It shook me up, right down to the bone, I tell you. I must have been in the freezer for a while, as all of a sudden I felt cold to the core. I wrapped her up again, best I could and went back to my cabin. No one saw me."

"What happened to her?" Carter said.

"Another boat came alongside the next day. Their crew knew where to go and took her off themselves. I don't know what they did with her after that, I can only guess. They wouldn't let us out on deck when they did it, same as when they dropped her off. Imagine old Black thinks it's easier that way."

We'd been taping the interview, and the old school miniature tape recorder took that moment to beep. We had digital recorders, but I liked the feel of something substantial. I replaced the tape with a fresh one, and Deacon took out another fresh smoke. I don't think Black had much to worry about, the way Deacon smoked, he'd probably die of cancer before too long.

"Was that the only time you took delivery of bodies?" I asked.

Deacon looked crestfallen as if his soul was telling us he was done. His face sunk into itself, dark rings under his eyes.

"No. There were others. Three or four at least."

"Did you ever look at the others?" Carter said.

"No. Never needed to. I knew what they was. One was enough."

We talked some more, wrapping up the details of when, where and so on. I was disgusted and giddy at the same time. Disgusted with the callous way Black treated my fellow humans like so much flotsam to be jettisoned into the deep. How Black could pretend to be above it all, never getting his hands dirty, I didn't know. And I was giddy that I could finally nail the son of a bitch. Giddy that I could exact justice for Paul, and Rivas, and Willis. Even though Willis was up to no good, no one deserved to be dumped unceremoniously overboard. No funeral. No peace. Just like a piece of garbage in the waves.

We made good on our promise and a Marshal showed up before we left. He was a big, hefty guy, and looked like he knew what he was doing. My last glimpse of Deacon was in the rearview mirror as we drove away. He was still sitting at the picnic table, smoking, looking into space with a vacant stare. I didn't feel sorry for him, he could have come in at any time, but it was a terrible situation. It was going to get a lot tougher for Black and his crew, though. Much tougher.

What I still didn't know was why the *Reel Lady* had dumped Willis and made it look like he slipped overboard. Surely, with the operation they had going it would have been easy enough to make him disappear. Perhaps it had something to do with the millions Willis had managed to squirrel away. Maybe Black thought he was going to get all that money. I bet he was surprised to find Rivas was getting it, but if he had her killed how would Black get his greasy, pudgy fingers on all that loot? It seemed that although we'd broken the case open, there were still many questions that had to be answered.

More worrying for me was how the SAC was involved. It wasn't as if I could go up to Lewis and say, Hi, sir. Hey, Carter and I were in the parking lot the other day, we couldn't help notice you gave George, who works for Black and is under suspicion of murder, an envelope of what looked like cash? Or was it plans for something, a future op maybe? He could deny it all. What proof did we have now the surveillance feed was deleted? Shit. I wondered if anyone else in the department was involved. How deep did the treachery go? One thing for sure, there was a lot of money floating around.

The Medical Examiner called on our way back, and since we'd pass right by, we decided to stop in, even though it was getting late. Mark also called, oh rather he sent me a cryptic text, which said, *must talk soon*. I texted back that we'd be in shortly, he didn't reply.

"Frank, good to see you again. And Jessica, is Frank treating you well?" Hutchins said as we walked into the morgue.

"He is, thanks," Carter said.

"What have you got, Doc?" I said.

"Come over here, and I'll show you."

We walked through to a different section of her lab, one I hadn't been in before. Where the business end of the morgue was all stainless steel and bleach, in here was microscopes and books. The room was lit by several lamps shining onto haphazardly placed piles of notes. It smelled differently too, less like formaldehyde and more like research lab and fresh ozone.

"How do you know which pile is what?" I said, waving at the notes.

"Frank, dear. Don't you worry about me. Now then," she said, pulling over a stack of papers and gesturing us to sit on two stools. "When you were in here before I told you I'd made an analysis of Mr. Willis's tissue samples and said he was frozen at some point before he was recovered from the water."

We both nodded.

"That was my preliminary finding, something quick to help your case. What I didn't know then is that the frozen samples left a residue that we could analyze. Most remarkable indeed. If I hadn't been looking closely, I might have missed it..."

"Come on, Doc. Don't leave us in suspense," I said.

She continued, "Quite simple really, but the residue comes from anhydrous ammonia."

"What's that?" Carter said.

"I can answer that," I said. "It's a chemical that's used for many things. Fishing vessels use it as a refrigerant, it's mixed with nitrogen to make ammonium nitrate which is a fertilizer, and it's also a component of meth. Highly toxic if inhaled."

The ME gleamed. "Quite right, Frank. It is used in fishing vessels, but it's not really a component of meth though it is used in manufacturing meth. It's also used to make the explosive of choice for your homegrown terrorist. You mix ammonium nitrate and diesel together, and it can pack quite a punch. Commonly called ANFO. That's what McVeigh and his accomplice used in the Oklahoma City bombing, back in '95."

"But the key point is that it's another link back to Black," I said. "It solidifies that Willis could have been frozen on board the *Reel Thing*. I don't suppose there's any way to match samples of anhydrous ammonia is there?"

"Possibly. If you get me a sample, I can try. One more thing, we have several Jane & John Does in here-"

"Cold cases?" I said.

"Shut up, Frank," Carter said. "Not funny, again."

"Sorry. Carry on, Doc."

"As I was saying," Hutchins said, "in the last year or so I've had several unidentified people in here. Seven to be exact."

"Is that a lot?" Carter said.

"It's not as unusual as one might think. Corpus is a big city and being so close to the Mexican border, we do get a lot of strays coming through here from time to time. We take samples before the bodies are cremated and store them for future reference. Mr. Willis's frozen sample matched all seven when I ran it through the database. They were all frozen at some point, all using anhydrous ammonia."

"Didn't you know they were frozen before?" I asked.

"No. As I said we have so many unidentified people passing through, standard procedure is to take the samples and close out the case. It wasn't something that I invested a lot of time in, nor expected my staff to either. Nothing about the bodies appeared unusual, and they certainly didn't show signs of freezing when they came in. That wears off pretty quickly. It's almost dumb luck that Mr. Willis was brought in so soon."

"Seven dead people. All previously frozen. Anything else, Doc?"

"That's it, Frank," she said, standing up. "I'll keep you guys informed if I discover anything else. Goodbye Jessica, lovely to see you again. I can tell you look more comfortable."

"I am, thanks. Bye, Doc," Carter said.

As we walked out, I said, "Jess, it makes more sense now."

"What does?"

"Why we found Willis's body."

"How so?"

"Remember who it was that called in the missing captain over the radio?"

I gave her a moment to think and then she said, "Paul!"

"Yeah. Poor dumb Paul. He radioed in for help. He was never supposed to. That's why they dumped Willis and then had to recover him again. If they didn't look for him it would be suspicious." I blew out a breath. "In the end, I think that's what made them kill Paul. He was a liability. They couldn't have him putting two and two together, or us, and the easiest way was for him to have an accident." I air quoted accident.

It made sense. They killed these people on land, or maybe another fishing boat transferred them to the fish processor who froze them, then transferred them to another fishing boat for burial at sea. The bodies would make an excellent snack for a hungry shark, but if they did wash up onshore, they'd be bloated, rotting, putrescent flesh. The ME would do a once over, and with no missing person's report or grieving relative, they'd be classed as a John or Jane Doe and cremated. Not unusual with all the coyotes transporting illegals across the border.

They probably didn't think twice about Paul being on board. Let him do his shift; keep him out the way while they dumped the captain. They probably make a few trips like that, and then when the new crew finds out what's going on it's too late, they're in too deep. Tell the authorities about us, and you'll end up the same way.

It was probably just dumb luck that the *Reel Lady* dumped their own guy. That was the mistake they couldn't cover. They had to go through the motions of finding him after Paul called the Coast Guard. They were probably shitting bricks this whole time. If only I'd known. I knew there was something wrong, just couldn't place my finger on it. I cursed myself all the way back to the office for not seeing what was in front of me.

We parked and entered the elevator. When the bell dinged, and the doors slid open on our floor, all hell was breaking loose.

# TEN

## *Oblivious*

When the elevator doors parted on our floor, there was a sea of federal agents in front of me. Nothing unusual in a federal building, except these agents didn't belong here, and their jackets were emblazoned with the bold yellow logos of the Alcohol Tobacco and Firearms and Drug Enforcement Agencies. Officers were carrying cardboard boxes towards the freight elevator. I stopped one of them.

"What's going on?" I said. He shrugged and carried on to the elevator. I weaved my way through the cubicles to my desk. My locked file drawer wasn't locked so much anymore and hung open and empty.

"Hey," I shouted. "What the hell?"

Smith came up behind me and put his hand on my shoulder. "Frank, keep it down. Come into my office. You too, Carter,"

I followed him in and slammed his door behind me, narrowly missing Carter and making the blinds shimmy.

"What's going on?" I said.

"Sit down."

Carter went to sit down but stood back up when I said, "No, I don't want to sit. I want to know why my desk is busted open and the ATF and DEA are here."

"If you sit down, I'll tell you," Smith said.

Smith waited. I looked at Carter and nodded, and we both sat at the same time in the two chairs facing his desk. Smith perched himself on the edge of his desk. "The SAC called and ordered us to hand over everything to the ATF and DEA. He said based on all the new information you two have uncovered, this case had to be referred-"

"Bullshit! You can't do that, Tobias. We're about to bust this thing wide open–"

"Yes, I can. Don't interrupt. The SAC's made his decision. It's done. The case was close to getting out of hand." Smith held up his hands in front of himself trying to placate me. "Not with your work, it was just getting too big for us. We're a small service with a narrow investigative focus. Gun running? Multiple deaths? All linked to Black's operations? This is beyond our mandate, so it was inevitable we'd hand it over. Listen, for what it's worth, you've both done some great work, and I know you've put in some long hours. Take some time off, relax a little, and I'll give you the next juicy case that comes in."

"You know this is still bullshit, Tobias. Lewis just wants to cover..." I caught myself.

Smith looked at me. "Lewis wants to do what?"

"Nothing, Tobias. Nothing." I couldn't tell him. I didn't know whose side he was on. It was certain though that the SAC thought we were getting too close. He'd made a deal with the devil and was whisking away all our evidence. I wouldn't be surprised if a few of those boxes were going to get conveniently lost en route. Black sure had his fingers deep inside our organization.

"Anything else?" I said.

"No. Nice work, though. I'm sure there'll be some arrests in due course. I'll let you know if they find anything out."

We stood and walked out without saying anything else, and I closed the door behind me.

"Frank?" Carter said.

"Hold on, Jess. It's not over yet."

We walked over to the DOMEX office. Mark had his eyes pressed to a microscope, his hands prodding at something only he could see.

"Mark?" I said.

"Oh hi, Frank, Carter."

"What did you text me about?"

"Doesn't matter now. I was going to tell you the DEA were in here with their big Gestapo boots. They took Willis's phone and all the evidence I had collected. I tried to tell you." Mark gave a little apologetic scrunch of his shoulders.

"Shit. So that's it then. No evidence, nowhere to go," I said.

"Well not entirely," Mark said. "What they didn't know is that I'd already cloned Willis's phone. When I saw them coming in, I slipped it in my pocket. It's activated and working. You can read all the old texts and look at everything that was on the phone. Even the deleted stuff I recovered."

"You're an angel, Mark. I could kiss you." I reached over as if to do just that, but he dodged out of the way.

"Hey. Enough of that," he said. "About that other thing, you asked me to look into." He looked at Carter.

"It's okay. She knows."

"Alright. I managed to use the feed from the backup camera. Whoever deleted the main one didn't do a thorough job. That or they didn't know about it. I recovered the missing few minutes. You were right," he lowered his voice. "Is that who I think it is in the feed?"

I nodded. "Best you forget what you saw, Mark."

"I put the feed on this thumb drive for you," he said, handing over a small envelope. "I hope you know what you're doing, Frank. I...I'd rather not be further involved." Mark gave a little shrug. "I hope you understand."

"It's okay, Mark. I get it. Thanks for all your help." We shook hands like businessmen, and by the time I was at the door, Mark's head was buried back in his microscope.

Carter and I decided the best place to camp out and come up with a game plan was Pete's. A friendly face I trusted to bounce around ideas wouldn't hurt and neither would a beer or six.

Smith asked us where we were going on the way out. I told him we were going to celebrate working a good case and have a few beers, no harm no foul. The answer seemed to mollify him, and he went back to his office. Through the slats in his blinds, I saw him picking up the phone as we left. I hoped he wasn't crooked. He seemed like a decent guy.

"Come on, Jess. Let's get out of here."

Carter greeted Pete like a long-lost buddy. He'd fixed the glass in his door since we'd last been in, and he told us he hadn't had any repeat visits from unsavory characters.

"Probably didn't like how he exited the bar," Pete said. "Head first."

"I thought you just pushed him?" I said.

He waved his hand at me. "He left, that's all I care about."

Pete got us a round of beers, and we sat in a booth at the back. Pete only has one booth; it's perpetually reserved, mostly for Pete. All the locals knew that was his, so they never bothered with it. Once in a while a lost tourist would try and sit there, but it didn't last long. The rest of the bar had a few tables scattered haphazardly, but most of the real seats surrounded the bar.

I filled him in on what had happened, including being taken off the case.

"By the way," I said. "Thanks for the shaman hookup. She made my boat better than new."

"The *Serenity* now, I hear?"

"Yeah. Word gets around, huh?"

"Only when my best customer does something different."

Pete got us another round of beers and then tended bar for a while, seeing to his regulars.

"What do we do, Frank? Where do we go from here?" Carter said.

I scratched my chin and thought for a minute taking a swig of my beer. "Honestly? I don't know. Nothing like this has ever happened to me before."

We sat in silence, both of us deep in thought. I couldn't think of a way out. I knew that Black and his crew were smuggling guns. We had or at least did have, until the gestapo took my files, evidence from Deacon that linked Black to the weapons. We had the testimony, again from Deacon that he'd seen bodies on board the *Reel Thing*. That they were transferred on and off by other fishing vessels, all owned by Black. Add to that the evidence the ME had that proved all the bodies were previously frozen by a product used on fishing boats as a coolant. It all added up, but I still had a few gaps. I didn't know what had pissed Black off enough to kill Willis, or what the other poor saps had done either. On the plus side, I still had a working clone of Willis's phone, so perhaps I could do something with that.

Pete came back to the booth with the third round of beers just as ours were getting empty. I wasn't worried about driving as I could walk to the *Serenity,* and besides, I didn't have anywhere to go.

Instead of talking about the case, Pete started to reminisce. I think it was his way of offering advice in the roundabout bartender way.

"Remember when you first came to work for me, Frank?"

"Yeah. Long time ago now." I took a swig of beer.

"True, but you were all mixed up then. If I remember rightly you were an angry man. Torn between serving your country, which was what you had joined for, and working for those numbskulls at your first unit."

"I remember. There was a trifecta of leadership bullshit. I can still remember their names as if it was yesterday, Chief Troy, Charlie Baker and Robin Man. It was hopeless. Everything I did seemed to be either wrong or not good enough. It wasn't just me, though; it was everyone in the department. They just mentally and emotionally beat us down. I was ready to get out."

"Couldn't you have reported them up the chain?" Carter said. "I mean, you could have seen your CO. People get relieved of command all the time for climate issues."

"Not back then," I said. "Things were different. That was an era we called the Old Guard when men were men and sheep were scared. Advancements and promotions weren't based on merit; they were based on the good old boy network. If I'd gone over their heads and reported the shit they were doing up the chain of command, it would have been their word against mine."

"I haven't heard much about the Old Guard, I thought it was all a joke. They were serious?"

"Yeah. It was just the way it was back then. Thankfully, it's changed a lot these days, definitely for the better." I took another swig. "But I think the pendulum has swung too far now the other way, what with micro-aggression training and if you look the wrong way at somebody they'll complain their feelings were hurt." I swirled the remaining beer in the bottle. "The good stuff, Jess, is that you don't have to worry that a man would get promoted over you or paid more, and you definitely shouldn't have to worry about being sexually harassed. That shit is right out, and I agree wholeheartedly, there's no place for it, there never should have been. It's hard to explain, but it sometimes feels as if they've taken the guts out of the Guard. We used to have fun at work; now everyone's head is buried in a computer, or up each other's ass, too nervous to say boo. I mean, Jesus, it seems like you have to get congressional approval to take a shit during work hours, for Christ's sake."

"You done?" Pete said.

I nodded.

"It is what it is. Times change. Perhaps it's time for you to move on, let these youngsters like Jessica here take over." He smiled.

"I'm not that old, or that much older than Jess," I said. Carter looked like she was going to say something. "And don't tell me I'm deaf, either." Carter closed her mouth. I reached over with my empty beer, and we clinked bottles.

"It's great to fix the world's troubles with you, Pete, but it doesn't help our current situation. I haven't got enough to go to above the SAC's head. All I've got on him is a few minutes of video, and all that shows is he gave something and got something in return. It doesn't prove anything."

"How about having our case reassigned?" Carter said. "Surely that means we were getting close to the truth?"

"Unfortunately there's a million ways Lewis could play that out too. He could easily say we were in over our heads—"

"That's bullshit, though," Carter said.

"Jess. I know it, you know it." I gestured at the bar. "The whole damn world probably knows it, but we don't have any proof." I slammed my empty bottle down on the table.

Carter sat back. "What then? We give up?"

"That's what I'm trying to tell you. I don't know," I said. "Look, I don't mean to get angry, I'm just frustrated. I'm sure you are too. We need a change of pace. Pete, I never work well on an empty stomach, any chance you could rustle up a ham sandwich or something?"

"Sure. Jessica?"

"I don't suppose you have a big fat juicy burger back there somewhere do you?"

"I don't usually serve food, but for you? I'll see what I can do; I might have something in the back of the freezer."

"Thanks, Pete. 'Nother beer when you get a chance?" I said.

"What am I, a bartender?" Pete said. He grinned and loped off into the nether regions of the bar.

We chatted for a while, Carter and me. I asked how her mom was doing, she said she had good days and bad days, I asked what her favorite color was, it was purple, and I asked if she wanted kids, yes six. I snorted beer out of my nose on that last one.

"Six?"

"Yes. No. I don't know, perhaps it has something to do with losing my brother. I want a big family."

She told me she didn't have anyone serious in her life right now. She asked about me, and I said I wasn't that good with relationships. Always seemed to find the wrong person. I said I wanted someone I could talk to, someone that I could share my thoughts with. Someone I could trust.

Perhaps the beer had gotten to me when I said, "Someone like you."

Pete chose that moment to come back, saving Carter from having to say anything and from me making more of an ass of myself. "Ham sandwich for you, and the best burger I could find in the freezer for you. Oh and a couple more beers. Bon Appétit!"

Around a mouthful of ham sandwich, I said, "Pete. Any bright ideas? You've been in that scullery for long enough to have written the Magna Carta."

"Slaving over the hot plate, you mean? Maybe I do, slide over." Pete sat down next to Carter. "Logically you should do what your ASAC, Smith said. You should rest, watch a movie, have a few beers, which you're doing very well on, by the way, and go back to work tomorrow. File this one away and hope to God the ATF and DEA don't screw it up."

"And not logically?" I said.

"Not logically, which is probably what you're going to do anyway, is you should pursue the case. Quietly. If you're right about Lewis taking bribes, then he probably got the case transferred 'cos you were getting too close. He was probably paid by Black to keep you out of it. All of this is supposition, of course, and I'll deny everything if anyone asks."

"Of course. Go on."

"You were warned away. They trashed your boat, left you cryptic messages. Got rid of Rivas. Shot at you. And you *still* didn't get the message. So Black probably ordered him to relieve you. I doubt he wanted to kill you, that would have drawn way too much heat, and Lewis wouldn't have been able to give the case away, too much visibility from up high, media too. It's not every day a Coastie gets killed. Would've been big news."

"It certainly felt like they were trying to kill us."

"Didn't actually hit you, though, did they?"

"No. I suppose you could be right," I said. Pete raised an eyebrow. "Okay. Okay. You *are* right. But that still doesn't help us."

"Doesn't it?" Pete asked. This time it was my turn for the questioning look. I just listened, and Pete continued. "I'm not going to rehash the whole case again. I think you've done that enough yourselves. But I believe you're missing something that's staring you right in the face. Why was Rivas killed?"

"But we've talked about that. We don't know," Carter said.

"How's that burger?" Pete said.

"Perfect, thanks."

"And my ham sandwich is great too, thanks for asking."

"I don't need to ask you," Pete said. "All you ever eat is ham sandwiches. Listen, I think you should follow up on Rivas, follow the money trail. Why did Willis leave her all his money? They got divorced years ago, and from what you tell me, it's not like she needed the money. You said the Fire Marshal was conducting the investigation?"

I nodded. "Yes."

"Well he's probably not in the – you're off the case - loop. So my suggestion is to talk to him or her and find out if they know anything. Maybe the cause of the fire will lead you somewhere. Do you even know if Rivas is dead?"

I stopped chewing and put my sandwich down. "Son of a bitch. I didn't even think to check. No one could have survived that. I was there. It was a raging inferno. We've been so busy..."

"It's okay, Frank, she probably is toasty barbecue, but you need to follow up all the loose ends you can. Especially if you can talk to people quietly. One last piece of advice, do what Smith said. Don't do it today; you've had too much to drink. Take it easy. Relax. Come up with a game plan. And then first thing tomorrow, act like nothing's up, and go about your business sharply."

I shook Pete's hand. I felt a bit like a dumbass. How could I have missed something like that? I was in such a rush to keep moving forward I wasn't thinking clearly.

"Right. First thing."

Pete left us to go about his bartenderly duties.

As soon as Pete was out of earshot, Carter said, "Frank? What you were saying before?"

"Before what?"

"Before Pete came back with the food. You were saying something about how you wanted someone to talk to…"

"It's nothing, Jess. Forget it. Just the beer talking is all."

"I don't believe that." Carter looked me in the eyes. "I think…I think that I would like to get to know you better. We do everything you said you wanted. We talk, I'm funny."

"You're funny?"

"Yes. You're not, you just think you are. I feel like we connected. Even Doc Hutchins said so."

"I don't know about the ME, but the shaman thought our souls were connected."

"You never told me that," she said.

"Must have slipped my mind." Really, it was the other stuff she'd said about Carter being in trouble and me saving her. That was what I didn't want to tell her. Why make someone worry unnecessarily? "What do you propose?" I said.

"One small baby step at a time. Why don't we go for a walk, shake loose this burger and those beers, and then maybe you can take me to a movie or something."

"I'd like that very much, Miss Carter. Barkeep? Check please." Pete ignored me, and I threw some money down on the table. I knew he didn't want anything from me, but it felt the right thing to do.

We caught a cab to the local theater and decided to watch *The Finest Hour*. It was based on a true story set in the 1950s, about a group of Coasties at a Coast Guard station on Cape Cod in Massachusetts. An oil tanker had split in two on one of the worst winter nights, with a massive Nor'easter approaching. Against all the odds the crew had gone out and rescued everyone on board, far offshore. Like any movie, some liberties were taken, but it wasn't bad, and it was just what we needed. I'd bought popcorn that we shared, and we messed around, acting like school children on a field trip. After the movie, we caught another cab back to the *Serenity*, and I offered Carter an evening cocktail.

"There you are," I said, handing her the drink. "Something special I made up."

"What is it?"

"Try it."

Carter took a sip. "Oh my gosh. Bubbles. This is excellent, Frank. What is it?"

"It's called a French 75. It's made from champagne and gin. I didn't really make it up, though."

"It's great. I don't care who made it up. I normally don't like gin, but this is fantastic."

We toasted ourselves and to a new day tomorrow, sparks of optimism finally heading our way. We had a couple more drinks, watched the sunset from the cockpit and then Carter asked me for a blanket.

"Just bring one this time."

I did. A big one we could both use. My back was against the bulkhead, and Carter snuggled up to me.

"This is breathtaking here, Frank. I can see why you would want to live on board."

"Did I ever tell you how I got her? It's quite an interesting story," I said.

"I'm sure it is. But I have another story that I think needs to be told."

She twisted in my arms and ever so delicately kissed me on the lips. I couldn't tell if the stars were coming out in the night sky or if I actually saw stars in my head. I kissed her back, savoring the tang of the gin mingling with the faint perfume of her lipstick.

"Let's go inside and continue this story in private," she said.

In the morning, I arose early and made coffee and a small breakfast and brought it into bed. I stood watching her sleep for a second, her chest rising and falling with her gentle breath. I woke her, and after she had freshened up, she returned to bed where we ate breakfast and drank strong dark coffee.

We agreed to meet back at the office. She needed to change her clothes and shower at home. She kissed me goodbye. I showered, changed and drove into work. It was a glorious morning, deliciously warm and the light seemed to glow all around me. I felt buoyed and happy unlike I'd ever felt before. If nothing good came out of this utterly sordid Black investigation, I'd at least found Carter. And if I was to die today, I could make peace with the world, a happy man.

But for me, peace seemed to be a conceptual endeavor. Something that bald professors with goatees and bow ties would talk about on late night TV. How such and such Armpit Country was at war again, and the civilians were caught in the middle, screaming and crying. Begging the stoic reporters on the other side of the camera for help except they've been down that path before and know it's of no use. I should have remembered what the shaman said as storm clouds were brewing in the mists overhead, but her warning was the furthest thing from my mind. I drove to work oblivious.

Happy for the moment, but oblivious.

# ELEVEN

*Fire Sale*

"Frank, you must have taken my advice to get some rest, you're looking relaxed," Smith said, as I walked into the office. It was quiet this time around; no marauding Federales.

"I did, Tobias, thanks. Felt good."

"Have you seen Carter? I wanted to reassign her to another case. Let her work with a few other folks; get a feel for how each shop works."

"I think she should be in soon, but I figured I'd show her how we input some of the casework, filing and so on. Thought now that the exciting stuff is over I'd show her the real side of detective work, case reports, and paperwork."

Smith laughed. "You're a hard task master, Frank. Okay, I'll give you a couple of days. Is that enough?"

I looked thoughtful for a second. "Yeah, that should be fine. Thanks."

"No problem. Just let me know when you cut her loose."

"Yeah, sure thing, Tobias."

After Smith walked off, I rifled through what was left in my desk drawer and found an old business card for the fire marshal. I casually glanced around on the pretense of stretching before I called the number and made sure no one was near me. I dialed the digits with the eraser end of a pencil, and he picked up on the third ring. We gossiped for a while about old investigations, and then I asked him about Rivas. He told me some interesting things about her fire and said we should be able to catch the arson investigator if we got out there soon.

I changed into coveralls, and as I was grabbing the keys to a G-ride, I froze as a meaty hand landed on my shoulder.

"Frank, going somewhere? New case already? I thought Smith would cut you a break."

I turned and put my game face on. "Mr. Lewis, didn't see you there. What brings you downtown?"

"Oh, just doing the rounds. Say, no hard feelings taking you and err..." He looked at me for help.

"Carter, sir," I said.

"Right, Carter. No hard feelings then?"

"Me? No, sir. I thought we were getting close to finally taking Black's operation down though. I don't see why we had to turn everything over, at least like that. You know they came in here and just cleaned us out? Didn't wait for me to brief them, or tell them what was important or not. It felt a little like the feds the media are always talking about, not like sister agencies."

Lewis's face contorted into an expression of concern, but it made him look like an afternoon soap actor rather than genuine care. "Is that the way it happened? Sorry, Frank. I didn't think they'd be quite that harsh. I'll have a word with their commander; see if we can't get the miscommunication sorted out. That's not the kind of interdepartmental relationship we want to foster."

He sure could talk the talk. I'd bet my bottom dollar that was exactly how he wanted things to happen.

Fishing, I said, "Say, sir. They cleaned out all the files on my desk. I had some private files in there; you know, medical information, that sort of stuff. Any chance I could go down there and retrieve it?"

"Let me see what I can do, Frank. I'll put a call in. If you let me know what exactly is missing, I'll let them know and get it sent back up here. That's probably the easiest way, better than wasting your time in their rabbit warren. Now, where did you say you were going?"

"Oh just tying up some loose ends on some old cases. Thought I'd show Carter how to do some real investigative work. Go through the motions, as it were."

Lewis looked pleased. "Good to hear it. I'll let you know about those files."

He walked down the corridor smiling and shaking hands with the other agents, occasionally stopping and saying a few words as he made his way to Smith's office as if he was a freaking movie star. Bastard. He didn't want me anywhere near those files. Just one more nail in the coffin, old man, one more nail.

Carter had come in while I was watching Lewis and I'd told her to change into coveralls too. Fire sites were usually stinky and dirty. We left quickly, before anyone else had a chance to stop us, and before anyone else soured my morning glow.

We arrived at Rivas's house, or at least what was left of it. The door still stood, but little else. I introduced Carter, and the arson investigator said his name was James London, "But call me Jim."

London gave us Tyvek booties to cover our shoes so we wouldn't trash them or contaminate the scene and he offered us face masks for the stench.

"Although they don't really help much," he said.

We made our way through the wreckage; some of it was still damp from putting out the fire; even several days later. It smelled like an old campfire. Gradually we worked towards what was the epicenter of the fire, treading carefully and talking. If I looked closely I could identify some pieces of furniture and appliances, but not much else.

"So this was what you'd call extreme fire behavior, most unusual for a house fire," London said.

I looked at Carter. "Before you get too far ahead, Jim, I'll stop you right there. You'll have to forgive us, but our training is woefully lacking on fire terminology. What's extreme fire behavior?"

"Of course. Extreme fire behavior is simply a fire that can't be put out with the usual methods, due in this case to a high rate of spread, meaning the fire was almost everywhere at once and especially intense. We had to call the local marine unit and borrow some AFFF, which is a type of foam they use in boat fires, and use that in conjunction with water. Kind of layering." London gestured with his hands. "The back of the house, where the kitchen used to be was the head of the fire, the side with the fastest spread."

"So you're saying this was where it started?" I said, looking at what he said was the remains of the kitchen. If you'd asked me what this room was without being told, I would have had a hard job.

He nodded. "Yes. Usually, on an incident, I would hesitate to say what the definitive cause was, but I can tell you, in this case, it was arson. A natural fire wouldn't have moved like this and left so much devastation so quickly without anyone noticing."

"What could've caused it?" Carter said.

"We've sent evidence out for analysis, but you can follow the burn line back here to the kitchen, and if you shine your lights over there," he pointed at a large lumpy object, "you can see the old granite kitchen counter. It stood up to the intense heat, only cracking in a few places, and luckily stayed more or less intact. If it had been Corian or tile or whatever, the counter would have disintegrated, and we would never have figured it out." He paused to retrieve a handkerchief and wipe the moisture from his face. "On the counter, we found the boilerplate of a drip coffee maker. That was the ignition point."

"What was? The coffee maker? How could that be arson?" I said.

"Because it wasn't being used to make coffee, it was used to make a superheated fire, one that can literally...burn a house down. The way it works is like this. The arsonist puts granulated chlorine, calcium hypochlorite, into the carafe, which is the same regular chlorine you'd use for a pool. You then pour regular dot 3 brake fluid, like you'd use in a car, which is polyethylene glycol, into the reservoir on top. It's stable for as long as the two chemicals remain apart, but when the coffee maker is turned on, and the brake fluid drips onto the chlorine, it creates an intense smoke and heat and within seconds shoots out a flame ten to fifteen feet high. It would have caught all these cabinets and taken off from there. It looks as if someone also left the gas oven on and ajar, lending itself to a further explosion. I've read your initial report, Frank, and the gas explosion was what you guys heard and felt."

"How do you guys ever figure this stuff out?"

London smiled and perked up some, a little gleam appearing in his eye. "Some of its experience. You follow a certified fire investigator around on some fires; some of its classroom stuff, learning how things burn, and a lot of bookwork and homework. But the fun part for me, I'm a hands-on guy, was the practical experience. You get to set stuff on fire and see how it burns, and you also try and figure out from staged fires where the ignition point is and so on. The old coffee maker trick isn't that common, but you can check out videos on YouTube. It's quite impressive."

"How would the arsonist escape?" I said, "If it goes up that quickly?"

"Well, that's the marvel of modern coffee makers. They have timers. In effect, you're making a bomb and can set the timer to go off whenever you want. In this case, from what you've told me about running into the culprit, it would have been a very short timer, a matter of minutes. Enough time for him or her to get away, but not enough time for anyone to discover the gas was on, and the coffee was going to taste burnt."

Another joker. "So he would have had to have gained access to the house somehow?" I said.

"I don't suppose the security footage survived did it?" Carter said.

"No. But as it happens the feed went into the cloud. Mrs. Rivas had quite a high-tech house all around. We've been able to retrieve part of it before the cameras burnt up."

"I'd like to see that, and get a copy if I can?" I said.

"Of course. I have it on my laptop in the truck; I can show you when we leave here. And of course," London said in passing as we walked back to the front of the house, "You'll probably want to talk to Mrs. Rivas as well, she's been nothing but helpful."

"Wait. What? She's alive?" Carter and I said together.

"Well, yes. Didn't you know? Your Special Agent in Charge called yesterday expressing his thankfulness that she was okay."

I felt chills down the back of my neck. "As this is an arson investigation and Mrs. Rivas was the target..."

"Yes, of course. We have that covered. She's under the protection of an armed Fire Marshal in a private room at the hospital. At least until we figure out she's not in any danger."

I didn't realize I'd been holding my breath until just then. I exhaled and said, "How did she ever escape? How bad is she?"

"She has some smoke inhalation and a few burns, but remarkably she's pulled through quite well. She had a panic room, upstairs. By the time the fire was raging, she said she didn't have enough time to escape, so she ran to her panic room and secured the door. What with the video feed and communications burnt out, and the fact that she didn't have time to get her cell phone, we didn't know she was in there for quite some time. She's super lucky as that part of the floor is one area that didn't collapse. The room wouldn't have saved her if that had happened."

Outside we reviewed London's laptop video of the security footage and got a good idea of who entered her house. It looked like he was wearing coveralls, and Jeeves, may God have mercy on his soul let him in, presumably to do repairs on something in the kitchen. We also now knew who had shot at us.

We thanked London for his time, stripped out of our coveralls, bagged them so they didn't stink up the car and headed to the hospital. Time for a chat with Mrs. Rivas.

Things were finally coming together. We had conclusive testimony from Deacon, footage of Lewis receiving a bribe, and footage from the arson.

I knew time was running out before Lewis, and Smith would become suspicious that we weren't actually following up on old cases and filing shit like I'd said, but we had a little wiggle room.

I high-fived Jessica, and we got in the truck and drove at warp speed to the hospital.

The nurse on duty was hesitant until I showed her our badges, and then she was delighted to help. She called ahead to the Fire Marshal to expect us, so I was confident that the security was as tight as it could be.

The elevator took us to the fifth floor, and when it dinged, we exited and walked down a long sparkling corridor reeking of pine sol. It was an interesting juxtaposition from the dank smell of burnt house.

The Fire Marshal watched us come down the corridor and checked our IDs when we got close. He let us in after knocking on the door and confirming with Mrs. Rivas that she was awake and presentable.

After what Jim London had said, I wasn't prepared for the state Mrs. Rivas was in. I thought she'd look better. She had bandages around her hands and the left side of her face, presumably from the burns. Most of the left side of her once beautiful hair was gone too. It looked painful, and I'm sure it was. She truly was lucky to be alive. All sorts of machines were beeping, and a glance told me her blood pressure and heartbeat were low, probably due to the morphine to control her pain.

She tried smiling when she saw us but then immediately grimaced.

"Mrs. Rivas, I'm so terribly sorry. I thought the worst when I saw your house. I was there; I tried to get in but the flames..." I said.

Joan Rivas spoke in a soft, raspy voice. It looked like it hurt when she talked and we moved closer so she wouldn't have to strain.

"...told you, call me Joan. And thank you for trying to help," she said.

"Joan. I know this was awful, but do you know why someone set that fire?"

I saw the look on her face. She wanted to tell me, only something was holding her back. I could see the inner struggle play out on her face, and then she relaxed, overcoming her inner demons.

She nodded. "Yes. Freddie came to me last week," she whispered. "He was agitated. I hadn't seen him for years, and there he was, on my front porch." As she spoke, her voice improved. "He was acting bashfully; he knew I'd remarried, but said he needed to talk to me urgently. I took him into the library, and he sat just where you did, Special Agent, when you came to see me."

I shivered. Almost as if I had been sitting in Willis's ghost's shadow.

"He told me that he thought Black was turning against him. He'd found out that Black had taken out insurance on him for two million dollars. He didn't know how he'd done it; he thought there was probably someone at the insurance company he'd paid off. He said that he thought Black might try and kill him and claim the insurance money...Do you mind handing me that cup of water, please?"

I handed it to her and helped her drink from the flexible straw. When she was done, I put it back on the table.

"Thank you. Freddie had a lot of money, and he said he had no one to give it to, he'd never bothered to change his will from when we were married, and I was the sole beneficiary of all his assets. He told me if something happened to him, he wanted to give it all to me for putting up with all his years of bullshit and for breaking my heart. Of course, when Freddie said he had lots of money, he never told me how much. I thought it was maybe a few thousand at most."

"Why didn't you tell us about this when we visited, Joan?"

"I don't know, Special Agent. I suppose I was a little flustered, what with Freddie dying. I didn't know whether it was that awful Black or what was going on. I would have come down to the Sector and told you. In fact, I was getting ready to leave the house when...this happened."

A big brutish nurse with a no-nonsense look on her face came in and told us it was time to leave. We said our goodbyes and the nurse followed us out. Outside the room, her demeanor softened, and she told us the prognosis was good and ensured me Mrs. Rivas was in the best hands.

I was happy that Joan was going to be okay, sad that Jeeves had perished; it surely was a horrible way to go, but forgive me please, I was elated we were closing in on Black and his crew.

We now had a motive. Willis must have had a falling out, and knowing Black had insured him, knew his life was on the line. In a last fuck you to Black, he'd given all his money to his ex. Black though, was still going to try to cash in on the insurance money. It made a little more sense now why they had dumped him overboard and then recovered him. Unwittingly, Paul calling the Coast Guard had legitimized their operation, as they now had a viable timeline. They needed a drowned and dead Willis; otherwise, the insurance wouldn't pay out.

What they couldn't have known though, is our crack medical examiner figured out he was dead before they dumped him, and as they say on packs of fish - had been previously frozen.

What we needed to do now was figure out if we had enough to make it stick. Finding some actual guns would be good, or even better, finding the place where they froze the bodies. I was sure they had it all set up in one place; it would be too hazardous for them to move that kind of operation around. If we could find it, there was sure to be some trace evidence or DNA we could find. That would be the final nail in the coffin. I couldn't help but wonder if the ATF et al. had done anything with the case or whether it was going to be buried deep inside some underground government vault. I wasn't big on conspiracy theories, but I did work for the government, and there were certainly some nefarious things goings on. I wondered how long the SAC had been on the take. Why would he anyway? He certainly earned an awful lot of money, much more than me. Perhaps it would be worth digging into his finances.

On that thought, we headed back to the office. Maybe I could get Mark to check the SAC out? I knew Mark was nervous about what was going on, and I didn't want to see him get in trouble. I'd see how it went.

As soon as the door to the elevator opened, I was out and went straight into Mark's domain. He was busy with some contraption, and his hands were stuck inside sealed rubber gloves inserted into the side of a clear cabinet. I could see he was manipulating valves, and a sudden cloud of smoke filled up the small space.

"Hey, Mark. Watcha doing?" I said.

"Oh. Frank. You really want to know?" Mark looked hopeful.

"Of course." Not really.

He pulled his hands out of the gloves and wiped them on his lab smock. "It's quite fascinating. I placed a piece of evidence in the cabinet from a case and the smoke inside - I won't get technical for you, it's a sort of vaporized glue – sticks to any residual oil from fingerprints. Then I dust the evidence using fingerprint powder, and if there are any fingerprints, the powder will stick to the glue. If we get any prints I can run them through CODIS to see if we get a hit. It works way better than the traditional methods and is admissible in court."

"That's cool," I said, peering into the cabinet. I couldn't see anything. "Couldn't you just dust for prints at the scene?"

"You could. However, this method is usually used when we don't get any hits on scene. It's more," Mark rubbed his chin. "It's better at picking up faint fingerprints that otherwise would be missed. You must have watched CSI at some point. That's one thing they actually got right."

I looked suitably impressed for Marks benefit and then moved closer to him and lowered my voice. "What I was wondering is if you could help me out with something."

"Why are you whispering? I'm not going to get in trouble am I?" He looked around me, out the door, as if expecting to see someone watching us. I almost looked too.

"No. Of course not. But I do need you to keep this on the down low."

"It's always something with you. Does it have anything to do with the case you and Carter were kicked off?"

"Indirectly. Look Mark, I'll be honest. There's a leak in the department. I aim to plug it. I don't know who else to turn to, no one else has the technical skills to help me out. I came to you. I don't think you're the leak—"

"Never."

"That's what I thought. See? I came to the right person after all."

Mark looked me over. "I'm not going to fall for your obvious flattery, Dalton. What is it you want?"

I told him as much as I could about my suspicions without giving away the whole enchilada, and then what I wanted him to do.

"You want me to what?" he said.

"Keep your voice down." I did look out of the office this time. No one was paying any mind. "I need you to search the SAC's finances. I know it's unorthodox, but if you don't find anything, no one's going to be the wiser. It's important. Can you do it?"

Mark looked pained. "I trust you, Frank." He let out a weary breath. "Okay. I'll do it."

"Thanks, buddy." I slapped him on the shoulder. "Call me when you get something - anything. Don't leave me any post-it notes."

I grabbed a coffee from the break room, sniffing it suspiciously to make sure it wasn't old when a bright red beetroot screamed at me.

"Dalton! I gave you a direct order to leave that case alone." Spittle was flying from Lewis's mouth; people turned to look at him. "You're a fucking idiot. You hear me? A fucking idiot. I can't be responsible for the consequences of your actions—"

"Mr. Lewis!" Smith hurried out of his office. "Perhaps this conversation would be better had in my office, sir?"

Lewis looked at Smith. Looked at me. He suddenly seemed to notice that people were staring, and strode across the room to Smith's office.

Smith looked at me. I hadn't said a word and the coffee was still raised to my nose. I slowly lowered the mug.

"You too," he said.

I followed them. The SAC started to pace back and forth, ignoring me. Smith sat down behind his desk after he closed the door.

"Mr. Lewis, I—"

"You will stand at attention when you are addressing a Special Agent in Charge, Special Agent Dalton."

Surprised? You betcha. I didn't move, momentarily frozen in mid-step.

"Did you hear me, Dalton?" The SAC said, his face still a dangerous shade of stroke red.

I slowly put my coffee mug down on the corner of Smith's desk and came to attention. "Yes, sir!"

Lewis circled me twice, looking as though he was trying to calm down. I kept my eyes in the boat, dead ahead, not blinking. He stopped right behind me and spoke into my ear.

"Do you understand what you have done, Dalton?"

"No, sir."

"I can't protect you anymore, Dalton. I'm not going to have this on my conscience. I ordered you off this case. Why did you disobey me? Speak, Dalton."

"Mr. Lewis, I didn't disobey you. I was just following up some leads on some old—"

"Bullshit!" Lewis walked around to face me. He was now a softer shade of pink. I didn't think I'd have to get the defibrillator out just yet.

"Smith. You did tell Dalton here to back off, am I correct?"

"Yes, sir," Smith said. "We had a conversation right here."

Turning back to me Lewis said, "Imagine my surprise then when I got a call from an old buddy of mine, Jim London. He was concerned you seemed not to know Mrs. Rivas was still alive and wanted to make sure there hadn't been a breakdown in communications. I assured him everything was okay and that you'd probably just missed my call."

"Thank you."

"Thank you be damned." Lewis sat down and put his head in his hands. He didn't say anything. I looked at Smith. He looked alarmed but tried to hide it. I couldn't tell if that was because of the SAC's breakdown, or if it was because I'd gone behind his back.

Lewis straightened himself in the chair, his face flip-flopped now to pasty and sweaty, his voice weary and modulated.

"You disobeyed a direct order; your conduct was unbecoming of an officer. I'm placing you on administrative leave until a formal investigation under Article 134 of the Uniform Code of Military Justice can be conducted. You are to leave this building immediately and not return until this shit show has been resolved one way or another. Are we clear?"

I stood ramrod still. The blood draining from my face. I felt weak.

"Permission to speak, sir?"

Lewis waved me to go ahead. "What is it?"

"Carter, sir. She had nothing to do with it. I just want to be clear that this was all my direction, she was just following my orders, following along. She's new, this would ruin her career."

"Do you see her in here with you? No, of course you don't. Don't try my patience, Dalton. I'll take your statement under consideration. I-" He paused for a moment, and a slow smile appeared on his lips. "Are you admitting the charges? I'll go easy on Carter if you do. We can clean this up quickly. Minimum of fuss. You're what? Nineteen years in?"

I clenched my jaw, my teeth grinding, and spat out, "Yes, sir. Almost twenty."

"Excellent. Plead guilty to the charges. I'll let you keep your retirement, but you'll be done in the Guard."

I felt like I was back at my first unit. I was being bamboozled. I'd lose my career, my job, my life. Everything.

Carter would be okay though, and with that thought the decision was easy.

"I have your word?"

"As an officer and a gentleman, you have my word that Carter will be looked after. ASAC Smith will be a witness."

"Sir," Smith said, silent until now. "This is highly irregular, you can't just—"

Lewis stood up, his almost purple now. "I'm the Commanding Goddamn Officer of this unit, and I can do any Goddamn thing I damn well please. Is that clear? If it's not, you can follow him out the door too."

This guy was off his rocker.

"No, sir. I mean yes, it's clear, sir." Smith looked apologetically at me. I didn't blame him. Perhaps I could trust him after all.

"Your answer now, Dalton. I don't have all day."

I felt even weaker. "Yes, sir. I admit the charges."

Lewis smiled a tight smile, almost a grimace. "Very well, Dalton. Your badge and gun. Put them on the ASAC's desk."

My heart sank even lower. I had no choice now but to do as he said. As I placed my badge on the desk, it felt like a small piece of my soul ripped and shredded. Inwardly, I was cursing his mother for ever having had sex with his father. I was impotent, there was nothing else could I do.

I left without another word. Walking like a zombie. Devoid of life. An automaton. I didn't hear Jessica calling my name. I didn't hear Lewis ordering her into Smith's office. I don't remember getting in my car. I don't remember the drive home. I was in a haze. The world was passing me by, but I wasn't in it. I was a passenger in life at this moment. On autopilot.

I sat on the back deck of *Serenity* and just drank.

# TWELVE

## *What A Shit Show*

"Frank? Frank? Wake up, Frank."

I was flat on my back, on the back deck. It was dark. I had an awful taste in my mouth. Beer bottles clinked as I tried to move.

"Jesus, Frank. How much did you drink?" Carter said.

"Mmmmffff." Was all I could say.

"Here take this. Drink it."

Carter propped my head up with her hand to help me drink, and a million small explosions bounced around in my skull behind my eyes. She forced three pills into my mouth, and blessed, refreshing, cool water, nectar of the gods washed them down.

"Aspirin. It'll make you feel better," she said, to my unasked question.

There was some clanking as Carter cleaned up. It sounded like she was throwing bottles and cans into a steel garbage can with all her might. I squinted but only saw her carefully placing empties into a white garbage bag.

"Noisy," I mumbled.

"Yeah." She placed a pillow under my head. "Wait until the aspirin kicks in. You'll feel better."

I felt my world spinning. Was the boat moving? Were we underway. The stars above were spinning. I made a clumsy attempt to stand, falling down the steps to the lounge in my hurry and lunging for the head. I vomited the vomit of many beers and no food. It felt as if my stomach was turning inside out, purged. I vomited the angst, the anger. The shame and fear. It all came out and was flushed away.

I sat back, sweaty and exhausted, but feeling oddly cleansed, somehow fresher. Jessica came in holding her nose, disavowing me of the fresher aspect and turned the shower on. When it was steaming hot, she ordered me to strip off and get in. The burning water surged over my head and aching body. I stayed in until my water tank started to run cold. Jessica held a towel out for me; she'd cleaned the toilet.

"You didn't have to," I said.

"I know. Don't be stupid. I made coffee. And toast. Get dressed and come out when you're ready."

I padded into my cabin wrapped in the towel. She'd even laid out clothes for me. How did I get so lucky?

A moment later out on deck, all cleaned up, with my darkest shades on to ward off the evil brightness of night sky, she handed me the toast and coffee. I carefully eased myself down to the deck seats.

"I don't think you'll need those sunglasses, it's night. How do you feel?"

"Much better, thanks to you. My headache's nearly gone. I think throwing up was probably the best thing. I'll keep these on for a few minutes, the dock lights are still quite bright tonight. At least we're not underway anymore."

"What?"

"Never mind. Thanks, Jess. Again." I looked out over the water. "How much did I drink?"

"Too much."

"Yeah. I'm so sorry, Jess. For everything. Dragging you into this shit show. I wasn't myself yesterday. What happened to you?"

"Lewis called me in and told me you'd been relieved. I'm the one that's sorry, Frank."

"Did he..." I started again. "Did he..."

"No. Nothing happened. Well, nothing bad. He yelled at me some and assigned me to Fredericks. Told me to thank my lucky stars, and that he would be keeping an eye on my future performance. You know, Fredericks is an annoying twat. All we did for the rest of the day was sit and input data into a computer. He wouldn't let me go until well after hours. I came here as quickly as I could, Frank. He can't get away with this, can he? The SAC, I mean, not Fredericks."

I shrugged. "He has so far, but no. I did what I had to do, but I'm not going to stop. I can't let this one sit. He's crooked, Jess. If nothing else, his manic tirade just proves he was trying to cover something up. It was a complete and utter overreaction." I looked at the sky for a minute, pleasant now it wasn't swirling and took off my sunglasses. "What did the others say in the office?"

"No one actually said anything to me. I'm still pretty new there, remember? I could see them talking though. Quietly, in corners. I think you'll have support if you need it. Apart from Fredericks though. He seemed like a wet blanket."

"Yeah. He is a little. He's solid though, just unimaginative. Don't hold it against him. He's got a ton of kids, I'm sure he doesn't want to get pulled into something like this. Don't blame him."

She shook her head. "What'll we do, Frank?"

"We? Nothing. Me, I'm going to carry on. I need to track these guns down; I need to find that freezer. I asked Mark before I left to run a check on the SAC's finances. I need you to be careful and go to work as normal. I don't want anyone thinking that you're anything but a loyal worker doing her job. No one knows about our relationship. No one can."

"I can't let you do this by yourself."

"You can, and you will. I don't need you to screw up your career too. Besides, I might need you to support me soon when I'm out of a job." I tried a smile on for size. "Let me talk to Pete. I think I have an idea of how to proceed. Just act normal, as best you can. I'll be in touch. I promise I'll call you when there's anything worth knowing."

She nodded. "I don't like pretending nothing's wrong. I'm not a good actor, but I'll do it."

We shared a blanket and sat in companionable silence for a while. Despite the coffee, I was getting tired, and we finally called it a night. We were both too emotional to do much else besides sleep, and I dozed off with Carter holding me in her arms.

I woke several times sure I could hear something, but nothing ever happened. In the morning Jessica was already gone. She left me a note next to the fresh coffee she'd made saying she had gone to work early, and that she'd be in touch. I was a fortunate man to have found someone as special as Jessica.

It was early, but I knew Pete would be up, prepping for the day's crowd, so I walked over to his bar and banged on the bar's steel back door. While I waited, I had to wave off the occasional fly that got me confused with the nearby garbage. I sniffed myself but couldn't detect any odor, so I didn't think it was me. I had showered again, after all.

Pete finally wrenched open the big door, the hinges squealing in protest.

"You could use some WD 40 on those bad boys," I said.

"You look like hell. Come in." He left the door open, and I followed, letting the door screech back in place, and sliding the deadbolt home.

"To what do I owe this early morning pleasure?" Pete said, nodding at a stool. "Coffee?"

"Please," I said, and sat.

Pete poured from a carafe and handed me a steaming mug of coffee.

"I'm in a spot of trouble, brother," I said.

"Figured this wasn't just a social visit so early. What gives?"

I told him what had happened after we had left here the last time. I glossed over my relationship with Jessica, but Pete was savvy enough to pick up on it.

"Hot damn. I knew you too would be good together. But that's not all is it?"

"No. Not by a long shot."

I told him how we'd found proof the fire was arson. That we'd seen the culprit on the video, and how I thought Lewis was involved. I finished with telling him how I'd been relieved of duty and how Jess had found me last night.

"She's going to be okay though?"

"From what she's told me, yes. I have to believe that Smith is a straight shooter, that he looked after her. I think he was genuinely shocked at Lewis's behavior, he looked it. He tried to speak up for me. Lewis shot him down and threatened his career too." I took a sip of coffee, blowing the steam away. "I've been thinking some. For Lewis to flip out like that he has to be under a lot of pressure."

"Maybe Black is turning the screws a little tighter. Now he's in the bag it wouldn't be difficult. Particularly with that George fella at his beck and call."

We talked it over some more, three mugs of coffee's worth, and then Pete said, "I might know someone who could help. Many people pass through this bar. I have a monthly visit from an old colleague. You don't know him; he was before your time. He's a retired Admiral, went into the security business. Does a lot of contract work for the government. From what I understand, and reading between the lines, he still has a lot of connections, some bigwigs in the DHS. He might be able to help."

'Thanks, buddy, I was hoping you might know someone."

"Yeah. You know though, what the SAC did. He can't legally do that. That was beyond his authority. Oh sure, he can book you, but when it comes to the court-martial, any lawyer worth their salt should be able to get you out."

"I figured that. You know what though? For all the years I've put into the service, all the long days and nights away from home, this brought me right back to my first unit and those shitbags that ran roughshod over me and everyone else. I thought the times had changed. I thought that that sort of bullshit was long gone."

"You know it's gone. This SAC of yours is running a different game. You can't compare the two situations."

"I think after all this wraps up I might just pack it all in. Take that trip on *Serenity* I'm always talking about. Go hang out in the Bahamas somewhere."

"And take Jessica with you?"

"Sure. If she'll come. I think she would. For a time anyway."

"Even if you do quit, she still has commitments you know. You can't run off into the sunset forever."

"I know, I know. Just an idle thought."

My pocket started to vibrate. I reached down to pull out my phone. It was a text from Mark.

"Who's that?" Pete said.

"It's a text from Mark. You know, the tech guy who's checking out Lewis for me? He wants to meet, soon. Thanks for your help, Pete. I've gotta go. Maybe this is the lead I need."

We shook hands. "Be careful," he said. "Do you need a piece?"

"No. I've got my backup in an ankle holster. I'll be careful. Thanks again."

I drove to where Mark said he wanted to meet me. It wasn't a place we regularly hung out in, which was probably the point. I pulled open the door and was assaulted with the heavenly goodness of freshly roasted coffee and baked muffins. Mark wasn't there yet, and even though I was floating to the gills with coffee, I figured one more couldn't hurt. I ordered a large coffee with skim milk, and scoped out a secluded seat in the corner where I could still see the door.

The gigantic flat screen television on the wall in front of me had the volume turned low, but I could read the subtitles. I was just getting engrossed in the ongoing dispute between the queen of pop Taylor Swift and her arch nemesis Katy Perry when Mark walked in. If only I could have the same problems those two had. What a world we live in, where news is a petty argument between two pop singers.

"Thanks for coming," Mark said.

"Sure. Can I get you a coffee?"

"No, I'm good."

Mark sat and took out a sheaf of papers he'd stashed under his jacket. He looked around before handing them over.

"It's okay. I've been here a while. We don't know anyone."

"Sure." Mark appeared nervous.

"You okay?"

"Not really. I feel sick. I think I'm coming down with something. Excuse me."

Mark dashed off in the direction of the bathroom, and I took a moment to look through the papers he'd brought me. A lot of it was just random banking nonsense, but Mark had taken the liberty of highlighting several entries. Besides the SAC's regular pay on the first and fifteenth of every month he also had a wire transfer of twenty thousand dollars. Every month, like clockwork. I flicked through the pages. It looked like this had been going on for a long, long time. I couldn't begin to grasp how bad this was. There was no earthly reason he'd be getting that much money every month. If it had been an inheritance or something we'd all have known. It would have shown up on his security clearance. If you have too much money, they'll discharge you. He seemed to have gotten around that problem. There'd also been a regular withdrawal to another bank. I didn't know what the code meant, but Mark had scribbled in the margin. Evidently, he'd tracked the withdrawals to a matching account in Lichtenstein. A so-called offshore account, in a land-locked country. Everyone knows about Switzerland being the capital of unmarked secret accounts, but Lichtenstein is also another, sometimes better, option.

Fuuuuuck meeee. He must have...I couldn't fathom the figure. I was sure it was small peanuts for a guy like Black to have the local Commanding Officer of the Coast Guard investigative Service in his pocket...But shit, it was riches to the likes of me. It made me wonder whether Lewis's buddies in the ATF and DEA were also on the take. It would explain how they'd just grabbed all my stuff. It would also explain how they could put the kibosh on any follow-up investigation. This was getting bigger than I had ever imagined. No wonder they didn't want me snooping around. It had probably made them all super nervous, which was why I'd been ordered off the case and they'd secured my files. When Carter and I carried on the investigation, it must have flipped their lids.

With my hands tied virtually behind my back, I would have to tread carefully. If they found out I hadn't given up, I might suffer those consequences Lewis had threatened me with. Surely they wouldn't try and kill me? I was a law enforcement officer.

I was lost in thought, so it was a while before I realized that Mark had taken an awfully long time in the bathroom. I collected the papers and threw my coffee out and went to the bathroom to check on him.

"Mark? You in here?" The bathroom wasn't large but had three stalls. "Mark?" I banged on the door of the only closed stall. "Mark?" The door swung inwards as I knocked, stopping part way. I looked down and saw a foot blocking the door. I pushed it open as far as I could. Mark was sitting propped up on the toilet seat, his feet sticking out at an odd angle.

"Shit." I pulled out my phone and dialed 911 for an ambulance. I hung up when they asked me who I was. I felt Mark's neck, his body was already cooling and there was no pulse. Mark had been strangled, and in an ultimate fuck you, the garrote was still around his neck, the killer not bothering to even try and hide the execution.

It didn't look like he'd struggled and there was absolutely nothing else I could do. While I was engrossed in the papers at the table, he'd been in here having his life stolen from him. Some Special Agent I was.

I backed out of the stool and kicked the next stool door as hard as I could. It rattled on its hinges and slammed backward. I wanted to scream and roar, but knew I couldn't. I couldn't afford to be in here with him when the EMT's came. I didn't need the hassle, the questions from the cops, why were you meeting him, Mr. Dalton? What did the two of you discuss? You say you're a Special Agent, where's your badge? I didn't need them to know anything. I went back in the stool and searched him quickly looking for any evidence that he may not have given me. I didn't find anything.

I opened the door to the bathroom a crack and poked my head out. No one was about, and I let myself out the back door just as the sirens were approaching. I'd parked around the corner, and I walked back to the car. I had the strongest urge to smoke, now I wish I did smoke again. I needed the distraction. What a fucking waste, Mark was an innocent. Once again, just like Paul, someone trying to do me a favor had ended up on the list of dead.

I was running out of time. I could feel the hempen noose that was swaying in the wind over my head. Whoever had offed Mark had probably seen me, which meant Black new I was up to something. The other thing that would catch up with me sooner or later was the video feed from the coffee shop security cameras. The cops would take a look at that and put a BOLO out for my arrest as a person of interest. Hopefully, the cameras were on the blink, but that wasn't something I could take for granted.

I was tired of playing defense, seemingly always playing catch up. I needed to stop this scratched record and go on the offensive. I needed to shake up Black, needed to take him down, to stop this senseless slaughter of people.

I saw a Stripes gas station ahead on the other side of the road and crossed over. I broke down and bought a pack of smokes. It'd been years since I quit, but I felt like I needed something. The first drag was long and glorious, the nicotine giving me a head rush, making me lightheaded. I smoked about half of it and then ground it out. I gave the rest of the pack to a passing bum.

I bent over, leaning on my car and coughed my guts up. Perhaps not my brightest move, smoking. I got in my car and drove. Where to, I wasn't sure at the moment. I had a feeling my subconscious would direct me where I needed to go.

I texted. Yeah, I text and drive, so shoot me. I needed to know Jessica was okay. She got back to me saying she was just stepping out for some lunch, and would I want to join her? I replied that I would, but couldn't right now. We agreed to meet at Pete's after work and swap developments. I didn't tell her about Mark, I didn't want her to worry, she'd find out soon enough.

I dropped the phone on the passenger seat and carried on driving listlessly. My subconscious evidently hadn't come through for me, as I still didn't have any clue as to where to go. I took back control, engaged my brain, and drove up to North Padre Island, accessing the beach by the Holiday Inn. The sand was always hard packed and ideal to drive on. I parked facing the Gulf and rolled the windows down to listen to the surf. I must have dozed off without realizing it as I'd lost track of time when my phone rang with an incoming call. I glanced at it. Smith. What could he want?

"Dalton," I said.

"Frank, you need to come into the shop." Shit. Surely they hadn't tracked me to Mark this quickly?

"What's up, Tobias? I thought I was expressly forbidden."

"Something's come up. I'm expressly telling you to get your ass down here."

"Listen, Tobias, I can explain everything. I didn't want to wait around; you know?"

"What in hell are you talking about? Never mind, I don't want to know. Just come into the office. Now."

"Yes, sir."

I drove off the beach, looking in the rearview at the waves with longing. I drove down South Padre Island Driveway at speed and got back to the office within a short time. I looked in Smith's office, but he wasn't there.

"If you're looking for the ASAC, he's in the Command Post," another Agent said.

"Thanks." I walked down two flights, preferring to kill a little more time and entered the code on the door.

Inside it looked like hell. Video streams were playing on all the monitors; Paper was strewn all over the large conference room table. I found Smith talking with a bunch of guys from the enforcement shop. They looked like they were prepped for business. Bulletproof vests emblazoned with U.S. Coast Guard on them. Rifles and riot helmets.

"What's going on?"

"Sit down, Frank."

I sat.

"As of forty-two minutes ago, Agent Carter's been missing."

# THIRTEEN

## *This is my Fight Song*

"What do you mean missing? She just texted me she was going out to lunch," I said.

"She did go out to lunch, but that was two hours ago," Smith said.

I glanced at the large twenty-four-hour wall clock. I'd misplaced some of the afternoon during my sojourn to the beach.

Smith continued. "Frank, she was on her way back to the office when it happened, stopped at a traffic light. A late model minivan pulled up alongside her car. We've pulled the footage from the traffic cam across the street. It happened quickly, she never had a chance to respond. The door to the min-van slid open, and two men wearing baseball caps pulled low, smashed her window, opened her door and pulled her out and into the van. The surveillance gets patchy after that, but we're looking. One of our guys was monitoring the scanner and heard the description of her car, that's how we got on this so quickly. Nothing yet. She was taken, Frank. Kidnapped. I'm sorry. I know you two were getting close."

I was numb. "There must be some mistake. It must be someone else."

"There's no mistake, Frank. Listen, I called you in to give you the courtesy before you saw it on the news, and also to see if you recognized anyone on the footage."

One of the monitors played the scene out for me. I could see how Carter was blindsided. Smith was right; there was nothing she could have done, nothing anyone in that situation could have done. Two people subdued her and bundled her into the van, and when one of them glanced across the street, I saw George's creepy features look into the camera. It couldn't have been a coincidence.

"George," I said.

"What was that?" Smith said. "Did you say, George?"

I looked up at him standing over me. "Yeah. George. He works for Black. He was probably the one that shot at us and the SAC..."

"The SAC what?"

I didn't say anything.

"If you know something, anything, you have to tell us, Frank. The enforcement guys are ready to roll they just need to know where to go."

I looked over at the group of well-armed professional Coasties. I had faith in these guys and gals. They knew what they were doing, and I wanted to protect Carter.

"I don't know where he'd be, and I don't have any idea where they could have taken Carter. I've been looking for their operating base, where they froze those people. That's where I'd look, but I have no idea where it is."

"Kidnapping one of our own is fucking stupid. They must know we'd pull out all the stops to get her back. Apparently, they're trying to scare you off, but this is ... Black isn't thinking this through, unless ... you must have been getting close. You must have scared them; this is a stalling tactic. Think, man, think. Where could they have taken her?"

"I am thinking, Tobias. I don't know. Don't you think I'd tell you if I did? I'd like nothing more than to see that fat bastard obliterated off the face of the earth."

Senior Chief Maritime Enforcement Specialist, Senior Chief Montoya broke away from his people and came towards us.

"What's up, Senior?" Smith said.

"We're ready to roll, sir," Montoya said, nodding to me. "Until we have better intel we're going to search the fishing docks around the *Reel Lady*, see if we can come up with anything. I don't like to keep my people standing around. They'll start breaking things. It's a bit like managing bulls in a china shop."

"Senior," I said. "You won't find anything at the docks. Black isn't going to be somewhere so obvious. He'll be holed up with his gang, somewhere we haven't located yet."

"That's probably true, sir, but we have to start somewhere. What if she is there? We'd look pretty stupid if we didn't try."

I shrugged, knowing it would be useless, but not having anything better to offer. "Sure."

The enforcement group, wrapped with Kevlar left the command post. "We'll be on tactical channel twenty-two Charlie," Montoya said, and followed his group.

Montoya was a good man. A reliable man. I couldn't think of anyone better to conduct the operation.

Smith looked around the room and gestured me to follow him into a side office. I wearily got up and followed, closing the door behind me. The room smelled stale. I knocked the dust off of an orange plastic chair and sat down. Smith didn't bother with the dust and just sat down.

Smith began. "I wanted to apologize for Lewis's behavior. It was inappropriate and uncalled for. There's procedure and protocol, and he didn't follow either. In his defense though, you did disobey his direct order to back off the case. And you failed me, as I told you too. That's something that we're going to have to address in due course. But..." Smith looked at me. "I've known you a long time, Frank. I know we're not social buddies, but I thought we had an understanding, a good working relationship. This isn't normal behavior from you, either. If the SAC orders you off a case, and I tell you too, that should be the end of it. There's a chain of command for a reason. You're not privy to everything that's going on, that's why we make the decisions. What's got your goat with this case? I know something's going on. Lewis's behavior is odd, and the numbers aren't adding up. Murder, gun running, people being frozen, and now this with Carter." Smith got up and started to pace in the small space. A plume of dust followed his movements.

"Dammit, Frank. What I saw yesterday, I've never seen before. I've known the SAC a long time. He has an excellent reputation. Everyone likes him, but he flipped his lid. That's not normal. Even if you did outright disobey him, it's an administrative thing. He didn't even ask you why. But I am. I want to know why Frank. I want to know the truth. And we're not leaving this room until you spill your guts. All of it."

He sat back down. I needed a moment to think, difficult while he was staring at me. I could feel the tension in the room, and if I'd had a knife, I could've sliced it six ways. I silently weighed my options. He could be grilling me to figure out how much I knew. If Black's operation was crumbling, he could be under orders to find out what I knew. He could be in league with Lewis. Could be taking bribes. Was I next to disappear? Would I end up in some storage freezer in some god-forsaken place, hanging on a hook while the life slowly leached out of me? Is that what was happening to Jessica while we sat around with thumbs up our asses?

On the other hand, he could just be a puzzled man. Wondering what was going on like he said. If so, he could be an ally of mine, he could help me. I could tell him about Lewis's finances. I absently fingered the files that were still stuffed inside my shirt. I should tell him about Mark. Poor Mark. I didn't know what to do.

My world had gone from that of wondering if I should sling my hook for a vacation in the Bahamas to almost being kicked out of the Guard. My new found soul mate was alone and frightened somewhere with that freak. And a litany of dead and injured people were littering the landscape. All in a few days. I pinched my nose, stifling a sneeze, the stale air and dust drying out my sinuses. I made my decision.

"There's something you need to know. Mark Malone has been murdered."

I told him of my meeting with Mark at the coffee shop and why I'd run. I said that Mark was working on a project for me and didn't want anyone to see us meeting. I told him I thought it must have been an inside tip that let someone follow Mark. We both would have picked up on someone following us. We're not that incompetent, so it had to be a leak. Someone had to have seen me talking with Mark before we left, or seen what he was working on. I didn't know if Mark had saved a copy on one of our servers, he was fastidious in his professionalism, so it was possible. It was also possible, thinking it through now, that someone could have accessed said server and figured it out.

Smith looked shocked but took it in stride, his professionalism and training taking over. We could mourn his loss later.

"Frank, I'll take what you just told me at face value. I have no reason to disbelieve you, and until proven otherwise, I have your back. I'll make a call to the local authorities in case that video feed comes to light. Tell them that you were working undercover. They'll probably still want to talk to you, but we can arrange it on our terms rather than theirs. I can get you some space. I need to know what Mark was working on though."

And that was the clincher. Mark was obvious. Mark's death probably wouldn't stick on me, but it sure would be a good way to get me out. A Special Agent on administrative leave, tormented with his loss of identity, his badge and gun gone. Yes, we know officer's, he left here saying some bad things about revenge and payback, that's why we took his weapon from him. No, he's never been like that before. Yes, he and Mark did argue before he left. Why yes, of course he knew where Mark took his morning coffee. Mark was always very routine. I just can't believe it, but I guess he must have flipped out. So sad, we never saw it coming.

And then I'd probably meet with a tragic accident while in lock up. Maybe I'd even hang myself with the belt and shoelaces that they conveniently forgot to take from me.

I wanted to trust Smith. I needed someone that had my back. I didn't want to be the only one holding these secrets. If something did happen to me, there was no evidence, nothing that couldn't just disappear or be explained away.

A phone started to chirp. It wasn't mine. I always have mine on vibrate. It kept chirping, the acoustics in the small room making it sound louder than it probably was. I looked at Smith, annoyed that he didn't answer it.

"You going to answer that?" Smith said.

I looked at him with surprise. "It's not mine."

"It is. It's coming from your pocket."

I pulled out my phone and showed him. "Look. No texts, the last call was from you."

The phone chirped again. I patted my pockets and pulled another phone out. Shit. I'd completely forgotten I'd been carrying around the clone of Willis's phone with me. It was that phone that was chirping. I clicked on the text message that had come through. As I read it I chilled, my resolve hardened, and I felt rage. The message said, *you know who this is. We have your girl. If you want her back in one piece, you'll hand over all the evidence.* Another text came through, and I clicked on that one. It was a photo. A picture of Jessica, tied up with her hands over her head, secured to a beam. She had a gag in her mouth and looked terrified. Another text. *Meet in one hour. Come alone.* What followed was the meeting's location.

Smith had been patient, letting me read the texts but his frustration came through. "Come on, Frank. Put the phone down. Texting isn't appropriate right now."

I felt awful. I was going to run out on him. I was going to leave him hanging. I thought he was on my side, but not after I did this.

"Don't hate me Tobias, but I have to leave," I said, reaching for the door.

Smith put his hand out and stopped the door from opening. "Frank! Don't do this. You need to tell me what's going on. I can't protect you if you don't let me help."

I yanked on the door. "Like you protected Carter?" It was a low blow, and I could see it in his face. His arm fell from the door and it gave me the chance to bolt.

I went straight to my car half-expecting Smith to have the security guard stop me, but I drove out unmolested.

I looked at my watch. I had time before the meeting to gather a few things from my safe aboard *Serenity*, and I needed to bring Pete up to date. At least one person needed to know what the hell I was doing, especially if I didn't come back. I needed some insurance. As I drove home, I kept a lively eye on my mirrors. I didn't need to be followed or ambushed. This was the last time I was going to get careless. I felt my resolve harden and a tentative plan form. It could work. I hoped it did.

I drove to the meeting. It was to be at an obscure, abandoned airstrip in Aransas Pass. I thought of Jessica. Her sweet caress, her laugh, the way she touched the tip of her nose when she was thinking, the lock of hair that kept falling across her eyes no matter what she did with it. I thought of our long conversations on the deck of the *Serenity*, her eagerness to learn. How she liked to listen, how she could point out the obvious problems with my logic.

I missed her with a yearning that made my heart ache. So help me God, if they've harmed one tiny little hair on her head, I'll destroy them all. Vengeance may be some omnipotent being's prerogative, but I would invoke my right of free will. I would make them all burn, burn in hell.

Rachel Platten's *Fight Song* came on the radio, and I turned it up. I thought it was appropriate for my mood. It could have been *Dancing Queen*, so I at least had that going for me.

Jessica would have laughed at my music selection, and that made me smile too, just imagining her fake halfhearted scorn.

I slowed down as I neared the airstrip. I could see that a gate had been wedged open and I nudged the car through the gap. This place was far away from any main roads so there was no fear of any security or police happening along. I followed the road straight to an old hangar. The roof was wind damaged, partly ripped off and missing. An old dilapidated sign, peppered with shotgun holes announced that this was the Aransas Commercial Strip and Hangar Number Two. I couldn't see any sign of Hangar Number One. Maybe that had blown away along with the roof, or perhaps it had never existed at all, the number two moniker making the airport sound bigger than it was.

I stepped out of the car and held on tightly to the envelope of evidence I had brought with me. I closed the door. It was unnaturally silent, the heat radiating off the tarmac. I took a breath, the faint whiff of jet fuel still permeated the air. The sun scorched the landscape and played with tumbleweeds as I walked into the hangar.

My eyes didn't take long to adjust to the semi-shade of the hangar as the missing part of the roof let in plenty of sun, and I saw Black sitting in a big brown leather armchair about half way in. The chair looked like the same one he had at the fishing warehouse. Maybe he took it with him everywhere.

Externally, I kept my expression neutral. I doubt Black could see what I was feeling, but internally I was on fire. I wanted to shoot him, punch him, scratch his eyes out in a girly way, piss on him—

"Special Agent. Stop right there," Black said.

I did.

"I'm glad you followed directions and came alone, it makes things simpler. As I'm sure you know," Black said, indicating the upper walkway around the hangar, "I didn't come alone. My associates have you well covered, and I imagine you're also aware that I have a supply of world-class weaponry at my disposal, so don't try anything cute. Just so we're on the same page, right from the beginning. If you fuck up in here, you won't see your lover again. I suggest you pay attention and listen carefully."

"Where is she? If you've hurt her—"

"She's perfectly fine. Although...I can't guarantee her safety forever. The boys do like to play rough now and again, and I can only stop them from having fun for a little while." His fat body wrapped in a neon green jogging suit jiggled up and down as he laughed. "I believe you have something for me?"

"What assurances do I have that you'll let her go if I give you this?" I said, waving the envelope.

"Absolutely none. But if you don't give me that envelope, you'll die right where you're standing. And then I'll take it anyway."

I kept my rage in check. "I might have come alone, but I didn't leave unprepared. If I don't make it back in two hours-"

His fat slithered over his body as he barked a laugh again. "Yes. Yes. Yes. And you've left written instructions in a particular file to be opened if you don't return, blah, blah, blah. You amuse me, Special Agent. You must be very special. Special in the head, no? What? Do you think we don't know about your friend Pete? Or perhaps you left a copy with your Assistant Special Agent in Charge, Tobias Smith? Could you have placed copies oh so carefully and reverently inside the safe no one but you knows about in your stupid boat? Men can be killed. Fires can be started. Boats can be sunk." He paused to light a cigar, the smoke wafting upwards as he puffed. "Come now. I am not a patient man."

"You'll never get away with this." I stepped closer. "You can't kidnap a federal agent and expect to get away with it."

"You sound like a broken record, Agent. You forgot to mention all the murders I've gotten away with. Come now, I've been playing this game a lot longer than you. Do you not think I have an escape plan? This game was getting tiresome anyway. If you'd just given me a few more weeks, we would never have had to have this conversation."

"Where do you think you're going to be able to hide from me on this planet? I'll hunt you down you egotistical cockfuck, and you'll dance the hempen jig."

"You're absurd. Hang? What are you? A pirate? Perhaps you really are special? Do you think I'm going to tell you all my plans like a sad actor in a two-bit James Bond knock off? Tie you up and expect the lasers and sharks to get you while I walk off into the sunset? Don't be stupid. No, you brought all this upon yourself, Dalton. You were supposed to back off. Don't you Coast Guard people know how to follow orders?"

"So Lewis really is on your payroll."

"Is that a question or a statement? Either way, I'm not answering, and you're trying my patience. Enough. Bring the envelope to me now."

I walked a few steps closer.

"Far enough. Just throw it from there."

"What makes you think I won't put a bullet in your eye right now and skull fuck you. Carter could be dead already, I've nothing to lose."

"Oh, but you do. What if she is alive? What then? You'd be killing her and yourself. You'd never know. And then think of the good Frank Dalton name. Frank

Dalton, U.S. Marshal, shot and murdered in a shootout. Fast forward a hundred years or so, and we have Frank Dalton, Special Agent shot and killed. Was he crooked? Did he murder that tech guy? Maybe he set fire to that bitch Rivas's house? Whatever good you've done in your career it'll all boil down to a media frenzy of bullshit. You'll be analyzed, chewed up and spit out. Your name will be nothing but dirt, and Carter will be right there with you."

For a moment I didn't blink, didn't move. And then I threw myself down to the ground and rolled quickly, coming up with my weapon drawn. Black-clad operatives rappelled down ropes that appeared through holes in the broken roof, machine guns chattering, bad guys falling to the ground. I put a bullet through Black's forehead, brain matter exploding out in an arc.

Of course, none of that happened, and I threw the envelope down on the ground and kicked it over. I'd thought that maybe, just maybe I'd have some options, could figure something out. I was used to improvising, but there was no cover in this wide-open space. No stash of secret weapons. No small thermonuclear bomb designed for one and concealed in the envelope. No laser watches or cigarette darts.

No, this was real life, and just as real life sometimes is, this was an entirely stinky shit show. Whatever grand plan I had was just that, a grand plan. Nothing I could execute. Fuck it all to hell and back.

"Helen Back," I said.

"What was that?"

"Nothing. Just a girl I used to run with." Jessica would have liked that. Or probably would have just groaned. "What now? You've got what you want."

"Quite. Now, you leave."

"And then what? What about Carter?"

"All in good time. You still have that traitor Willis's phone?"

I nodded and tapped my pants pocket.

"Good, keep it close at hand. We'll be in touch with where you can collect Carter. Goodbye, Special Agent. It was entertaining, but there are things I must attend to. A few loose ends to tie up, as it were."

"And I walk out? Just like that?"

"Of course. We're not barbarians, just businessmen. And I have business to attend to. Good bye."

Black didn't move. I turned and started walking out, to light, to sanctuary. I glanced up at the walkway and saw a few shadows shaped like men. I expected a shot in the back of the head before I made it to the sunlight.

# FOURTEEN

## *Loose Ends*

left the hangar without dying. I walked to the car and let out a long breath. Black now knew everything I did about the case. Sure, I'd made copies, but he was spot on with where I'd put them. I shouldn't have been so obvious; it was evident Black had had eyes on us all along.

I got in my car, scorching myself on the sun-heated pleather seats and slammed the steering wheel over and over with my fist. I rammed the car in gear and peeled out.

My phone vibrated as I was back on the road. A text from Smith. It said that the enforcement guys had turned up a blank. There were a few fishing vessels there, but nothing was going on. He also told me to call him. I was relieved he'd let me know what was going on, especially after the way I'd left. I didn't respond though, call me callous, but I had my own motives. I knew where Black was, but if I told Smith, they'd be long gone by the time anyone could get there. And still, if they did manage to track him down, we still didn't know where Jessica was. I couldn't see Black suddenly spilling the beans. He still had the upper hand, temporarily though, I hoped.

I was running out of leads. I screamed in the car. Screamed and yelled at the injustice. At a traffic light, the young woman that pulled up next to me glanced over and immediately looked away. She took off as soon as the light changed, no doubt wanting to put some distance between her and the crazy guy. The car behind me honked, and I looked in the mirror giving him the finger and slowly moved on.

I called Pete and told him to watch his back. He said not to worry; the place was buttoned up tight. I asked him to keep an eye on my boat, and he said he had it covered, whatever that meant.

I ran through the options in my head and decided to give Deacon another visit. This was one guy that had worked for Black, maybe he knew of a hidey-hole where Carter could be. It was worth a shot; I didn't have much else.

I drove out to Calallen again, the flat landscape fitting for my mood. Halfway down Deacon's dusty driveway, a U.S. Marshal's car blocked the way. The Marshal got out of his car, hand on his sidearm and walked cautiously towards me. I turned the engine off, rolled down my window and placed my hands on the steering wheel. Didn't need to get shot. As he edged closer, I saw it was the same guy from before. I didn't have my badge anymore, so I showed him my military ID.

"Where's your badge?"

"Must be in my other jacket," I said, patting my pockets.

He gave my ID the once over, looking from its picture to my face and back again. After making me sweat for a moment, he handed it back to me without another word and walked to his car. I wondered if he was going to let me through, but then his car started and he backed it out of the way. He eyeballed me as I drove past, and then I saw him in my rearview mirror move the vehicle back into place, blocking the driveway again.

Deacon looked as if he hadn't moved since Carter and I had left him. I'm sure he had, but a large pile of smokes lay piled up on the floor next to the picnic table, and he was still staring off into space, a vacant look on his face.

I sat down. Deacon still hadn't moved. I snapped my fingers to get his attention, even though I was right in front of him. His eyes slowly focused on me.

"Agent." He nodded at me.

"Deke. How've you been?"

He shrugged. "Just waiting for Black to come get me."

I froze. Was he coming here? "What do you mean?"

"Black always gets his way. Expect he'll send someone to take me out. I know how he works," Deacon said.

I relaxed a fraction. "I wouldn't worry about him. From what I hear, he's probably leaving the country. His operation is compromised, he has no out, except to leave. I doubt he's concerned with you."

"Maybe. Maybe not. You never worked for him, did you?"

"Deke, you remember that nice lady I had with me the last time we visited?"

He nodded and lit another smoke.

"Black has her. She's been kidnapped."

Deacon internalized this new piece of information for a moment and then said, "Told you there was no escaping. She's probably dead."

"Cut the self-pity, man. She's not dead, and neither are you. I need to know where they have her stashed. Rack your brains, Deke. You could help save her."

Deacon took a long drag on his smoke, letting the ash fall on the table to join the large heap already there.

"She's probably on a boat. Black owns lots of them. Take one out to sea. Safest place there is. You'd know if anyone was comin' near you. Could move out the way. Or dump her body. Move on."

"What boat, Deke? What boat would they use?"

He shrugged again. "Don't know. If it was me, I'd use a big one. Black only has two biguns. One I worked on and her sister ship. What I–"

Deacon didn't finish his sentence, nor would he ever. His head exploded, splattering me with blood and chunks of brain matter. I heard the report from the tree line. I dove for cover under the table, pulled my piece from my ankle holster and returned fire. I looked behind me for more protection and ran to the side of the house, weaving as I went. The marshal got out of his car, and I waved him down. He was no dummy and used his car door as a shield.

There were no more shots. I knelt down low and peeked around the side of the house. I saw Deacon slumped over the table but could see nothing behind him. I shot into the trees anyway.

Nobody returned fire. I saw the marshal on the radio and signaled I was moving out. I ran to the shed that we'd seen Deacon come out of on that first trip. Still no shots. I peeked around. Nothing. I didn't feel safe running across open ground to the tree line, I'd leave that to the crime scene people. The shooter had accomplished his goal and Deacon was gone. Black was evidently cleaning up. No loose ends. Guess Deke was right after all. Shit and double shit.

The marshal tried to stop me, saying he needed me to wait to give a statement. I told him I didn't have time and to call the ASAC if he needed me. He wasn't happy but moved his car out of the way. I spun out of the dustbowl.

Another one dead. Had Black no respect for humanity? No, stupid question. He felt above the law. He operated so far above us mere mortals he thought he was unreachable. But, thanks to Deacon's last words, I had another clue, a starting place. Two ships. Two ships where Jessica might be. I needed help on this one. I called the office and told Smith I was coming in.

Smith cursed at me when I told him Deacon was dead. "This is becoming a habit, Frank."

In the command post, we pulled up the list of Black's assets and found the two large fish processing vessels he had. A check of the automatic vessel tracker, AIS told us where they'd be; luckily they were far apart from each other. If we could secure the radio room on the first one, they wouldn't be able to call out any warnings to their sister ship, and as we didn't know which one Carter was on, we might have to take both ships. We accessed our law enforcement database, found some old files and got the large-scale scantlings of the ships up on the screens.

Senior Chief Montoya gave the brief.

"We're going to take the two new stealth helos. They're regular sixty-fives that have been equipped for covert ops. They have a sniper station and fifty-cals mounted, and we'll be able to execute vertical insertions. One helo will hover over the stern deck, and that team of six will secure the engine room then check the cargo spaces. The other helo, which I'll be on with another team, will hover over the bridge and secure that and the cabin spaces. We plan to take off at dusk, putting us on scene when it's fully dark. We'll make two passes with night vision, and if there are any armed unfriendlies, we'll take them down first. Any questions?"

"I want to be on your helo, Senior," I said.

Montoya hesitated for a second and then said, "We can talk about that in private after the brief is over, sir. Any other questions?" Montoya looked around the room. "Very well. Wheels up in one hour. Get some rest."

After everyone had filed out of the room, I approached Montoya with my question again.

"Absolutely not, sir. You're not trained for this sort of counterinsurgency op. We need to come down quickly and quietly. I know you want to be there, but you'll hold us back, impede our mission. No offense, sir, but I don't have time to be your babysitter."

I bristled but realized he was right. I never had dropped out of a helicopter on a piece of string. Now wasn't the time to try. If I was on the mission and screwed up, I'd never forgive myself.

"Sir, if it's any consolation, we'll have live streaming of the whole evolution from our helmet cams. We'll even have tactical comms set up in here so that you can hear what's going on."

"Thanks, Senior," I said. He turned to walk away. "Senior, one more thing."

"Yes, sir."

"These boats. Some of the people on board are just going to be fisherman. Only one boat has Carter, the other is just a fish processor, doing their job."

"Understood, sir. We have that under control."

"Thank you, I didn't mean to step on your toes," I said.

"No offense taken, sir. If she's there, we'll get her back."

Sometime later the video feed spooled up and the comms channel opened.

"Radio check. Montoya one to base."

An Operations Specialist Petty Officer was manning the radios on our end.

"Montoya One, base. Read you five by five," he said.

We watched the unnatural green glow of night vision optics on the monitors. The large televisions were split into six quadrants so we could watch each team member individually. It was eerie, a little like watching someone play an Xbox game, only this game had genuine consequences, and there were no extra lives.

Sometime later, the radio crackled to life again. "Base, Montoya One. Target acquired."

"Montoya One, base. Understood."

One Coastie zipped down the line extending from the hovering helicopter to the ship below. This person would check out any immediate threats and neutralize them if possible. It was easier than have everyone else come down in a rush. That usually resulted in an epic cluster. The Guard had learned a lot in the aftermath since 9/11. Our mistakes are fewer, and the few that are, are less forgiven.

The all-clear was given, and the remaining five team members from each helo zipped down the lines. They wore black tactical gear but with the night vision goggles on each member and the feed on the screens here, we could easily see what was going on.

They made short order of clearing the ship. There was a small crew of eleven, no sign of Carter, and no sign anything was wrong.

Senior Chief Montoya took off his camera and looked into it. "Sorry, Sir. No sign of her." It was a nice gesture.

They left one team member on board to ensure no one used the radios and call the other boat. In an ideal world we would have hit both vessels at once. But even here, budget cuts were present.

The helos winched the teams back up and with little fuss and they were underway for the next vessel with an ETA of twenty-two minutes. This was it.

I went and grabbed a cup of coffee. This one was cold, so I shoved it in the microwave for a minute. I added powdered creamer I found, we couldn't seem to keep milk fresh. I tasted the coffee, and yep, it sucked ass. But it was coffee, and I needed something.

Smith came and joined me. "We'll get her, Frank. We have too."

I nodded, unsure of what to say.

"Listen, it's rough on all of us, having one of our own taken, and especially with what happened to Mark. It's...it's not something we're used to. She'll be okay." He tried to console me by patting my shoulder.

"Are you telling me or hoping?" I said, shrugging him off. I wasn't in the mood. "I hope she's okay too, but I don't see why Black would keep her alive. He's killed nearly everyone else, why would he keep her alive?"

"He's killed a lot of people, you're right, but he hasn't killed any federal officers."

"What about Mark?"

"He was one of us, of course he was, but he wasn't an agent, I think that's the difference. Mark was a civilian working in the department."

"That's an asshole comment, you know."

"I'm grasping at straws here, Frank. Just trying to come up with reasons, a theory. I don't know for sure, but it's the only thing that makes sense to me. Come on, let's get back, they should be getting on scene right about now."

In the conference room, the feed was once again live. I was nervous, biting my nails. I paced up and down. The team went through the same evolution, one person from each team securing their areas. In short order, the other team members had rappelled down. There were no shots fired, no angry voices. The team secured the crew on the back deck and searched the spaces. Nothing. No Carter. No evidence she was ever there.

"Sir?" Montoya said. "We've searched the vessel with neg res. She's not on board. The crew look like regular fisherman. There are no weapons on board, nothing out of place. Sir, I don't think she was ever here."

Two ships. Two ships. Our only clues before Deacon died. His dying breath all but worthless now.

It was time I filled Smith in on Lewis. He'd been in the wind since trying to bust me down. It was a long conversation. Smith listened well and made a few notes, his initial disbelief turning to resignation and then anger. I gave him copies I'd made of the video feed from the underground lot, the copies of the bank statements, all the stuff that Mark had helped me retrieve.

"And add his peculiar behavior, and the fact that Black pretty much confirmed it for me, he has to be taking bribes. He's also the inside leak, he's the one that's been feeding Black information, that's why we can't get to him or find Carter. I don't know if there are any more informants in the department, that's why I've been playing this close to my chest, it wouldn't surprise me to know that Black's got his fingers into more than one person."

"You didn't trust me?" Smith said, half joking. When I didn't reply he said, "Seriously? Me?"

I shrugged. "I didn't know who to trust, Tobias. I knew I could trust Carter. And Mark. That was it. I didn't know who else was in on it. Black's reach seems to be everywhere."

"It's a lot to take in, Frank. Very well. We'll send agents around the SAC's house to pick him up. It's time we had some answers."

I breathed a long sigh of relief. "Thank you. I'm sorry I ever doubted you."

"Forget it. Buy me a beer sometime. Let's go back to my office, and I'll give you your badge and gun back."

It was liberating to get my badge back. It felt like a part of me was home again, which made me wonder if I was too wrapped up, identifying with the job. Perhaps the job did define me, not the other way round, but I shook that thought off. Introspection could come later.

It wasn't long before the agents assigned to bring Lewis in reported he wasn't home. They said the door was unlocked, and I could imagine how they'd opened it. A brief search discovered a messy bedroom and it looked like some clothes were missing from his closet and drawers. It seemed as if he'd hurriedly packed for a trip out of town. There was no sign of a struggle, so we had to assume he was tipped off and made a quick escape. With the amount of money he had, he could probably get safe passage out of the country from many sources, if not Black himself.

In order to stop his escape we had a judge order the banks to freeze his accounts. The offshore bank was a little more trouble, but our liaison team was working that angle. We put out a BOLO on Lewis and alerted the Port Authority and TSA. Customs and Border Patrol was notified and flagged his passport. He wouldn't get far.

What I got was redemption. There was a chance Lewis could have tried to bluster his way out of this, and although the evidence was damning, he still had some authority. On that note, the DOD was notified, and they flagged his military ID card and his badge. With no easy access to money, and no legal way out of the country we were hoping to keep him somewhat contained. The local police were networked in, and we linked his name to the possible suspects of Mark's murder. Neither Smith nor I thought he'd gone that far, but it ensured the police would keep an extra special eye out for him. We needed him to come in. We needed to know what he might know. Some of it was also for his protection. There was no way of telling how far Black would go, whether Lewis was operating in his inner circle or whether Black would decide he was another loose end, now that he had no use. I couldn't really give two shits if Black decided to off him, though. Callous? Perhaps.

The big problem, of course, was that we still didn't know where Jessica was. I prayed and hoped she was okay. She was a tough cookie, but I couldn't see why Black would keep her alive now, couldn't see what use she would have for him. It didn't stop us fighting for her though. It wasn't over until it was over.

Smith looked weary, he was slumped in his chair.

"Hey, Tobias,", I said. He looked up at me, bleary-eyed. "You should go home, get some rest."

"No. No, I can't, Frank. I know Carter's your friend, but she's my people. I failed her, Frank. It's my job as her supervisor to make sure she's safe. I failed."

"Hey. No one could have predicted what that nutter was going to do. I mean, Jesus, this all happened in the space of a few days."

"I hear what you're saying. Thanks. But ultimately it's still my responsibility...No, I'm going to use the ready room here and rack out. If anything happens...you should go though."

I weighed the pros and cons of staying here. Honestly, there wasn't anything I could do. We were in a holding pattern.

"I'm going to go home, get a fresh change of clothes. Maybe I'll think of something. If anything happens, call me."

"You know I will. Likewise?"

"Sure."

I headed out and headed home to *Serenity*. I really did need to change, I'd washed my face as best I could, and changed out of my Mark encrusted clothes into coveralls, but still, I needed to shower.

I ran the water hot, scalding, trying to sear the skin off my body, to feel pain, to lose myself for a moment. When the water ran cold, I got out and toweled off, moving to the bed. It seemed like weeks since Jessica had been here, helping me get dressed, making love. Everywhere my eyes touched reminded me of her; a hairbrush, an item of clothing carelessly left in a corner. I started to spiral into despair, my heart banging against my ribs, feeling lightheaded. I couldn't afford the self-pity; I couldn't afford the emotion. It was crippling. I sat down and took some deep breaths, centering myself. The emotions would have to stay deep down for now. I needed a clear head and control. I closed my eyes and pushed the last lingering thoughts of what if's and what could be's out with every exhalation, breathing in positivity and focus with every inhalation. I could do this.

# FIFTEEN

## *Take a Seat Admiral Jones*

few minutes more and I had myself under control. I dressed and walked over to Pete's. I didn't need a drink, but I did need the company.

As I pushed open the door, I saw the bar was more crowded than usual, bar stools all occupied. I stood on the precipice, unsure. I wanted to talk to Pete but wasn't sure if I could do crowds. Thankfully, Pete spotted me and motioned me to the back where the sole booth was. Decision made.

I walked over and saw an older gentleman already there. He was sitting with remarkable posture, an amber colored liquor in front of him with no ice. Probably bourbon or whiskey. Pete introduced us.

"Admiral? This is Special Agent Frank Dalton. Frank, this is Admiral Jones, the man I was telling you about," Pete said.

We shook hands. He had a firm grip and dry hands. I looked at him and immediately felt I could trust him. He had steely gray eyes and a prominent nose. Although older in years, he still had a full head of hair, black but heavily streaked with silver, cut in a tight buzz. If I didn't know who he was, he would be easy to peg as ex-military or law enforcement.

"Pleased to meet you, Frank," he said, "but please call me Robert. I haven't been an Admiral to any that care about that sort of thing for a few years now. And I've told you before Pete, call me Robert."

"Old habits die hard, sir," Pete said.

"Please sit, both of you," Jones said.

We squeezed into the booth and got comfortable. I abstained from a drink when Pete offered, then Jones began.

"Pete has told me about your particular predicament, Frank. Are there any new developments?"

I told him about the recent deaths and brought him up to speed on the search for Jessica and my meeting with Black.

"And we've alerted the relevant authorities to be on the lookout for Lewis."

Jones looked pained and swilled the whiskey around in his glass. He'd been patient while I narrated the story, limiting his questions to a few succinct points.

"So you've put a BOLO on him then?"

I nodded.

"You know; I knew your SAC. I didn't know him well mind, but the Guard is so small you either know someone or know someone who knows someone. I was in the latter group. I'd heard some rumblings a few years ago before I got out of the service, but nothing anywhere near like this, like what you told me. It fills me with a deep sadness that someone could bring such discredit upon the Coast Guard. It seems almost impossible that he's apparently gotten away with it for so long."

"We're conducting an internal review. There's a possibility that Lewis wasn't the only one. It looks like he's been on Black's payroll for many years."

I filled him in on some of the details we'd been able to find out already, bits and pieces that seemed to fit. Smith had been busy, pulling every available agent to work on it.

"It appears to have started years ago when Lewis was a junior grade lieutenant before he crossed over and became an agent. Back then, Lewis was in charge of fisheries enforcement, and Black's operation was in its fledgling status. After Black's boss was indicted, he took control of a fleet of thirty fishing vessels or so, in Palacious, just up the street a ways. Each one was operating on a quota system. Quotas were, or are, supposed to protect the fishing industry from over fishing a species and promoting sustainability. Each boat is allotted a quota they can catch of each particular fish. If you happen to catch more of one type of fish, or not enough, you could buy or sell your boats quota. And when the quotas are full, you can't fish anymore. It's really called a catch share program, but everyone calls it a quota. The jury is still out on whether it works well or not.

"Anyway, what Black was doing, was this. If you have a quota to catch say Red Snapper, what Black was doing was calling everything he caught Red Snapper. Whatever the fish was, they called it Red Snapper. There are checks and balances to prevent this. You have to report the catch to NOAA and the wholesaler of the catch has to report what he gets. There are random spot inspections, Coast Guard boarding's, National Fisheries observers on board every now and again and so on.

"Black isn't stupid though. He owns the wholesaler, so of course, it tallied with what the vessels brought in. This worked for the captains, because if they had a quota for say King Mackerel, that allowance is small. Once you've caught, and I'm making these figures up as examples, two hundred pounds of King Mackerel, the trip is done. You have to go back and unload. But if you call everything you catch Red Snapper," I shrugged. "Well, you carry on fishing. The captains on the boat got paid the price for Red Snapper, which is a cheaper fish, maybe a dollar a pound, but they could bring in thousands and thousands of pounds. So it worked for them. Black would then sell the fish to a fish broker, but this time he'd label the fish as the correct species and sell them for a lot more money. Usually for cash. He had a deal set up through the airport too, had a TSA agent paid off and got the money to Mexico."

I paused to take a swig of water. "And this is where that young lieutenant comes in. I'm sure you know this part. The Coast Guard does fishery boarding's and verifies at sea that the catch is good, within quotas and so on."

Jones nodded. "I'm familiar."

"Good, I won't get into the weeds then. So, Lewis was the commander of a small cutter that did boarding's. If Lewis couldn't alert Black of a boarding ahead of time, and the boat got boarded, he would have the boarding reports run through him for approval and then doctor them to make everything look kosher. We believe that's how Lewis got involved initially. It probably didn't happen overnight. Coasties don't make much money, and maybe he had a gambling debt, or a new family and was maxed on credit." I shrugged. "It happens. It's a small community, and maybe Black offered him a way out. Do me this favor, and I'll help you out with your debt. Who knows?

"Anyway, by the time Black moved into the more profitable gunrunning business, Lewis was already used to the wealthy lifestyle, and just sunk deeper. Once in, it's hard to get out. Maybe Lewis didn't want to. Many people have tried and are now fish food. He'd know that. Once Black has his hooks in you, pun intended, it's tough to get out."

"That's really quite fascinating," Jones said. "And he's been doing this for years?"

"Yeah. Every time we get close, the informant seems to get cold feet, or disappears. Like I said, Black's smart. Until now. He made a mistake with Willis, and it brought down his empire. This is a rapidly evolving case. We just had to connect the dots."

Jones sat back and looked lost in his thoughts. I took that opportunity, made my excuses and went to use the head. When I came back, it was evident that Pete and Jones had been talking.

"Frank, the Admiral wants to make you an offer. I think you should consider it carefully before you answer."

"As you know," Jones said, "I now run a security firm. I have at my disposal a well-trained, elite team, made from various ex-Special Forces members.

All hold Top Secret clearances, and all of them have been tried and tested in the field. With my work for the DOD, sometimes we're called on to perform operations that, shall we say, couldn't be seen to be handled by our government."

I nodded, unsure of where this was going. Pete slid out to get me another glass of water and to sling a few drinks to patrons. He probably didn't want to hear all of this either.

"I'm deeply concerned that your unit has been compromised. From what you and Pete have told me, and from what I could find out at short notice, you may be right that you have more than one mole. It strikes me as odd that in this day and age of modern technology, counter-terrorism, and so on, that Black could remain in the wind. He has to have had or still has some outside help. What I'm proposing to you is that you consider using my team for an extraction should you find actionable intelligence on where your Carter may be. Naturally, we would keep this in-house and would need your assurance that there would be no interference from the Coast Guard. I don't want friendlies in the crossfire. That's unacceptable and non-negotiable."

"So you're asking me to keep this quiet."

"I know it's a hard decision. I think it's the best shot you have of getting Carter out alive. They wouldn't know we were coming, there would be no tip-off. It's up to you how you play it later, but you cannot mention us. We weren't there."

"And if it should go wrong?"

"We still weren't there. But we don't lose. And we don't have a mole."

"Why are you doing this for me?"

"I'm not. I'm doing it as a favor to Pete, and I'm doing it for your agent. The Coast Guard was good to me. I want to help in any way I can."

Jones made to leave. "Here," he said. "This is my card. Call me if you need assistance. You merely have to tell me you're in, and I can have my operatives mobile within minutes. I'll put them on standby now, just in case."

"One more question, sir. If and when I call you, I want to be in on the operation. I want to be there when we rescue her."

Jones looked thoughtful. "I can't answer that. I'll not have the operation jeopardized by a love-sick puppy."

"Now hold on a—"

Jones held up his hand. "But I will put your request into my operations Chief. It'll be go, or no go from him. That's as far as I'm prepared to stretch."

"Very well."

We shook hands, and Jones left, walking with the same posture as he had sat, upright and assured. Pete came back; the bar had emptied out some while we were talking.

"Are you really sure I can't get you a drink. One shot of something. It might help you sleep."

"No thanks. Listen, I'm going to get going. And buddy," I gave Pete a big hug, wrapping my arms around him. "Thank you. For everything."

He slapped me on the back. "Always."

I walked back to *Serenity*. I wasn't tired, wasn't sure what I was going to do, I was just going through the motions. Without paying any mind, I started to prep the boat for a trip. I did the basic engine maintenance, checking the oil, transmission fluid and so on. I double-checked the lines weren't frayed, did a radio check, figured out what provisions I might need for a few days' trip. In the back of my head, I was preparing for the voyage I had vaguely planned when all this had started. I wanted normalcy. Something to calm me. The Caribbean was a bit of a stretch, somewhat of a haul from Corpus, but we could always go down to Mexico, that wasn't too far. Hang out around Cozumel or somewhere. If we floated along following the coastline, we'd keep safer and pull in if the weather turned.

I eventually hit the rack. It was a restless night. I kept imagining what was happening to Jessica. It wasn't anything good. I awoke early, before first light. I wasn't going to get any more sleep. I obsessively checked my phone while I was making coffee, getting dressed, taking a shower. I was paranoid I'd miss a call or text, or my reception or Wi-Fi would suddenly stop working.

I couldn't delay any longer and went into work. Smith looked like hell. He hadn't shaved, his clothes looked rumpled.

"Anything?" I said.

He shook his head. "Nothing. Except for this Fax that showed up right before you walked in," he said, hiding a smile and handing it to me.

I took it. "What is it...?" And then I started to read. It was a departmental Fax from Doc Hutchins. She'd faxed over the preliminary results from some loose fibers she'd taken from the Jane & John Does. She'd also written that she'd e-mailed, under secure password protected files, the full results.

I went to log onto a computer and look at the results, but Tobias stopped me. "Here," he said, "I already got them."

I took them from him, looked for somewhere to sit down and fell heavily with a bone-numbing weariness into the nearest chair. I scanned the several sheets of paper, trying to work around the doctoral terms.

"This is good?" I said, not completely understanding.

"Yes, it's good, Frank. It means we have actionable intelligence. After I saw this e-mail, I walked over to Mark's replacement in DOMEX. I told him this was a top priority."

"What did he find out?"

"We know where she is, Frank. We know."

When I let go of my breath, I realized I'd been holding it in. My stomach flipped, and a glimmer of hope raced through me. We knew where she was.

It was going to be a close thing. Thanks to the work of Doc Hutchins, we had a break in the case, a huge break. The fibers she found were so small they couldn't be seen with the naked eye, but they were taken from scrapings under the fingernails and various other parts of the body that held onto transferred particulate. The fibers had then been sent to a forensic lab, but because of their backlog, and the fact they were labeled as Jane and John Does, there was no rush on the analysis. The results had shown up in an unassuming e-mail to the ME, without even a follow-up phone call. As soon as she realized what it could mean, she'd sent over the fax, the e-mail and even called Tobias to ensure he had them.

From the work DOMEX had done, we'd linked the analysis to the freighter that we had boarded just a few days ago in Ingleside, *The Bold Endeavor*. The link came from something to do with the metal used in the shipbuilding process. Not many people outside of shipbuilding realize, but each ship that's built, the steel has to be a particular grade. That steel has to be tracked from manufacturer to end product. The reason for this is so inferior quality steel is not used in shipbuilding. This helps prevent new reefs from littering the ocean when they sink. On this occasion, it helped us. The fibers picked up were particulates of steel and rust, from the inside of the freighter. When analyzed, we could tell which schedule of steel was used, and trace that back to the origin. Luckily for us, this schedule was a one-off. Something happened in the smelting process that gave this steel a unique identifier. That unique identifier was now in the form of a freighter en route to the Cayman Islands in the Caribbean.

As I said before, though, it was going to be a close call. We were going to divert the *Glorious* to board the vessel, but they were still about eighteen hours out.

I slipped away and called Admiral Jones and gave him the word. His team would take off in a company jet and land in the Caymans. From there they would use a high-speed launch to intercept the freighter. The timing shouldn't be an issue. If everyone kept the same course and speed the Admiral's group should be there several hours before the Cutter *Glorious*. That's if everyone kept to their schedule.

I asked the Admiral's group if I could go. They were willing to let me accompany them on the jet and the boat, but when they boarded the freighter, they wanted me to stay on the launch. I could come aboard after they secured the ship. We were expecting to take some heavy fire on this one, what with Black in the arms trade.

I'd agreed to any restrictions they imposed just so I could get there, but I wasn't going to stay put. The tricky thing was convincing Smith that I was going to disappear for a couple of days, without him wondering why. He knew I'd want to know what was going on and the only way I could do that short of getting on the

Cutter, which wasn't going to happen, was to be in the Command Post. It would be another kick in the gut to know I'd sidelined the Coast Guard on this op, especially if something went wrong.

I had to come up with something convincing, something where he wouldn't be suspicious.

"Tobias. Where's the *Glorious* going after they rescue Jessica?" I said.

"They'll probably head for St. Thomas. It's the closest U.S. port. We can get Carter back on a flight from there quicker than any other way."

And there I had it. "I'm flying down to ST. Thomas then. I want to be there when she gets in."

"Frank, be reasonable. What if she isn't on the vessel?" He looked at me. I gave him my best beseeching Boy Scout look. "Oh, what the hell. Go. Let me know when you get there. We'll get some orders cut to cover expenses."

"Thanks, Tobias." That solved my immediate problem, but once we had Jessica, I'd have to figure out how I suddenly happened to be on the freighter. I put that thought out of my mind for now and got myself out to the commercial airport where I was to meet the Admiral's people.

The Lear jet had seating for twelve, plus pilot and co-pilot. There were ten operatives. I made eleven. I sat at the back by myself, apparently after the initial meet and greet everybody had their way of prepping for a mission. That was all right by me. It gave me a chance to think things over. The operatives were in an entirely different class from our enforcement guys. It was no disrespect to our guys, but the ones on this plane were hard. Just looking at them, they looked like they'd all seen a lot of action. The weapons they carried seemed to be more of a personal choice than issued gear. They did all have one thing in common though, they all wore black, even their faces were blacked out, and when the cabin lights were dimmed after takeoff, I could have sworn that the plane was empty. No noise, no light, no reflections, no flash of skin to give them away. It was eerie.

# SIXTEEN

*Todderific*

When we touched down, I lifted my head with a start, drool down the side of my mouth. I hadn't realized I'd fallen asleep. With the restless night, the stress, the dark and the constant white noise, uninterrupted with annoying announcements to put up your tray table, I had dozed off.

I worked the crick out of my neck and looked at my watch. We'd been in the air for around three hours. I took a deep breath and followed the silent troops off the plane and into two passenger vans. One of the guys pointed at the second van so I got in that one. I sat in the back again, out of the way. The less they thought I was a hindrance the more they'd forget I was tagging along. At least that was my plan. I could tell from the glances a couple of them gave me they'd have sooner dropped me out of the plane and picked me up again on the way back, but they had their orders just like everyone else.

We drove to a secure facility co-opted by the admiral's agency. It was still dark, but I could just make out the narrow road, palm trees dotted along the side of the single lane road. The driver was pushing the speed limit but somehow able to see perfectly well, always dodging potholes. Once through the security checkpoint, we drove straight down to the dock, where bright lights lit up two boats, about forty-five feet in length.

The boats were prepped and running, the coxswains already at the helm. I was silently motioned to one of the two vessels.

The coxswain of my boat introduced himself, at least this guy was talking to me.

"Special Agent? My name is Foster. The Admiral said to make sure you were kept in the loop."

"That's mighty kind of you, thanks."

"I know where you're coming from, sir. I used to be in the Guard before I got out. I was a BM2. I've been working for the Admiral ever since - well for the last few years."

Foster didn't look a day over thirty, so he must have signed up at an early age. He continued, "We've been keeping tabs on both the vessels of interest, the freighter and the Cutter. The freighter has slowed some, which makes our trip out a little longer. It also means though, that the cutter has closed the distance."

"Foster leaned out of the cabin window and shouted to his crew. "Clear line one."

"Line one, aye. Line clear." Came the reply from the crewmember forward.

"Clear line four," Michael's said.

"Line four, aye. Line clear. All lines clear."

Foster gunned the engines, the Rolls Royce jet drives burbling smoothly, and set an intercept course for the freighter. Our ETA was about two hours at twenty-seven knots, the cruising speed for this Coast Guard Response Boat clone. Maybe it was one. They were fairly new boats for the Coast Guard, I couldn't imagine them being surpluses yet, but the Admiral seemed to have his hooks in all the right places. Either way, I was glad of the efficiency of the boat, crew, and the operatives who were slumped down in the cabin chairs.

I walked out to the back deck, careful to avoid the warm sea spray, I didn't feel like getting wet right now. For what it was worth it was a beautiful night. The speed of the boat blew away the Caribbean humidity, and the moon was waning, which would be good for the op. I saw a shooting star and made a wish.

I didn't know what to expect. I had no idea what condition we'd find Jessica, but we had a medic on the team for immediate triage. I hadn't yet come up with a plausible reason why I would be here and not in ST. Thomas, hopefully, it would come to me.

After a brief reverie, Foster called me in. "Sir, we're picking up the *Bold Endeavor* on the radar, she's cruising at about six knots, so the boarding should be seamless."

"About that," I said. "This isn't my usual game, but I'm assuming they're not going to just lower the gangway or a Jacob's ladder and welcome us aboard. How do we get on?"

"That's those guy's problem," he said, gesturing to the operatives. "I just drive the boat. What I've usually seen though, is that we'll make a wide turn and come up from their stern. Lookouts on vessels often lookout to see where they're going, not what's coming up behind them. We have a version of stealth technology so they won't be picking us up on the radar. We'll come up close. If there are any unfriendlies on the stern we'll take them out, and then probably use a pneumatic grappling hook. There are usually plenty of spaces on the stern to attach ourselves to, and then they just climb aboard. I understand you'll be staying with the boat, so we back off until we get the all clear."

"Yeah. I'm not okay with that plan though. I want to get on that freighter."

Foster looked at me. "I don't know about that, sir. You'd have to clear it through Wardwell, the lead tactical guy. Did you talk to him?"

"No, not yet. I'll have to do that," I said.

"Okay, contact in two minutes," Foster announced. When I turned around to look at the guys, expecting them to still be shaking off sleep, or still slumped over, they surprised me as they were all standing up on the back deck, weapons ready. I hadn't heard them move, nor even the door opening.

I walked out with them, gradually able to make out the shape of the freighter ahead in the darkness. They were running with all the proper complement of lights on, so they weren't trying to hide. Or maybe they were just trying to look innocent. The lead boat slowed speed to match the speed of the freighter and we matched that, staying back about two hundred feet.

I saw a man-sized shape on the deck of the *Bold Endeavor*, and I was about to shout a warning to the lead boat somehow, but the figure crumpled and pitched into the sea. They obviously didn't need my help. It was also obvious since they had taken him out we finally had the right boat. Thank God for small mercies.

I couldn't see exactly what was going on, they hadn't offered me any night vision goggles. I was, however, well-armed and had the foresight to bring my Kevlar vest with me.

In short order, the guys from the first boat made it on board. The plan was for them to find cover until everyone was on board.

I knew satellite images showing us the heat signatures of all those aboard were beamed directly to Wardwell, but it wouldn't show us if someone was deep inside a hold, or in the bilges, possible places Jessica could be imprisoned.

Our boat moved into position. One... two... three... on board. I positioned myself in the last spot. "I'll untie the grappling line for you once you're aboard, so we can clear out," I said to the fifth guy.

He nodded. Four on board, five on board, and as soon as he reached the freighter, I launched myself up the line as quickly as I possibly could. Luckily each team member was finding cover and paid me no mind. I came over the stern onto the deck, keeping as silent as I could. Number five saw me and violently gestured for me to get back. I shrugged, ignored him and found my own cover. I saw him press a finger to his throat mike, no doubt telling Wardwell what I'd done.

I didn't care, I wouldn't put anyone's life in danger, but I needed to be here. I let them creep forward, only hand signals from now on.

The plan was essentially the same idea that Montoya and his people had used. Secure the bridge and communications stations, secure the engine room, secure all the crew on the stern and then do a systematic search for Jessica.

While I was reviewing the plan in my head, a crewmember passed near where one of the operatives was hidden. He stopped to light a cigarette, the match flaring, a machine gun slung over his shoulder. The operative used the moment when the crewmember was temporarily blinded by his flaring match to take him down. He silently dragged him backward, and in a quick motion snapped his neck. He shoved him behind a crate, and I quietly followed. Two bad guys down.

Five members of the team entered the superstructure and climbed the stairs to the bridge. I couldn't see what was going on, didn't have a radio or anything, but when the guys moved forward I followed in their footsteps quietly and rapidly, in a piggy-back motion, one person moving forward while the other covers, two each side. I was kind of stuck looking out for myself. Up ahead as the first two passed a bulkhead, a door popped open, and another crewmember came out.

"Assiz? It is your watch. Assiz, you idiot, where are—" He caught sight of one of our guys, simultaneously trying to bring his rifle up to shoot, use his radio and retreat through the door. In his cluster fuck rush to do everything at once, and achieving nothing, a silenced round burst through his throat, blood spraying in an arc, surging in time with his beating heart. As he sank to his knees, gurgling through the frothy, foaming blood coming out of his mouth and neck, another operative kicked him in the head to seal his fate. Three down. I wondered how many there were. The crew didn't seem to be particularly professional. I hoped it stayed that way.

We pressed on. The guys on the bridge radioed that all was secure. No casualties and no shots fired. There were only three people on watch on the bridge, so that was quickly taken care of.

I followed as we weaved in and out of containers stacked two and three high, each container made of steel and forty feet long by ten feet high. If they were keeping Jessica in a container, it could take a while to find her. About amidships we came to a sort of clearing. A row of containers flanked the port and starboard sides of the vessel leaving a space in the middle, away from prying eyes.

I tapped the man in front of me on the shoulder and motioned that I wanted to talk and needed them to slow down and stop for a second. After the message was passed, the group of five agents huddled around with me in the middle. We crouched down, close to a container to provide cover and security. Three of the five were facing outboard to protect our flanks, continuously monitoring the area.

"Make it quick," one of them said.

I motioned them in closer. "Those containers over there," I pointed at the ones in the middle. "I don't know how many container ships you've been on, but there's no way a ship would have rigged them for passage from Corpus like that. It's just a useless waste of space, and if they should hit rough weather, they'll fall overboard." The containers in the middle were stacked two high, but arranged in a rough circle.

The operative caught on quickly. "If it's a circle, then that means there's some space in the middle."

"Exactly. These are standard forty-foot containers, so you'd have to figure the circumference is about two hundred feet give or take, the way they're overlapping. Stacked two high, makes them about twenty feet tall. There has to be a reason they would be like this, it's possible they're trying to hide something. This isn't a regular stow plan."

"Okay. We'll check it out." He hesitated, and then said, "I'm still not happy you're here, but thanks for the Intel. The name's Wardwell."

Wardwell gave quick orders, and in a few movements three of his team had scaled the containers and lay prone on top.

Wardwell held his left ear. "Team reports that there's one, approximately twenty foot, single stacked container in the middle of this circle formation."

"That has to be it," I said. "That has to be where they're keeping her."

He nodded and then pressed his fingers to his throat mike, radioing instructions to his team. The three prone team members dropped down from atop the containers into the clearing. The next few moments felt like forever. I wanted to be on the other side of those damn containers, but there was no way for me to scale them.

There was still something bugging me, something else that didn't make sense. I started to walk cautiously around the containers, away from the team. I was mindful of the danger posed on board the ship, and I had my gun held loosely at my side, safety off, finger outside the trigger. What was it? What was bugging me? I stopped, crouched down and turned, some internal Spidey sense tingling. I was about fifty feet away, just over a containers length from Wardwell. Then, just as one of the sealed container doors cracked opened right in front of me, I figured out what it was that was bothering me.

I felt like slapping my forehead with my hand. There had to be a way in. You wouldn't build a fortress of containers and then not have a way in.

The door, the one in front of me, slowly inched open on well-oiled hinges. It was just sheer dumb luck that I was in the right place. I saw Jimmy's fat gut squeeze out first, followed a half second later by the rest of him, and then Ricky appeared. If there was any doubt we were on the wrong ship, it was immediately and irrevocably erased as their two ugly heads looked around, blinking in the darkness. They carefully stood up and took aim at Wardwell and his partner still crouching where I had left them, not noticing me lurking in the shadows.

"Hey!" I said. "Fucktards! Over here." I didn't give Ricky a chance to turn more than a quarter before I shot him. I turned my aim to Jimmy, but my warning shout had got the attention of Wardwell, and Jimmy was soon leaking blood like a squished mosquito.

I raced through the container door the two fishermen had opened, and ran inside the container. A crude hole was cut through the sheet metal of the container, leading the way to the inner sanctum.

I carefully poked my head through the hole, not wanting friendlies to shoot me. The three operatives were just exiting the twenty-foot container in the middle. They motioned me over.

"It looks like she was in here, sir. Or at least someone was, but there's no sign of her now."

My heart came crashing down. Switching on my flashlight, I entered. It reeked inside. Reeked of fear and sweat. I saw the makeshift torture chamber and matched the beam across the ceiling from the photo Black had sent me. There was blood on the floor. Not a lot, but enough. I hoped it wasn't Jessica's.

I wanted to collapse on the floor of the container. Curl up and cry. But I couldn't. Jessica was still out there somewhere. She still needed me. Not until I was certain she was dead would I ever give up the search.

The rest of the crew were rounded up and interrogated. They all pretended they knew nothing. Still at large were Black, George, and Lewis, if he was with them. God help them when I catch them.

I walked back towards the bridge and into the captain's office. The captain of the *Bold Endeavor* was seated at his desk, hands secured in front of him.

"Remember me? Where's Black," I said.

He ignored me for a moment and then shrugged.

"I don't think you realize the situation you're in Captain. We know how the guns were smuggled, and we've figured out how the missing people were frozen. Refrigerated containers. Very clever. We'll have a forensics team on soon, and the evidence will be conclusive. You, my friend, are going down for a very, very, long time." I leaned forward on his desk, looked right in his eyes. "There won't be any lawyers for you, no protection, no trial, no rest, no escape."

The captain returned my stare. "I am international shipping cap-it-an. Protected by international law. And you are not in U.S. waters. Your threats," he shrugged. "They are idle. You do not frighten me."

I smiled, my mouth wide. "I think you're forgetting one small thing, Captain." I spat out the word. "You're now a terrorist, as is Black and his entire operation. So let me think." I tapped my fingers on his desk. His eyes flickered to them and then back to my face, gauging me. "Where do we send terrorists we capture? Hmm." I could see the light dawning like the early morning sun in his eyes.

"That's right. You've got it now. That little slice of heaven in Cuba called Guantanamo Bay. What with Donald Trump as the President, it'll never, ever close down. You'll rot in there forever. Is that worth it, Miguel? Is it worth it, to protect Black?" I slammed my fists down on the table, making his ashtray jump half an inch. "Is it?"

I walked out and slammed the cabin door, letting him stew for a minute. I went to the galley and made myself relax, poured a cup of thick, black coffee, the spoon nearly standing up on end.

I didn't say anything when I came back in, merely walked over to the large cabin window and looked out, sipping my coffee, letting the aroma fill up the room. It didn't take long for him to bite.

"When you say that Guantanamo Bay. You are serious?"

Miguel, hands still zip tied together, clumsily tried to reach for a cigarette on his desk, some foul looking Turkish blend. I knocked the pack out of his hands, cigarettes scattering, several rolling onto the floor.

"You might as well quit now, you won't be getting those where you're going," I said.

He stood up. "You cannot talk to me this way. I am not a U.S. Citizen, and we are not on U.S. soil when the vessel owners hear of this—"

"Sit down and cut the shit, Miguel. I *can* talk to you this way. I *am* talking to you this way. Don't for one second think the owners of this boat are going to support terrorism, support you. They'll drop you so fast...give up Black. Once we have him, we can talk about what happens to you. It can be bad, maybe it can be not so bad."

I could see his mind ticking over, processing the information. "Bad I know. What is not so bad?"

"Perhaps, you can still be a captain? But you'll be banned from the U.S."

"So. No more America?" He shrugged. "It is just. Okay. I tell you. First though. My cigarettes? Yes?"

I pushed them across to him, helped him light one, figured the gesture might help.

He took a drag and then said, "He has an island. Small. Not far from here. A launch picked him up a few hours before you got here. Took him, that crazy George person, and the girl."

I stiffened. "What was her condition?"

He shrugged again. "I am no doctor."

"Miguel, tell me how she was, dammit. Or we can revisit our deal."

"She was alive. That is all I saw." He lifted his hands in supplication.

I raised my hand as if to smack him. He scooted back and hurriedly said, "I do not know, truly. I only saw her from a distance. She was walking by herself. She did not appear hurt. Her hands were tied behind her."

I motioned him to a chart of the area, and he showed us where the island was. Wardwell called in for satellite reconnaissance, and we figured we could be there via our boats in about an hour. We made the crew set the anchor, and when it was safely secured in the depths below, we locked them all in the medical office, the only lockable and sterile place on board that would fit them all.

The *Glorious* was en route, with an ETA of about an hour minutes. Their small boat would be on us soon, so we left swiftly, figuring the crew could claim pirates or some such thing. I warned the captain not to tell the truth otherwise our deal would be off.

# SEVENTEEN

## *Get Some*

We were back on our two vessels, with zero casualties. I was in the lead boat now, having passed some sort of test, and the group decided I might be more of an asset than a liability.

The coxswain turned into the waves and increased speed to thirty-eight knots. Wardwell hunkered down and gave us a quick brief of the upcoming operation.

We made good time, and it was still dark when we were within sight of the target. For a personally sized island, this thing was immense. Perched atop a small outcrop was a tropical looking mansion, lit up like Bastille Day or the Fourth of July. Black, evidently not bothered with any thought of secrecy. That was good, meant he didn't know we were coming. Or maybe it said he didn't care? I pushed the thought from my mind.

We were surveying the island from a distance through optics, expecting some reactionary or defense force. If Black could afford an island, he could afford to hire a team to protect him. Either they were way better trained than his regular guys, or he didn't have any, as there wasn't anything obvious.

With the engines of the forty-fives carefully burbling away at a little over idle speed we approached the island on the darker side, away from the lights and mansion. The aroma of fried shrimp and the occasional faint note of big band music drifted across the water as we made our approach.

They'd lent me a spare pair of night vision optics so I could see what was going on in the dark, but I still couldn't detect any movement. Our boat went first, paving the way for the other. If we encountered any enemy fire, they would know where to focus.

We didn't meet any resistance and beached our boat, securing it via a line to a friendly palm tree in case the tide turned. The tree didn't seem to mind the imposition. We signaled the other team the all clear, and once they were beached as well, we moved out in teams of two.

Although I'd been given temporary honorary status, they still made me bring up the rear. I couldn't tell if that was a good thing or not, but the two guys in front of me were constantly monitoring our six, so it was a moot positional point.

We followed what could have been a goat path through the brush, careful to keep the noise to a minimum. We could hear the sounds of the music getting closer and closer as we moved forward. It sounded like he was having a goddamn party. Maybe he was. He'd managed to sneak out of the country. Undoubtedly he was exceedingly happy with his fat, tubby self.

My mouth twisted into a rictus of a bitter smile. I couldn't wait to get my hands round his fat neck and squeeze. I calmed myself. First, though, we had to get there.

We surged up a small slope, shale and sand falling behind us. Still no resistance. At the top, we lay prone and again assessed the situation. This was a lot for me, I'm more in tune with going in guns blazing, but I appreciated the steady as she goes sentiment.

We couldn't have been more than three hundred yards from the house. For all its vastness, I couldn't but help admire the landscaping and attention to detail. As we had come up on the rear of the house we could look down into the courtyard and the large pool, everything tastefully chic.

There didn't appear to be any walls surrounding the villa, but there would surely be some motion detectors or floodlights, as we got closer. Wardwell signaled for his electronics guy, who crab crawled up to us and hauled a small black box seemingly from nowhere and did his magic, looking through some sort of scope.

I surmised that he was scanning the area, and then he held up three fingers. Three minutes? Three guards? Three motion detectors? I wish I knew what their code meant. It was a little like learning to read for the first time, but then being given a book in complicated French. You might be able to stumble around and make the odd correct guess, but that would be sheer dumb luck.

"Motion detectors," Wardwell whispered, seeing my confusion. "He'll set up a jamming signal. Everything's all interconnected these days. Actually makes our job a whole lot easier."

We crept forward some more, keeping close to the ground. I never heard the gunshot, more of an overhead echo, and then a ka-thunk into a tree behind me.

"Get down," Wardwell hissed, pulling me into the sand beside him. "Terry, find the sniper."

Someone, presumably Terry, elbowed his way across the sand, staying low and set up his rifle. We waited for the shooter to take his next shot. The shooter waited too. These were professionals. Terry, trying to draw them out, sent out a three round burst, aiming at the most likely area. One of his shots must have ricocheted off of something as a narrow plate glass window overlooking the entire length of the pool cracked and shattered. Immediately the thump of the bass was louder. I could hear some muffled shouts, and the music stopped.

The place lit up around us. Floodlights came on; shots were thumping into the palm trees above and beside us, shredding foliage. Wardwell said a few things into his throat mike, and then the floodlights went out one by one, as they were shot out. We moved now, the advantage of surprise gone, having to make the best of it. We dodged and dived, inching our way to the house. We couldn't afford to be pinned down. It was hard to figure out how many people were shooting at us, and then we heard the high-pitched whine of an aerial drone.

"Goddammit, they've got eyes in the sky," Wardwell said.

The drones were too small to take out, and too fast, but they were getting a real bird's eye view. What was I saying about technology helping us? Just ignore me.

Not having any other choice, we moved closer, some fifty feet from the house. We were still taking fire, but from the angle we were now to the house, it was apparently harder to get a cleaner shot. I saw a tinted glass door open near the pool and the barrel of a rifle nudge its way out. I patted Wardwell on the shoulder and then pointed at the door. Two quick shots later and a human-sized shape slumped against the door and slid down, smearing blood along the glass, the rifle clattering to the floor. This was our chance to get in the house. Signaling his men, Wardwell and I rushed to the door, weaving and zigzagging. Coming up fast against the wall I flattened my back, and shimmied up to the door, careful that there was no one else inside ready to leap out. Confirming it was clear I was about to enter when I heard something skid across the nearby sandbank we had been on and land with an empty oomph. One of our guys had taken a hit. I could see him trying to crawl towards us, but one of his legs was twisted a weird way. Without thinking I ran out, hooked my elbows under his shoulders and backpedaled. I knew this was hurting his leg like a motherfucker, but it sure beat the alternative. I hoped he thought the same thing as I dragged him and his bleeding leg towards the house. He'd passed out by the time I got to the house, probably a good thing, and one of the other guys took over, giving him a shot of something.

I ran to the door, stepped over the dead guy, and almost shot my reflection in the mirror, my finger twitching on the trigger. I hadn't recognized myself, covered in blood and grime, I looked like some deathly apparition ready to reap vengeance. The reckoning was coming.

Through the door I found myself in a tiled hallway and stepping softly, followed it to the kitchen. I could have easily tracked where I was going as the aroma of shrimp was strong down here. As I came through an archway, I heard an ululating scream, and a massive meat cleaver swished through the air where my face had just been. The scream gave me enough time to avoid having half my face looking at me from the floor. The guy with the cleaver - June, he was not - ran at me again. Ala Indiana Jones, I just shot him and dodged out the way as he crashed into the wall. Score one for the good guys, too bad about the chef. Those shrimp smelled heavenly.

I heard the pitter-patter of almost silent feet behind me, crouched and turned, my gun held in a firing stance. Wardwell skidded to a stop a few feet from me, his gun aimed at me too. We slowly lowered our weapons.

"Got the drop on you," I said.

"I knew it was you," Wardwell said.

We left the kitchen and went through what looked like a dining room. It didn't appear as if it had been used recently, and dust bunnies skittered around the floor at our feet. We rounded an archway, and I saw a winding staircase leading to an impressive landing. The staircase looked like it was made from marble, I wondered again how Black had managed to ship everything here and get it built. There was the occasional sound of suppressed fire from nearby, so I knew the team was still fighting in close quarters.

We moved carefully, as silently as could be managed, shoes occasionally squeaking off the tile floor. I was on the third step up the stairs, when I heard a scraping sound from behind me. Instinctively I stepped to the side and crouched down, turning. George that Goddamned wraith man had a knife to Wardwell's throat.

"Shoot him," Wardwell said.

I took aim but didn't have a clean shot, George was in too tight to Wardwell, using him as a shield. George smiled, the first expression I'd ever seen him have. This couldn't be good. He started to back off down a corridor, Wardwell in a tight grip, subdued by the knife.

Fuck.

I followed.

"George. Don't do this," I said. "Come on, George. I can get you out of this. You can go back fishing. No one will have to know. I can fix it. You just have to stop now, George. Just stop. It'll be okay."

George kept moving. When he was near the kitchen door, he made his move. He sliced the knife across Wardwell's throat and shoved him towards me. I couldn't let him fall to the ground, but couldn't let George get out free either. Shit.

Training kicked in, and I caught Wardwell, laying him down, applying pressure to his wound. He was struggling with me, and I had to play the delicate role of applying pressure to his throat to stop the bleeding without actually choking him. He continued to struggle, and then with one great heave scissor-kicked his legs and bucked me off of him and rolled away.

"Fuck. Off me," he said.

"I have to stop the bleeding. You're in shock."

"Not in shock, not bleeding." He sat up and pulled down his collar. There was a slice in the collar, but his neck was clean. "Must have nicked the top of the Kevlar. If he'd tried to stab me it would have gone straight through, but sideways the Kevlar fibers slowed his knife down."

Wardwell got on the radio and warned his men George was on the loose and most likely coming out the poolside door. We started back up the stairs.

The tactical glasses we had showed thermal images, and we scanned each room on the second floor. Two heat signatures were coming from one of the rooms ahead, one stationary one scurrying to the side. We crept into position, one of us either side of the door and signaled to each other. I was to go low and left, Wardwell was to go high and right. If anyone was going to shoot us, they'd probably aim for the center of the door, and we could take them out without getting killed ourselves. At worst, they'd only have time to shoot one of us.

Wardwell took a step or two back and then slammed a booted foot into the door near the lock. It was only a normal house door, nothing fancy and the wood frame split, the door banging open. We slid in, and I scanned the room. No shots. No one was firing at us. The room was immense and overlooked the ocean. A large king-size bed with red sheets occupied one end of the room through a set of double doors. On the other side of me was a well-stocked bar with a mirrored back, and in front of me two over-sized, comfortable looking leather armchairs. In one was a disgustingly large fat man wearing a neon green set of velour pajamas. On the floor, next to an ashtray that had been knocked over, ash besmirching the carpet, was a still smoldering cigar, the thick stank filling up the room. In between the two chairs was a small square table, the tablecloth also on the floor, as well as the remains of two steaks, and two broken wine glasses, the red wine slowly spreading to form a sopping puddle next to the table.

I took all of that in at a glance, but what really caught my eye, was the thick steak knife jutting out of Black's massive chest. Blood was oozing from the wound.

"Jessica! It's Frank. Where are you?" I said, scanning the rest of the room.

I didn't hear anything. Wardwell went to look around, keeping one eye on the door. I made a beeline for Black. I could tell he was breathing, but shallowly, as his large chest was slowly rising and falling, the knife moving in concert.

I pressed down lightly on the knife. Black's eyes shot open with the increased pain. "Where is she, Black?"

He gurgled back to me, bubbles of frothy blood mixed with his spittle, his mouth working, but no words coming out. He also looked like he was trying to laugh. I pressed down some more, maybe a half an inch, barely touching him, but just enough, and his laugh-gurgle stopped, the life leaving his eyes, his chest ceasing to heave. I stared at him a for long moment, the bitterness I had coming up as bile, and I spat in his face.

"Fuck you," I said. "Fuck. You." And I spat again, tapping the knife for good measure.

"Frank," Wardwell said, coming out from another room. "You need to get over here."

# EIGHTEEN

## *Wait. What?*

followed his voice into the bathroom. In the shower, seemingly oblivious to the battle that was waging around us was Jessica, wrapped in steam, and singing a soft song to herself.

I motioned Wardwell out and said softly, "Jessica?"

Her singing stopped, and shortly after, so did the shower. The door slipped open, and a dripping hand stretched out. "Be a darling and hand that gorgeous fluffy towel to me would you?" she said.

Flummoxed. A million questions racing through my mind. I found the towel and handed it to her.

"Thanks, doll."

I stayed outside of the shower, averting my eyes, more from habit than courtesy. I wanted to see her, wanted to hold her, wanted...This wasn't what I wanted, the reaction I was expecting, and it threw me. "Jessica. It's okay. You're safe. We're here now. We...we got here as quickly as we could. I'm so sorry, baby. We didn't know where you were. Trust me, we didn't give up. Are you, you know, okay? He didn't hurt you did he?"

She stopped rubbing her body for a second and peeked around the frosted shower door, holding the towel in front of her like a shield. "Me? Of course, I'm okay. Why wouldn't I be?" And then she continued humming the same nonsense tune, toweling off again.

I stood rooted to the spot. "It's alright," I said. "Black...his crew, they're all dead or secured. You're safe. You don't have to worry anymore."

She finished drying herself, and came out of the shower, wrapped in the towel.

"Why would I be worried? Honestly, dear, I don't know what you're talking about. Be a darling and hand me that other towel behind you." I gave it to her, and she wrapped it around her head.

My words weren't reaching her, weren't getting through, so I went to hug her, to show her it was over, to hold her. She moved out of my reach. I stood back nonplussed. I suppressed a shiver that was crawling ever so slowly but steadily up my spine, trying to find a home in the short hairs on my neck. Trying to freak me out.

"Jess. It's me, Frank."

She didn't reply, just looked through me with a thousand-yard stare, semi-glazed look. Shock, I guessed.

"Black. He's dead. I finished it. He's never going to hurt you again," I said.

She paled, her eyes focusing for a moment. "Dead? I thought...No, that can't be."

She pushed passed me, rushed out to the other room, and looked at Black as if seeing him for the first time, the knife stuck in his chest. For a moment nothing happened, Jessica frozen in place. Then somewhere deep inside her head the images her eyes were sending her brain finally registered. She screamed and rushed over to him, her hands alternately reaching for the knife then changing course and flying back to her mouth, not wanting to touch him, but needing to do something, fluttering. A rictus of distress played on her face, at odds with some deeper, hidden emotion I could sense but not see.

"It's okay," I said, moving to her again, lightly touching her shoulder. "He can't hurt you anymore."

"He didn't hurt me. He was nothing but an angel to me." She sat and sank heavily into the other chair opposite Black, tears rolling down her face. "He was my protector."

Wardwell looked at me, shrugged and walked out of the room, crushing the still smoldering cigar underfoot as he went.

"I'll be outside, Frank," he said. "Shout if you need me."

I knelt down beside her chair and tried to turn her face away from Black. She resisted, so I didn't push it.

"What happens to me now?" she said.

Not knowing what she meant I said, "We'll get you checked out by the medic and back to the States."

"No, you fucking idiot. What happens now? You've ruined it all, you bastard. I didn't kill him. He was fine when I went to take a shower."

"I–"

"You killed him." It was a statement, not a question. She pulled her knees up towards herself and hugged them, finally looked at me. "We were going to live here in harmony together. Just the two of us. We were going to be happy together."

She stood up suddenly, went over to Black and yanked out the steak knife, a slurping sucking sound coming as she did so. She collapsed on top of him, holding onto all his massiveness and started crying again. Huge racking sobs shook her body.

I turned, pained, looking for help to the door, but Wardwell was nowhere to be seen. I didn't know what to make of this. I wasn't a psychologist. It tore my heart. What sort of fucked up shit was this?

As I was looking at the door, Jessica leaped from Black and lunged for me. The steak knife was in her hand, aiming for my heart like a spear. I backpedaled but tripped on the ashtray and landed sprawled on my back. Jessica came down on top of me, stronger than she looked, knocking the wind out of me, still trying to ram the knife in my heart, in my guts.

"Jessica! Stop. It's me, Frank.'

"You've ruined it all," she hissed.

I struggled. Tried to keep her hands away from me, but they were slippery with Black's blood, and the knifepoint slowly dipped lower, passed the point where I had the leverage to get her off. I didn't want her to kill me. I didn't want to hurt her either. The towel on her head slipped off and fell on me, covering my eyes. I thought this was it. I was going to be killed by the very same person I'd been trying to rescue. The woman I'd fallen in love with. My Jessica. Somehow warped by Black and now trying to kill me.

As I felt the tip of the knife pierce my skin, my mind blanked. I didn't feel my life's story flash behind my eyes, I didn't beseech any deity with lifelong devotion if they helped me out. I struggled to push Jessica away, and the only thought that rattled around my head was that I wouldn't have a chance to say goodbye to Pete, get that dog I'd always wanted, read another book, sail into the sunset.

The knife sank in another quarter inch and then suddenly the pressure eased off, and I heard a scuffle.

"Get off me. Going to kill him. Kill you. Get. Off."

I whipped the towel off my head, put a hand to my chest where the point had gone in, and a trickle of blood squeezed through my fingers. Wardwell had her in a bear hug.

"Give me a hand," he said, struggling with an out of control Jessica. She still had the knife in her hands and was trying to stab Wardwell, but she couldn't escape his arms wrapped around her waist. The towel slipped down exposing her chest and torso, and my heart gave out as I saw the bruises. She'd been tortured, cigarette burns on her breasts, small cuts along her ribs. Some of the bruises were already yellowing, some purple, others black.

"Help me," he shouted.

I pried her hands apart, and the knife fell to the floor with a dull clatter. Together we manhandled her down to the floor, pushed her onto her stomach. Wardwell produced a zip tie from a back pocket and made to tie her hands behind her back.

"Do we have to?" I asked.

"Would you rather she stick you again?"

I shook my head, too choked up to say anything. Tears flowed freely down my cheeks, unnoticed as Jessica continued to writhe on the floor, screaming and raging.

# EPILOGUE

## *Into the Sunset*

I don't remember how we left the island. Didn't know how we'd gotten back to the boat. It was a blur, a mental block, the mind shutting down to allow for recovery, perhaps the shock of seeing Jessica the way she was, beaten and lost. Black's death, easy and useless, was almost a disappointment. The cold dish of revenge, once served, more tepid than expected.

When the haziness cleared, I was sitting in a stiff plastic chair, my back aching, not sure how long I had been sitting, staring across at Jessica who wasn't moving. She was lying in a hospital bed covered up to her shoulders with crisp white sheets, folded back with stark precision, her arms laying still and lifeless.

A nurse told me we were in a hospital in St. Thomas. Jessica had had to be sedated, so she didn't hurt herself. I beat myself up, sitting in that chair, glad for the discomfort and cramping, a small penance for not finding her sooner. I grieved for Jessica. Grieved that I couldn't get to that island any quicker, couldn't help her.

Different nurses came in from time to time, shifts changing, the hospital always moving forwards, time always moving forwards, but Jessica and I seemed stuck in a cocoon of solemn never-ending, never-changing, plastic chair hell.

Her vitals checked, blood pressure pumped and released, heart rate monitored by pocket watches and stethoscope. Notations scribbled with cheap ballpoint pens on a clipboard attached to the foot of her bed. I barely stirred. Jessica didn't move.

She was hooked up to various IVs, filled with clear liquids some smaller than others, no doubt antibiotics, and pain meds. Her face and shoulders peeked out above the sheets and had some thick bandaging, small nicks and cuts already healing. I remembered the bruises, the cigarette burns.

I was wallowing deeply in self-pity. I knew it. I could feel it, see it, but I didn't want to move. I was responsible for this, for Jessica lying here, for what she went through. So I stayed.

I told them I was her fiancé, not wanting to lie, but needing to know what had happened. She didn't have any family that could visit, her brother was dead, her mother with Alzheimer's. I felt that someone should know, someone that cared for her. The doctors, hesitant at first, but when no one else arrived, they looked at each other, whispered and shrugged, gave in. They told me she hadn't been sexually assaulted, but she had been horrifically abused. They found burn marks, big enough to have been from a cigar, in places that only the softest lace should ever have laid. Bruises from repeated beatings, some older, some new. Bruises on top of bruises.

Each bruise punched me deeper in the gut. My melancholy bottomless. They didn't want to send her home. Her injuries weren't life-threatening, but the doctors thought she'd be better off where she was.

The Coast Guard sent a chaplain, asked if he could say a prayer. I shrugged. I'd take all the help I could get.

Night changed to day, the tropical light streaming through the blinds. Light fading, moonbeams chasing the sun. I sat through it all. I held her hand, motionless.

"Mr. Dalton? You really should get some rest. Jessica is going to be sedated for quite some time," Doctor Adams said. "The mind is a fragile thing, it needs time to heal, as much as if not more than her body. We're constantly monitoring her, and when the time is right, we'll slowly bring her back, make an assessment." He rubbed his face, looked like he wanted to say more, but turned instead and left.

When the time was right, they'd bring her out of it and see if Jessica was still inside, see if the damage was permanent. Prepare yourself, they said. Is there anyone we should call?

Tobias had come to see us. Flown out especially. He wasn't angry, god knows he had every right to be, but he'd had time to process. Admiral Jones had spoken with him and with some old colleagues and given them as much of the picture as he could to smooth things over.

It wasn't all bad. Black was dead, his crew captured and a mole in the agency had been uncovered. All the unnecessary deaths swept under the cover of official secrets, stamped, closed, locked up, and maybe in fifty years someone would dust them off and write a book.

Tobias told me that they'd found George. It had looked like he'd managed to escape the Island, but he must've only been wounded. The team had found him slumped over the wheel of Black's boat, puddles of blood seeping through a makeshift bandage. They hadn't found Lewis. He was still in the wind, but they wouldn't stop looking. Somehow he'd slipped out of the country. The last intelligence had him somewhere in South America. It was a big place, but he'd surface eventually. The rat-fuck couldn't hide forever.

Tobias left. Other people came.

They told me to leave, get some rest. They gave me pamphlets on surviving attacks, on how to care for someone that was abused. I couldn't read them, didn't want to, didn't want to admit it happened. I felt that reading them would somehow solidify it all; make it less a dream and more like reality. I didn't want this to be the reality. I wanted it to be a dream, needed it to be a dream. Just one fucked up night, surreal and bizarre, and I'd wake up in a cold sweat and shake my head. Drink some coffee, sit on my back deck, laugh at how ridiculous it all was. But no. It wasn't a dream. It wasn't one of those cheesy endings from a high school English class where the ending was a scribbled, 'and then she woke up and it was all a dream.'

Someone brought me a change of clothes when they realized I was never going to leave her side again; others brought me food, offered me a pullout chair. You'll be more comfortable, they said. I didn't move.

I looked out the window and saw palm trees, swaying in the island breeze. Couldn't work up the enthusiasm to give a fuck. Time went by.

When she first woke up, I was asleep, slumped over in the unforgiving hardness of my self-imposed plastic hospital torture.

"Frank? So thirsty."

I was immediately awake, brushing the sleep from my eyes, quickly standing, muscles screaming, contracting. I ignored it all, smiling through my tears. Hoping.

"Here. I'm here, Jessica. You're safe. Don't talk." I handed her a plastic bottle with a straw from her bedside table so she could drink. She took a few sips and then melted back into the bed.

"Jessica?" I said, but she was already asleep.

She didn't say anything for another two days. The doctors said that was normal; it was a good sign. The body resting after the sedation had worn off, repairing. More nurses, the occasional doctor filtering back and forth through the door. Lights shining in her eyes, blood pressure cuff humming and inflating every quarter hour, touching her, checking her pulse. Notes made, pens clicking, occasional brief, tight smiles, pats on the shoulder. We'll know soon, they said. So clinical, so efficient, just numbers on a chart. I'm sure they truly cared, but I was past the facade, past caring what they thought. I wanted my Jessica back. The waiting, worrying, wearing me down.

I started to come out of my stupor, now that there was some hope. Showered, shaved, changed clothes. I even found the cafeteria and ate some soup. I'd gone to the bathroom, taking the time to assess. I looked like I'd aged a thousand years from what I remembered my face should look like. The tan had paled; the bags under my eyes heavy and dark. My skin was ashen, replaced with the color of the great unwashed and fluorescent light king. That was me.

When I shuffled back to the room, she was awake, and I stopped in the doorway for a second to take her in. Her eyes seemed clear, those incredible, brown eyes. The sallow reflection of hospital and pain, replaced by something else, something only a living person can give.

"Frank," she croaked. "What happened?"

"What do you remember?" I said, moving to the bed and sitting on the edge, taking her hand in mine and kicking my plastic chair away.

Doctor Adams came in, paged by a nurse. He was all business and smiles, motioned me off the bed. Checked her vitals, her bandages.

"Jessica? I'm Doctor Adams. Can you tell me your full name and date of birth? Where do you live? Who's the current president? Do you know where you are?"

"Doc, give her a chance, will you?" I said.

"Cincinnati," Carter said.

Adams frowned and looked at me, not quite sure how to take her answer, about to say something.

"It's okay," I said, smiling through my tears. "It's her. She's herself." Cincinnati was an old joke. She'd told me before that had been her safe word as a child. She was going to be okay. Adams said it would still take time and therapy. Time for the physical wounds to heal and hide, time for the emotional trauma to recede. She needed a stress-free environment, somewhere the brain and body could heal. He said some big ten-dollar doctor words, but I had stopped listening. I knew what she needed. She needed to be out of here, and away, away from it all.

Over the next few days, there were more assessments, preparations for travel. Jessica told me awful things. Purging, mending. Things I wish I could unhear. But that was unfair of me. She needed compassion and understanding. It didn't matter a damn how I felt. It wasn't about me, none of this was. She said she remembered being taken, dragged from her car, something over her mouth so she didn't struggle. After that, it was a haze, snatches. Some real, some not. She felt the familiar rocking motion of a ship. Images of cigars, Black leaning in close and laughing. Pungent body odor, stale cigarette smoke. Peripherally, she knew what was happening, understood she was being abused, but the specifics weren't there. The memories might come back, or they might not. I was hoping not. It was probably better that way. I let her speak, let her get it all out. The sobs broke my heart. I held her.

As soon as they cleared her for travel, we set off for Corpus, a plan in mind. Jessica was on official convalescent leave, and I cashed in my chips with Tobias and took some extended vacation time. No one was going to argue with what we had been through.

We set sail the following week. *Serenity* was well provisioned and packed, fueled up and ready to go, thanks to Pete. Jessica cast off the lines while I spooled up the motor and we headed out of the dock and to parts south, parts unknown.

Pete mock saluted and waved as we motored past.

"Bon voyage, my friends," he shouted.

Jessica's light spring dress flowed in the wind as she stood on the bow, her hair streaming, shimmering like gold from the sunlight. If you looked carefully when she was close, you could still see the faint outline of the last of her bruises, barely showing.

It was going to be a long journey, a journey of discovery, a journey of forgiveness and healing.

I blasted the horn in reply and didn't look back.


THE END


"Fair Winds and Following Seas."

# AUTHOR'S NOTES

Thanks for taking the time to read *To Dance the Hempen Jig*. I hope you enjoyed it. If you did, please consider leaving a review on Amazon. Every single review really does help. Why don't you do it right now, right this second, before you forget? Thanks.

Questions about the book? Comments for the author? Typo's? Fan mail?

Send to: todancethehempenjig@gmail.com

Printed in Great Britain
by Amazon